GARY GIBSON

Doomsday Game

# Contents

IV   The Long Fall

V   Doomsday Game

VI   Eight Years Later

I

# A Choice of Catastrophes

# Kip

Everywhere Kip looked, dead seagulls lay scattered across the headland in their hundreds. Soldiers in hazmat suits moved amongst them, scooping up their small limp bodies with thick padded gloves and depositing them into heavy plastic sacks. A mound of sacks, every last one filled to capacity, had been steadily growing next to the coast road since dawn. One of Major Howes' men, equipped with a flamethrower, stood waiting next to the mound with a bored expression.

Kip nudged a seagull with the tip of one shoe. A wing lifted briefly, caught by an ocean breeze, then fell again. He picked out a handkerchief and kneeled down, carefully wiping the patent leather clean. He stood again, moving to replace the handkerchief in the breast pocket of his suit, then hesitated. At last he gestured to a soldier wielding a sack to come closer, depositing the crumpled silk into the sack as the soldier held it open for him.

Stepping up to the edge of the cliff that marked the end of the headland, he looked down at the shore below. Yet more

3

dead birds lay scattered across a pebbled beach. When he lifted his eyes to look out across the Pacific, he saw that the water had a deep red hue to it, as if the rising sun had suffered a mortal wound and had bled its essence into the ocean.

'A "red tide", one of the marine biologists called it,' said Major Howes, stepping up beside him. 'Something to do with algae and neurotoxins in the water.'

Kip felt a dull ache in his right cheek and reached up to touch it: the bruise had been livid when he woke that morning. 'Remarkable to think,' he said, 'that something so small could wipe out an entire civilisation.'

Howes shrugged. 'Unrestricted pollution will do that.'

They both turned inland on hearing the sound of an engine approaching. Past the coast road, a row of *Moai*—statues built long ago by the island's original inhabitants—regarded them with what Kip imagined to be faint disapproval. A jeep came rolling across the grass towards them with Preston Merritt, Kip's new second-in-command, at the wheel.

Merritt got out of the jeep and walked towards them. A thin moustache clung to the man's upper lip in an attempt at gravitas entirely at odds with his boyishly plump face. He gazed briefly at the multitude of avian corpses, then nodded to Kip. 'Director.'

'Shouldn't you be back in Washington?' asked Kip.

'I would,' said Merritt, 'if my stage privileges hadn't suddenly been rescinded for reasons that entirely escape me. I cannot do my job, Director Mayer, if I'm required to file a travel plan every time I want to use a transfer stage!'

'Someone's been taking unauthorised trips to off-limits alternates, and we need to put a stop to it,' Kip replied coolly. *Something that started as soon as I was forced to accept you as my*

4

*second-in-command, as a matter of fact.* 'Until we figure out who's doing it, that's the way it has to be.' He glanced at Major Howes, his face as blank as any one of the ancient statues. 'We can't risk some idiot on a cross-universe joyride carrying killer bugs or doomsday devices back to our home alternate.' He favoured Merritt with a brittle smile. 'But if it's affecting your work,' he added, 'then of course I'll look into it.'

He caught a hint of malice in Merritt's gaze, there and gone in an instant. 'Thank you,' Merritt replied. He glanced around, as if seeing the dead gulls for the first time. 'If your hands are full, I could take charge of the investigation myself.'

'Major Howes here is already looking into it. What I *do* need you to do is to take charge of the curfew. Some of our people don't take the weather here as seriously as they should.'

'Four of my men were hospitalised last night,' said Howes.

Merritt glanced towards him. 'They got caught in the rain?'

'A sudden squall,' said Kip. 'They were unprotected, unfortunately.'

Merritt stared at Kip's face. 'Your…'

Kip reached up to touch the bruise. 'One of the men broke free from his restraints and assaulted me when I visited the clinic yesterday evening. He died earlier this morning and he probably won't be the last.'

'We need to be extra vigilant from now on,' said Howes. 'Lives are at risk.'

Merritt's eyes narrowed. 'It had been my understanding before I was transferred here that we were safe on this island.'

Kip shook his head. 'We *were* safe,' he explained, 'due to some peculiarity in this alternate's ocean currents. Unfortunately, that's no longer the case.' He nodded at dark clouds edging the horizon. 'There's a storm coming. We need to tighten the curfew. That means nobody allowed to venture outside unless it's on essential business, and then only with appropriate protective clothing.'

They both turned at a loud *whoosh* and watched as the soldier wielding the flamethrower torched the mound of plastic bags. Tendrils of black, oily smoke rose quickly into the morning sky. Kip wrinkled his nose at the scent of roasting flesh.

'I expect you can take care of the details of the curfew, Mr Merritt,' Kip added without looking at him. *And maybe it'll keep you too busy to go on any more unauthorised excursions.*

'Of course.' Merritt nodded to Kip and to the Major. 'You're sure I can't persuade you to make an exception regarding the stage permits?'

'I can make arrangements to process your requests more quickly,' said Major Howes. 'But the rules have to apply to everyone.'

Merritt's mouth worked for a moment, then he turned and stalked back over to his jeep without saying another word. Kip watched as he performed a half-turn before driving back onto the coast road. Kip didn't speak until he was entirely out of sight.

'When Senator Bramnik was last here,' said Kip, 'he mentioned that the people responsible for hoisting Merritt on us are the same ones advocating we search for another Hypersphere.'

'We're watching him closely, sir,' said Howes. 'Randall Pimms and Oskar Boche are already on Delta Twenty-Five. If Merritt really is taking any unauthorised trips there, we'll know about it soon enough.'

'Good.' Kip adjusted his tie and nodded to the Major. 'I'll leave you to it, then.'

Howes nodded. 'Sir.'

Kip got back in his own jeep and guided it onto the coast road, driving south. His hands tightened on the wheel: that anyone in Washington could be so idiotic as to want to retrieve another Hypersphere...! The thought alone was enough to chill his blood, and further proof, were it needed, that there were forces back on his home alternate willing to risk everything in order to acquire one of the devices.

Before long, he entered the island's single town, most of it as abandoned and ramshackle as the day explorers from his own universe had found it. The low, dark slopes of Rano Kau rose above the rooftops, while the corrugated iron roof of the main transfer hangar was just visible past the old air strip. Closer to hand stood the original research station built for Katya Orlova, now superseded by the far larger facility on the Authority's home alternate.

Strange as it was, Kip had come to regard this island, as desolate as it was, as his home. It tore at his heart to think of finally abandoning it, even though the increasing number of red tides showed that, soon enough, they must. As for Randall, Oskar and the rest of the Pathfinders, rendered largely obsolete by Orlova and her stage-building *nous*, he couldn't help but fear what might become of them once the settlement of Nova Terra began in earnest.

He drove past dusty palm trees lining roads half-overgrown with weeds and dropped the jeep off at a carpool near the docks. He began to walk to Government House, a small, two-story building in a nearby street which had once served as the island's political centre, then stopped beside a jetty. The waves at the island's south-western tip weren't red, but they sparkled as if reflecting starlight—which was strange, given

7

that it was now late in the morning.

Kip stepped onto the jetty to take a closer look. Rather than stars, he realised with horror, the ocean was filled with uncountable dead fish, their iridescent scales reflecting the light of the rising sun.

# Katya

*Experimental Transfer and EM Storage Facility, Old Horse Springs, Authority Home Alternate*

Katya watched from the relative comfort of the arrivals building as the Sikorsky dropped onto the facility's helipad. Colonel Armington, apparently oblivious to the freezing temperatures in his light uniform, stepped up towards the helicopter, holding onto his cap with one hand to keep it from being torn loose by the rotor wash.

Once the ground crew were out of the way, the Colonel greeted each member of the congressional committee and their associated advisors as they disembarked. Apart from the inevitable secret service agents—identifiable not only by their dark suits, but by the way their gazes drank in every detail of their surroundings—Katya noted the presence of several Senators. Typically, she observed with distaste, there was not a single woman amongst them.

Damian Kuzakova, standing next to Katya, pulled his thick wool coat closer around his shoulders and shivered. 'It would be nice,' the physicist said in Russian, 'if you could spare a little of that immense budget of yours on central heating. I feel like my feet are submerged in ice-water.'

Katya glanced sideways at him. 'Some Russian you are,' she replied in English.

Damian made a *brrr* sound. 'Give me sunny days and stupidly elaborate cocktails any day. I still miss that island.' There was a touch of wistfulness to his voice. 'I was never cold once when we were stationed there.'

*Not many cocktails around here*, thought Katya. She couldn't remember the last time she'd been on Easter Island—or rather, the Easter Island that existed on Alternate Alpha Zero, base of operations for the Pathfinder Project. She decided not to remind Damian that her own time there had been markedly less positive and considerably more dramatic.

'What do we know about them?' asked Damian.

'According to Senator Bramnik, we need to keep an eye on Kinnison and Holmes in particular.' She pointed each one out in turn. 'Holmes hates Russians—he assumes we're all spies until proven otherwise. He chairs the congressional oversight committee. Kinnison will act the fool, but he's dangerous.'

A pager on her hip beeped loudly just then. 'More problems?' asked Damian.

Katya suppressed a sigh and glanced around. 'If I can find a phone, I'll tell you.'

'I'll check it out,' said Damian, turning away. 'You have work to do.'

He headed for a wall-phone as Armington guided the delegation in through the entrance. They talked and chattered as they came in from the cold, stamping their feet while their breath misted white. Even though the facility was technically a civilian operation, Katya had quickly found such visits went

10

better if Colonel Armington, who commanded the facility's security deployment, was on hand to greet arrivals.

Katya stepped towards the gaggle of visitors, who were still talking amongst themselves and with Armington. She cleared her throat loudly enough that most of them looked her way. 'I'd like to welcome you all to the Old Horse Springs Experimental Transfer and EM Storage Facility.' She gestured towards Damian, still talking quietly on a phone. 'Over there is my colleague and chief engineer, Damian Kuzakova.' She flashed them all a practised smile. 'And I am Katya Orlova. I know you're all very busy, so I'll be brief. We'll take a tour of the facilities, then break for lunch. After that, if you have any questions, I'll be happy to answer them as best I can.'

A man with thinning hair carefully arranged over his bald patch regarded her through thick-rimmed glasses: Senator Kinnison. 'Thank you,' he said, and gestured towards Damian. 'But if you could rustle up some coffee while we talk to your boss, I'd be very grateful.'

'Actually,' said Damian, turning to look at them with one hand over the mouthpiece of the phone, 'Katya is the Director of Operations for this entire facility. Without her, it wouldn't exist.'

Kinnison chuckled with apparent disbelief. 'Well, that can't be true.' He looked around at his fellow visitors as if seeking their support. 'This little girl can't be out of her twenties!' He turned back to Katya. 'All I'm saying,' he said in the voice of an elderly uncle talking to a child, 'is that it's an awful lot of responsibility for someone so young. If we had someone more senior in charge…'

Katya felt a sudden warmth flow up her neck and into her cheeks. 'I assure you,' she said, carefully brushing down the sleeves of her jacket, 'that I am the only one qualified to be in charge of this facility.'

Kinnison chuckled and shook his head, and she saw smirks on the faces of several others. She opened her mouth to make a retort, then felt Damian's hand close over her arm. 'Perhaps,' he said to the gathered dignitaries, 'we should get started.'

\* \* \*

Katya let Armington take the lead, guiding the oversight committee towards a bank of elevators. She let herself fall to the rear with Damian at her side.

'I really thought you were going to lose your temper there,' Damian said quietly. 'I see what you mean about Kinnison. The man is a snake.'

'Just tell me what the phone call was about,' she said, still seething.

'It seems the South-West Quadrant containment systems suffered a near-breach overnight,' Damian explained, drawing a startled look from Katya. 'Our backup generators took over in time, but if not, the result could have been very nasty indeed. As soon as we're done here, I want to run a full analysis and safety review on all our storage facilities. Something isn't right.'

A *near-breach*. Katya shuddered at the thought: just one-thousandth of a gram of stored anti-matter was sufficient to power a transfer stage for a year—but were it to come into contact with ordinary matter, the result would be devastating.

'We should look into it immediately,' she said, then nodded at the cluster of men up ahead. 'Perhaps that would be a good excuse to cancel this visit.' She started to move towards Armington—it would be better if such news came from him—but Damian caught her arm again and pulled her back.

'Wait,' he said. 'You don't want them thinking anything's gone wrong.'

She regarded him with confusion. 'Things *are* going wrong.'

'And wouldn't that be just the excuse they're obviously looking for to take all this away from you?'

She laughed under her breath. 'Idiots. *Kretin*. I'd like to see them try to run this place without me!'

'Katya, please.' Damian was unable to hide his exasperation. 'Your engineers are entirely capable of dealing with whatever happened, so go ahead and give these people their grand tour so they can be out of our hair that much sooner.'

They started walking again. 'So many of our integral systems are not up to the required standards,' she said. 'And do you know why?'

'Yes,' Damian nodded wearily. 'You have said this many times. They insist on giving construction and design contracts to the—'

'The *lowest bidders*,' she hissed. 'Can you believe these people sent men to the moon on board a craft built by contractors who provided them with the *lowest bids*? And we wonder why our systems fail so often, or turn out to be junk! Why, I—'

Damian touched one finger to his lips and nodded up ahead. Only then did Katya realise she had been getting louder and louder.

'By the way, I've been in touch with Aleksi,' he said under his breath. 'He's spoken to the Chinese. They've already broken ground and they expect to complete construction within nine months.'

Katya nodded. *At last, some good news.* 'What about Brazil?'

'They responded positively. So have Kenya, but it's going to take time before they can begin diverting rare earth shipments without alerting the Americans.'

'Of course,' said Katya. 'We'll speak more of this later, but not here.' She glanced towards the committee members up ahead and smiled to herself: they weren't nearly so much in control as they imagined. 'We should catch up.'

\* \* \*

An enormous cargo elevator carried Katya, Damian and the congressional committee several stories down to a long, well-lit underground tunnel with an arched ceiling. The tunnel stretched into the distance, and formed part of a labyrinth that ran beneath the entire complex, which itself sprawled over fifteen square kilometres. Men and women, some in white coats, moved here and there with apparent purpose.

'Looks like some super-villain's underground lair,' said Senator Holmes. 'Is this really what we're spending all this money on? When are we going to see some actual results?'

'We've been working around the clock to get this facility up to full production capacity for nearly two years now.' Katya spoke in what she hoped were reassuring tones. 'We expect to begin mass production of transfer stages and the fuel necessary to power them within the next six months.'

Holmes regarded her with clear skepticism. 'If you can convince me we aren't just pouring billions into a hole in the ground, maybe I won't worry so much about having a commie in charge.'

That got a few more half-suppressed chuckles. Katya felt

her face grow warm. 'I am neither a communist,' she said, 'nor am I a citizen of the Soviet Union.'

'To be precise,' added Damian, 'Katya comes from an alternate universe where Russia remains under the rule of an imperial Czar.'

It was easy to tell by their glazed expressions who amongst the gathered dignitaries hadn't paid attention during their briefings. 'Well, that's where I get lost,' said Kinnison. 'Other universes! It don't make sense to me, even after I visited Nova Terra last month. If God invented more than one universe, you think he'd have at least *mentioned* it in the Bible.'

'An unfortunate oversight,' Katya agreed, indicating a row of electric carts, some the size of a small bus. 'If we may continue.'

Colonel Armington herded them all aboard several of the carts and took the wheel of the lead vehicle. They soon arrived at one of thirteen cyclotrons used to generate anti-matter as well as other, even more exotic forms of matter necessary to open passageways between universes. Afterwards, they returned to the surface, and Katya caught a glimpse of snow-shrouded mountain peaks through a window. It had been a long, hard winter in New Mexico—the worst so far, according to the climatologists: glaciers had already reclaimed most of Canada along with vast swathes of Northern Europe and Russia, and they were creeping ever faster across the continental United States.

Katya guided them on foot across a factory floor large enough to accommodate a dozen jumbo jets wingtip to wingtip. The ceiling, far overhead, was largely hidden behind a tangled mass of conduits and pipes. Cranes and other lifting gear attached to rails suspended from that same ceiling carried pieces of machinery high above the floor. Kinnison and the other committee members soon found themselves gazing upon a dozen transfer stages in varying degrees of completion, some almost as large as a football field. They were of a modular design, so that once construction had finished each stage could be broken down and shipped to different locations.

'The energy required to power these stages is enormous,' Katya explained. 'Yet the logistics of evacuating most, if not all, of the human race to Nova Terra represents an even greater challenge.' She gestured to Damian. 'Russia, of course, has been extremely cooperative, hence their willingness to lend us their best scientific minds.'

'I was told full evacuation plans had been drawn up for all of the United States,' said Holmes. 'Surely that means any logistical problems have already been solved?'

She stepped towards a completed transfer pylon that towered far overhead and laid one hand against it. It felt cool to the touch, and she felt a very faint vibration from somewhere deep inside it. 'For America, yes—but not for the rest of the world. And beyond that remains the question of housing and feeding so many millions of refugees on a parallel Earth that has none of our infrastructure. The only way to avoid mass starvation and panic is to stage the evacuation over a period of twenty to thirty years.'

'And the cost of all this?' asked Holmes.

Katya felt her muscles tense. 'What we are attempting,' she said, 'is, without doubt, the greatest work of human and social engineering your world has ever seen. This alternate will soon be in the grip of a new ice age, and unless immediate action is taken, hundreds of millions will die and countless species will become extinct. If the *cost* is really your concern, then instead of hoarding all this technology to yourselves, share it with other nations and allow them to build their own stage factories. That way you'd share the financial burden and reduce your costs to a fraction of what they otherwise would be.'

'I can tell you right now,' said Kinnison, 'that President Stanton isn't going to share all this with anyone else.'

'He shared it with the Russians,' Damian pointed out.

'Because this little lady made it a condition of her cooperation,' said Senator Holmes. 'But we can't go handing out technology like this willy-nilly to just anyone who wants it!'

'Wasn't there some classified report,' asked Kinnison, 'about how you'd all found some other machine that could instantly transport people from one universe to the other without digging trillion-dollar holes in the desert?' He glanced around the assorted Senators, advisors and secret service agents with a wide-eyed look. 'I don't see why we can't just go get some more of those.'

'You are referring,' said Katya, 'to the Hypersphere.' She fought to keep her voice level. 'Such devices devastated one civilisation within a few days and nearly wiped out my own. Acquiring a Hypersphere would be tantamount to suicide.' She walked up close to the Senator, her expression fierce. 'Knowledge of its existence requires a high level of clearance—and nobody here but myself and Mr Kuzakov have that level of clearance. May I enquire, Senator Kinnison, as to how you learned of it?'

Before Kinnison could form a reply, a low vibration rolled through the floor beneath their feet. Far off in the distance an alarm began to blare.

She shared a look with Damian, who blinked rapidly then retreated to another wall-phone. He put it against his ear and began to speak urgently into it in Russian.

'What just happened?' asked Holmes, clearly alarmed.

'Perhaps we should head back the way we came.' She looked towards Armington. 'Colonel, can you take care of our visitors?'

Armington nodded. 'Of course.' He turned to the delegation. 'Gentlemen, if you'd please follow me.'

Once they had left, Damian hung the phone back up. 'We've lost contact with the South-West Quadrant,' he said.

'"Lost contact"?' She stared at him. 'Do you mean communications are down, or...?'

'No idea,' Damian replied, his face drawn. 'But we need to evacuate the entire facility until we know just what we're dealing with.'

Katya nodded, her lips pressed tight together. 'Do it.'

'It's already done, Katya.'

She nodded again and pushed a hand through her hair. 'I need to get to the Comms building, coordinate from there. Otherwise I'd feel like a captain abandoning his ship.'

'We're not at fucking sea.' Damian had to shout as a series of voice alerts echoed out across the shop floor. All around them, engineers either shut down their machines or abandoned their posts. Another vibration rolled through the floor, much stronger this time.

'Come on,' said Katya, grabbing Damian's arm. The rumbling grew in volume as they hurried towards the nearest emergency exit. Just before they reached it, the ground lurched hard, followed by a thunderous boom that left her ears singing.

Katya glanced towards a nearby window, seeing a column of dust and flame reaching high into the sky where the South-

West Quadrant had been. *Containment breach*, she thought, her belly squirming with horror. She turned to Damian, who stared slack-jawed out through the glass.

'Run!' she shouted, grabbing hold of him and tugging him once more towards the emergency exit. Her own words sounded muffled to her ears.

Then the ground rocked beneath them with such force that she lost her footing and fell on all fours. She struggled to get back upright, and glanced upwards in time to see cracks spidering across the factory ceiling and growing wider. She turned to shout a warning to Damian just as the building came tumbling down on top of them both.

# Randall

*Alternate Delta Twenty-Five*

'No sign of them yet,' said Randall, squinting through his binoculars. 'Maybe they're running late.'

'Maybe Kip made a mistake and they're not on their way here at all,' grouched Oskar. He crouched next to Randall, peering across a wide, sunlit glade from behind the cover of long grass. 'Could be we're sitting here wasting our time.' He rubbed at his ankle and groaned. 'Now my damn foot's gone to sleep.'

On the far side of the glade from them, a huge, rectangular and ancient stone structure rose up from amidst a dense and alien-looking forest. Its exterior walls were covered in intricate carvings, all of them entirely incomprehensible to the two men. Other ruins were murkily visible in the distance, thanks to shafts of light that found their way through the forest canopy. An opening set in the side of the building facing them was wide and tall enough a transcontinental truck could drive through it. Beyond the opening, a passageway sloped down into unlit subterranean depths.

Randall dropped his binoculars back down around his neck and gazed fixedly at the building as if trying to make sense of its carvings. 'Quit whining,' he said. 'I don't like being here any more than you.'

'I'm just tired of waiting,' Oskar sighed. He pulled out a dark cloth and used it to mop away sweat. 'And it's too damn hot. All I'm saying is that it'd be easier to set the girls on patrol here.'

'Bad idea,' said Randall. 'Can't interrogate a corpse.' For about the thousandth time, he glanced up at the tree from beneath which they kept a watchful eye on the building—although maybe *tree* wasn't the right word; it looked more like an overgrown seaweed stalk, with whiplike branches and leaves that, when seen out of the corner of one's vision, resembled nothing so much as long, tapering claws. The way they moved in even the slightest breeze made it look like they were reaching out to grab you.

Oskar, despite Randall's reservations, had insisted there was no such thing as a man-eating tree in this alternate or any other they'd yet visited. Randall had pointed out that, well, Oskar wasn't a goddamn botanist, so what did *he* know? So they had argued about that for a while, at least in part because seven hours sitting in this weird-ass forest with nobody's company but each other was enough to drive both of them batshit crazy.

In the end, Oskar won the argument and they both remained hidden next to what still looked one helluva lot to Randall's unpracticed eye like a man-eating tree, were such things to exist. By way of reassuring himself, and in case the damn thing made a move on him, he kept his pistol holster unbuttoned.

It didn't help any either that everything was the wrong colour. The grass was pastel blue and the sky a shade of

21

bilious green. Every now and then, as if to emphasise just how far from home they both were, clusters of tiny airborne creatures that looked an awful lot like toy balloons drifted through the glade. Closer inspection revealed veiny bubbles with minuscule, wiry bodies suspended beneath each by a thin cord of gristle.

'Hang on,' said Oskar, peering through the long grass. 'I think I heard something.'

Randall groaned. 'You said that ten times already and there wasn't a damn thing.' He lifted his binoculars back up regardless and peered at the building. He felt a surge of shock on seeing half a dozen men, all in camouflage gear and all carrying rifles, emerge from around the side of the structure. They had torches zip-tied or duct-taped to the barrels of their weapons.

Oskar rose up just high enough he could lift a long-lens camera to one eye and start taking pictures.

The voices of the men drifted across the glade as they walked purposefully towards the building's shadowy maw. They came to a halt, and Randall heard the crackle of a walkie-talkie. The men scanned the glade around them, and Randall and Oskar both hunkered back down.

Randall peered at them through the long grass, his hands trembling from excitement or fear or maybe both. They were all armed with rifles, except for one guy with what looked like an M24—a US Army sniper rifle. He couldn't be sure, because it had some kind of weird modifications to the barrel like nothing he'd ever seen.

The men spread out and began hunting through the glade.

'Maybe they're looking for us,' Oskar whispered urgently. 'Maybe somebody tipped them off we were here.'

'Don't be ridiculous,' Randall whispered back. 'Only ones know we're here are you and me and Kip.'

'If they get too close,' said Oskar, touching a bracelet-like device on his wrist, 'I'm calling in the girls.'

One of the men approached to within a few metres of their hiding place. He peered up into the branches of the tree beneath which they hid like he was looking for something. Then he turned and walked back the way he'd come, stopping at each tree and peering up into their dense foliage. He stopped at one in particular, hanging his rifle over his shoulder by its strap and reaching up to a branch. He pulled himself up off the ground and started to climb.

Randall tried to keep an eye on him, but there was too much foliage in the way. He belly crawled around the far side of his own tree until he could clearly see where the other man had settled on top of a wide branch. Fortunately, he was looking the other way, so couldn't see the two of them down below. The man took hold of a video camera that Oskar had placed there weeks before, its lens angled so it had a clear view of the building entrance. He opened it up, removing its memory card and replacing it with another. Then he closed the camera back up and replaced it precisely where he had found it.

By the time he had climbed back down, his compatriots had all returned to the building entrance. He went to join them.

Randall crawled back over next to Oskar and told him what he'd seen. 'Well, that clinches that,' said Oskar. 'There wasn't a glitch in the footage at all. He must have swapped the memory card for one with footage of the glade with nobody around.'

'Told you we should have used one of those micro-cameras we found on Kappa Sixty-Seven,' said Randall. 'Remember them? They look like goddamned flies, tiny things with wings

23

that can land on your finger. No way they'd have found one of those.'

'And I told *you* the Authority have their heads up their ass about tech from other alternates,' Oskar growled back. 'We shoulda stole some and kept them for ourselves.'

They waited several more minutes before an open-top truck with huge tires came rumbling out of the forest from the same direction the men had come. It pulled up outside the building entrance and all of the foot-soldiers climbed on board. It then drove inside the building, tilting downwards as it disappeared down the steep incline, its headlights illuminating the tunnel's roof. Randall waited as Oskar snapped more pictures.

Oskar stood and stretched once he'd finished. 'Any sign of Merritt amongst them?' asked Randall, standing to join him.

Oskar shook his head. 'Not that I could see. But looked to me like there were a couple of guys inside the truck. Couldn't see well enough to make out their faces.'

'The main thing,' said Randall, 'is now we have pictures—and proof they've been screwing with our cameras.'

Oskar sucked his teeth. 'Except Kip needs proof that Merritt is involved. A bunch of snapshots of random grunts isn't going to prove that.'

'But it's *something*.'

Oskar regarded his friend carefully. 'It's not enough to prove he's been sneaking around alternates he's got no business being on.' He glanced towards the building entrance. 'Although I guess we could follow them down there and see if he comes out of that truck.'

'Risky,' said Randall. 'What if we get caught?'

'Let's try not to.' Oskar patted his camera. 'This takes infrared as well. If Merritt is down there, we can get the

24

proof.'

Randall made a face. 'Fuck it. I'm willing if you are.' He looked around, feeling an urgent need. 'One second—gotta take a leak.'

He wandered back around the far side of the tree and unzipped, grunting with pleasure as he emptied his bladder. Vast, cyclopean ruins, shrouded in vines and dark masses of vegetation, loomed in the forest depths. Delta Twenty-Five, he thought, not for the first time, would make a terrific location for a horror movie.

Something moved through the branches overhead just as he zipped himself back up, sending leaves and debris tumbling down. The fading sunlight streaked red through the foliage and, as he looked up, it revealed the outline of a beast at least three meters in length. Dagger-like spikes lined its spine, and its tail twitched back and forth like a cat. Branches and leaves were blurrily visible through its semi-translucent body.

It opened wide, reptilian jaws, and leapt.

Randall threw himself to one side with a shriek as the Chimera landed close to where he had been standing, a foul stench emerging from deep within its gullet. Then Oskar was there, hissing at the creature, even as it towered above them both.

'*Bad* Veronica,' Oskar shouted at it, his voice full of outrage. '*Bad* Veronica—don't go sneaking up on Uncle Randall like that!'

'God*damn* it!' shouted Randall. 'Will you *please* keep the damn things under control!'

'Keep your panties on,' Oskar snapped, touching his fingers to the bracelet on his left wrist. Immediately, the Chimera sank down until its huge head rested on its forepaws. 'She's not going to hurt you,' said Oskar, tapping the bracelet and grinning. 'Not unless I tell her to, anyway.'

Randall's heart was still beating at a hundred miles an hour. 'I really thought the damn thing was going to attack me this time!'

Oskar scowled at him. 'I told you, Randall—you need to take more lessons in how to control them. You've seen me do it: being scared of them is just ridiculous once you know how to talk to them.'

'You know I don't—' he paused momentarily, seeing the Chimera's gaze swivel towards him '—*like* the damn beasts,' he hissed. 'And where the hell is the other one!'

'Betty?' Oskar glanced around. 'Somewhere nearby, I guess.'

Randall sometimes thought Oskar had forgotten just how horrifying their first encounters with the two beasts had been. The Chimeras were semi-biological entities native to Delta Twenty-Five, created by whomever—or whatever—had also constructed the vine-drowned city amidst whose ruins they stood. As killing machines, they were enormously efficient: indeed, they had slaughtered a considerable number of people before Oskar had stumbled across the mechanism by which they could be controlled. And ever since Oskar's dog Lucky had passed away of an aneurysm, the Pathfinder had effectively adopted the two Chimeras as pets.

Enormous, terrifying pets that could turn invisible and rend you limb from limb before you even knew they were there.

'Let's just get moving,' Randall muttered, grabbing up his backpack from where he'd left it hidden in the long grass.

Oskar did the same, and they jogged across the glade. Soft, warm air gusted up from deep inside the tunnel entrance like the breath of some enormous sleeping animal.

* * *

The two Pathfinders kept to one side of the tunnel as they made their way down, and it wasn't long before Randall's shoulders ached from the weight of his backpack. The two Chimeras followed behind, and Randall tried hard to forget the close proximity of his throat to their dagger-like fangs.

It took them fifteen minutes to reach the bottom of the sloping tunnel, where it opened out into a cavernous, high-roofed chamber filled with ancient machinery. Some kind of bioluminescent bacteria in the cavern ceiling gave off a faint green glow just barely bright enough to allow the two Pathfinders to navigate. Up ahead, from far across the cavern, they heard the rumble of a truck's engine.

The chamber was so crowded with engines of unknown purpose that it afforded them plenty of shadowy nooks and crannies in which to hide as they crept closer. A faint vibration through their boot soles suggested the continuing activity of yet more machines, in yet deeper chambers somewhere far beneath them. There were doors which might lead to those lower chambers, except nobody had yet found a way to open them. There had been attempts to cut them open with plasma torches, or even explosives to blow a hole open, but for all their efforts the doors had been barely scratched.

Even so, they could both see one of these doors illuminated by the truck's twin headlights.

Randall and Oskar jogged through the darkness, taking care not to go crashing into anything as they headed towards the truck. Soon, they could hear voices from just ahead, and slowed down before creeping cautiously forward.

They stepped around the side of some ancient machine and

saw three doors in a row set into the cavern wall, each one twice as tall as a man and hexagonal in shape. The doors were coloured the same dull bronze as many of the machines populating the chamber around them.

The truck had been parked in a narrow alleyway formed by the gap between two neighbouring machines. Randall and Oskar watched from nearby in the shadows as three figures disembarked from the truck and walked up to the middle door. Two of them played their torches across the door, illuminating it.

Randall lifted his binoculars. The torch light was just enough to allow him to get a good look at the third man, who wore a dark-coloured suit of the type favoured by Authority bureaucrats and politicians. Randall immediately recognised him as Preston Merritt. He'd met him just the one time, after Merritt had been made Kip's second-in-command. He watched as Merritt stepped up close to the door, pressing a hand against it and turning to say something to the two soldiers accompanying him.

'Got your camera ready?' Randall whispered to Oskar.

Oskar had crouched down to change lenses and stood up again, placing the camera against his eye. 'I wonder what they're up to,' he muttered as he took several pictures with an infra-red lens. 'They don't think they can actually get through that door, do they?'

Randall glanced back towards the truck. Several of the soldiers stood next to it, apparently poring over what could only be a map, spread out over the vehicle's hood. One of these men then turned to point towards a long line of metal cradles situated not far from the doors. All of the cradles were empty, except for one that held the shattered remains of a

Hypersphere.

Randall grinned to himself. *Talk about red-handed.* If Merritt really believed he could find a way through that door, it was almost certainly because he thought there might be an intact Hypersphere somewhere beyond it.

Oskar lowered his camera as Merritt and his companion quickly returned to the truck. 'What the hell are they up to?' he muttered. 'Ain't nothing short of a nuke's going to get through that door, and even then I wouldn't bet on it.'

Another of the waiting soldiers got into the back of the truck and began tossing out white bundles to one of his compatriots, who passed them out to the rest. Soon, Merritt and all the rest of them were dressed in baggy white costumes with hoods and clear visors. ABC suits, Randall reckoned—the ABC standing for Atomic, Biological and Chemical.

Something sour roiled deep inside Randall's belly. The soldier with the weirdly modified sniper rifle had hunkered down on top of a nearby machine, while all of the others went and crouched behind the truck, covering their heads with their arms and hands.

'What's with those damn suits?' whispered Oskar. 'They look like they're waiting for some kind of nuclear explosion or—'

An idea hit Randall with such force it nearly drove the air from out of his lungs. He grabbed Oskar by the shoulder, dragging him back into the shadows and further from the cavern door.

A roar filled the air loud enough that Randall could feel its pressure beating on his ear drums like an angry husband trying to break down a motel-room door. He opened his mouth and yelled, but his own voice was lost in the chaos. He clamped his hands over his ears and squeezed his eyes shut against overwhelming brightness.

The ground swayed beneath them hard enough Randall thought for a moment the cavern was about to collapse. He coughed hard, his lungs full of smoke and gritty ash that burned. For a moment, he couldn't see and could hardly hear, although he was vaguely aware of Oskar beside him shouting something that sounded tinny and distant to his ears.

Eventually the light faded, but it was still bright enough that Randall could see his surroundings much more clearly, despite the smoke and debris.

A new light shone in his eyes and he blinked, putting a hand up to shield his face. The light moved away again, and he heard a shout.

Randall blinked, his eyes tearing from the dust, and realised that the light of the explosion had placed him and Oskar in plain view of the men crouched down behind the truck. One of them was shining a torch on them.

Randall still couldn't hardly think straight, but he had the wherewithal to reach for his pistol.

Several shots echoed across the cavern. Beside him, Oskar staggered backwards, red blossoming on his shirt. His camera went tumbling from his grasp.

One of the shots pinged off a machine next to Randall's head. Randall froze, his pistol still halfway out of its holster.

Two of Merritt's men appeared right in front of him and Oskar, shouting something he still couldn't quite make out. The view he had of the wide bore of their weapons, however, spoke far more eloquently than words ever could. He let the pistol fall to the floor of the cavern.

He glanced down at Oskar. With immeasurable relief, he

saw that his friend was still alive, although he clearly had a bad shoulder wound. He was leaning sideways against one of the machines, a hand clamped over the afflicted arm. He looked up at Randall, his face bright with sweat, and gave him a sharp nod.

Shoulder wounds weren't necessarily fatal, but the sooner Oskar got attended to, the better.

One of the soldiers kicked Randall's pistol out of reach. The light had faded to a dull red, and the air still tasted of burning smoke and ash. After-images danced across his vision, but rapidly faded.

He looked back over at the hexagonal door. To his amazement, the machinery that had been closest to it had been destroyed. The door was still largely intact, but now, he saw, a huge crack had opened in it, growing from a narrow line near its top to a gap wide enough at its base that a man could easily pass through it. After another moment he also realised the dull heat he could feel down one side was coming from the door, although its temperature seemed to be dropping.

How, he wondered, could a sniper rifle do something everyone thought was impossible?

One of the figures in white stepped towards them and the soldiers moved out of the way. Randall saw through the clear plastic visor that it was Preston Merritt. He stared at Randall for several moments until recognition sparked in his eyes.

'Randall Pimms,' he said, his voice slightly muffled by his hood. He peered down at Oskar. 'And you must be…Oskar Boche?'

Oskar didn't say a word. Merritt nodded and shifted his gaze back to Randall. 'You're Pathfinders, right? I think we met one time. Now how about you tell me what the hell you're doing creeping around down here like a couple of spies?'

'None of your damn business,' Randall spat. 'And I ain't saying one more thing until you do something to help Oskar. There was no reason for you to shoot at us.'

'You're not supposed to be here,' Oskar grunted. 'This place is off-limits to everyone.'

'Then I guess neither of you are supposed to be here either, are you?' said Merritt.

'Sir?' said one of the soldiers. 'They had this with them.' He passed Oskar's camera to Merritt, who studied it for a moment before handing it back to the soldier.

'Destroy it,' he told the soldier. 'And make sure you also destroy any memory cards inside it.'

The soldier fiddled with the camera until a memory card popped out of a slot. He snapped the card in two, then dropped the camera on the ground before smashing it with the butt of his rifle.

'The only reason for you to be sneaking around down here,' said Randall, 'is if you're looking for a Hypersphere.'

'And only a lunatic would go looking for one,' added Oskar, strain showing in his voice. 'We've seen what happens when a Hypersphere gets used. *This* happens,' he said, indicating the chamber around them with his chin. 'Or didn't you ever wonder what happened to the people that built all this?'

'I wonder if either of you,' asked Merritt, 'are aware of the accident that took place at Miss Orlova's stage-building facility?'

Randall frowned. 'Sure we heard. What about it?'

'I hear Miss Orlova's recovering in hospital,' said Merritt, 'but nearly a quarter of her facility was destroyed. It's set the Authority's evacuation program back by years. I know what

32

the Hypersphere can do if it's mishandled, but that doesn't mean the same thing would happen if we found another one. And under the circumstances, we badly need one, or a lot of people are going to die.'

'If you manage to find one,' Oskar grunted, 'dying is the one thing that's guaranteed to happen.'

'For God's sake, help him!' Randall shouted. 'He could bleed to death if that bullet hit an artery.'

Merritt put up a finger to shush him. 'You've visited my home alternate, haven't you, Mister Boche?'

'Once,' Oskar admitted. 'It's been a few years.'

'America—*our* America, on our alternate—is facing a new ice age. Whole cities have already been ground to dust. The projections of the number of fatalities if we don't act decisively and quickly to evacuate our civilian population to a new alternate are staggering. Tell me, Mister Boche, if you could get your hands on a device that could solve all your problems in an instant, wouldn't you be just a little bit tempted?'

Oskar said nothing. Randall had the sense he was breathing with difficulty. He opened his mouth to say something more, then noticed that Oskar's right hand was draped over his other arm in such a way that it touched the bracelet on his left wrist, his fingers moving in barely discernible but long-practiced patterns.

'No, he wouldn't,' said Randall, his voice flat and dismissive. 'And neither would anyone else with a shred of goddamn sanity. Why waste time, Merritt? We know you're going to kill us.'

'I don't want to,' said Merritt. 'Fortunately, there are alternatives.'

Randall exchanged a look with Oskar. 'Such as?'

Merritt shrugged. 'It's true I can't let you go back to that island,' he said, 'but there's no reason I can see why you shouldn't work for me instead.'

Randall couldn't help but laugh. 'And why the hell would we do that? Don't you think Kip and the rest of them would get to wondering what happened to us if we never went back there?'

Merritt shrugged. 'He won't be around for much longer, and neither will your Pathfinder friends.' He looked between the two of them. 'This way, you don't end up the same way they will.'

Oskar's fingers stopped moving for a second. 'What do you mean, exactly?'

Merritt looked down at him. 'For one, that precious island of yours is soon going to become just as uninhabitable as the rest of the alternate it belongs to. And there are plans to shut the Pathfinder Project down, probably within weeks.'

Randall stared at him, stunned.

'No way,' said Oskar, his voice full of scorn despite his injury. 'Kip wouldn't keep something like that back from us.'

'How many curfews have you had in the last six months?' asked Merritt. 'It's getting like you have to go into hiding every time it rains. It's as good as uninhabitable already, and the fact is you're all excess to requirements now Orlova's given us the means to build our own transfer stages.' He nodded towards the half-cracked door, which no longer glowed with heat. 'But I know how skilled you people are in environments like this. You help me find a working Hypersphere, and the both of you can name your price.'

'No,' Oskar muttered.

Randall shook his head. 'Same goes for me.'

34

Merritt stared down at them with undisguised contempt.

'Sir?' A soldier came running over from where some of them had been investigating the door. 'The door's not hot any more—in fact, it's already cool to the touch. Private Ross just walked through the crack and took a look around. It seems like there's more machinery back there, same as here.'

Merritt glanced towards the cracked door. 'Remarkable.' He turned back to Oskar and Randall. 'I think maybe the two of you need a little more time to think about what you're saying.' He pointed to two soldiers in turn. 'Marcus, Grant. Stay here and keep an eye on them until we get back. We're going to do a quick reconnoitre and see what we can find.'

Merritt and the rest of the soldiers left the truck where it was and headed towards the cracked door. 'Hey!' Randall yelled after them. 'What about Oskar? He's in bad shape!'

Merritt stopped and turned. 'That's up to you,' he called back. 'Have you changed your minds?'

Randall said nothing, his face full of barely withheld fury.

'That's what I thought,' said Merritt, turning away again.

Merritt and the soldiers accompanying him had to squeeze through the crack in the door one after the other, leaving Randall and Oskar alone with their two guards.

'So what's with that fancy gun you used on the door?' Randall asked one of them.

'How about you shut up?' the soldier replied. 'Wouldn't upset me at all to put a bullet in both your heads.'

'That,' mumbled Oskar, 'would be an awesomely bad idea, asshole.'

The second soldier frowned at him. 'Say what?'

'All that noise you and your buddies made,' Oskar explained. 'I'm thinking you woke something up.'

'What the fuck is he talking about?' said the first soldier.

'There's more down here than a bunch of artefacts,' said Oskar. 'There's something alive, and it eats people.'

The second soldier scowled. 'Bullshit.'

'You must have heard the stories,' Oskar continued. He coughed, then winced at the pain in his shoulder. 'People torn limb from limb. One time, something on this alternate killed a whole bunch of people over at Site A. When their relief came through, they found nothing but blood and guts scattered all over the place like they'd been butchered by something insane.'

'If there was anything like that,' said the second soldier, 'we'd have known about it already.'

'Hey, Marcus,' said the first soldier. 'I *did* hear a story about something like that.'

Marcus glared at him. 'Are you just completely fucking stupid?'

'I'm just saying,' said Oskar, 'because I'm sure I heard something moving around while me and Randall were keeping an eye on you folks.'

Marcus's expression shifted from contempt to anger. 'Now you're pissing me off.'

Randall glanced down and sideways at Oskar. If Merritt or any of the rest of them had bothered to pay enough attention, they might have seen the way he stroked the bracelet on his left wrist with precise and careful movements. For the first time he was glad the caverns were as dark as they were.

'I heard something too,' said Randall, returning his attention to the two guards. 'Just now.'

Marcus took a step towards him, his expression darkening. 'Why don't you the two of you just shut the f—'

Randall heard a soft *thump* from somewhere close by in the

36

darkness, followed by a low, drawn-out growl.

The second soldier—Grant—swung his rifle around, the beam from the torch duct-taped to his rifle flashing across dust-laden machinery. 'The fuck?'

Randall shot another quick glance at Oskar. His lips were twitching, forming subvocalised commands. Oskar had worked hard to teach those same commands to Randall, but the Chimeras just creeped him out too goddamn much.

Both guards were swinging their rifles to and fro, and appeared, at least for the moment, to have forgotten about their prisoners. Grant made a sound in the back of his throat when his torch revealed the outline of one of the Chimeras: he fired at it, the noise abrupt and overwhelming in the silent darkness.

The Chimera leapt upwards and back out of sight. Randall pushed himself upright and threw himself at Grant, slamming the soldier's head against the side of a machine. He slumped, groaning to the ground.

Then Randall turned, only to find Marcus's rifle aimed straight at his heart, his finger whitening on the trigger.

Something flowed out of the dark and crashed into Marcus, sending his rifle spinning out of sight. The chimera took hold of the soldier's head and upper shoulders in its jaws and shook him like a terrier shaking a rat. It dropped him again, and he lay unmoving in the dust and ashes.

Randall snatched up Marcus's rifle and swung it around so he could shine its torch on Oskar. He looked far too pale for comfort, and he was slumped to one side against a thing that looked like a giant-sized radiator, but he was still sliding his fingers across that goddamn bracelet and muttering things to himself, his eyes focused on something that Randall couldn't see.

Randall heard one of the two Chimeras pad up behind him, making snuffling noises. Its warm breath touched the back of his neck and he fought the urge to run.

'See?' Oskar croaked. 'Just a little practice pays off.'

Randall knelt next to Grant and checked his pulse. He was breathing, but unconscious. His head was dark with blood where it had hit the side of the machine, but he wasn't going to die of his injuries. Probably.

'We need to move,' said Randall, standing back up. 'They didn't go that far. Chances are they heard the shooting and they're on their way back.'

'That weird-looking rifle,' Oskar mumbled. 'I don't think they took it with them. We need to take it back with us.'

Randall didn't argue. He ran over to the truck and glanced inside the cabin: the rifle they'd used to blow a hole in the cavern door was lying right there.

*Idiots.* He pulled the door of the truck open, grabbed the rifle and dropped back down. A quick glance towards the cracked cavern door revealed the light from approaching torches.

Randall briefly contemplated using the nuclear-or-whatever-the-hell-it-was rifle to blow either them or the truck to smithereens, but until he had some idea how it worked he didn't want to run the risk of blowing himself up instead. Instead he used the regular rifle he'd taken from Grant and Marcus and shot some holes in the truck's tires.

The sound of the shots echoed loudly through the cavern. *Well, if they didn't know something was up before, they sure as hell know now.*

Randall shouldered the nuclear whatsit rifle and kept the conventional one in his other hand so he could use the torch to find his way. 'C'mon,' he said, hurrying back over to Oskar and taking hold of him by his uninjured shoulder. 'Time we got out of here.'

Oskar nodded, his skin damp with sweat and blood and his face pale enough the sight of it stabbed at Randall's heart. Even so, he managed to get himself upright with a little help. 'I set the chimeras on patrol,' he managed to croak. 'That'll slow the fuckers down.'

Seeing Marcus all chewed up like he'd got into a fight with a shark would probably give them pause too, thought Randall. He switched the torch off and oriented himself by a faint grey patch amidst the darkness that revealed the location of the tunnel leading back to the surface. Adrenaline gave him the energy he needed to get moving fast, even with Oskar leaning heavily against him. The fact that Oskar didn't utter one word of complaint was a strong indicator of just how badly he was hurt.

'You okay there, buddy?' Randall asked as they hurried along.

'Need to rest,' said Oskar, the words barely comprehensible.

'Gonna get you some sexy nurses, Oskar,' Randall panted. 'Gonna have a hell of a party in the hospital.'

'Sure.' Oskar made a grunting noise that might have been a laugh. 'An' maybe some tequila.'

He could hear Merritt and the others somewhere behind them, shouting to each other. Their truck grumbled into life, the roar of its engine loud and terrifying in the darkened spaces.

A moment later it crunched to a halt, followed by more shouts. Then came a long, echoing animal screech, followed by sporadic gunfire, followed, in turn, by very human-sounding screams.

'Veronica,' said Oskar, his breath intermittent and warm on Randall's neck. 'Good girl.'

'Just keep moving,' said Randall. The tunnel entrance looked closer now. *One foot after the other, buddy*, he told himself. *Easy as pie.* And who'd have thought a skinny little runt like Oskar could weigh so damn much?

Somehow, someway, they got to the bottom of the tunnel, the sound of gunfire and screaming and animal roaring fading behind them. It was dark outside now; Randall could see stars up past the tunnel entrance.

Behind them, the tunnel lit up the way it had when Merritt blew a hole in the door. A sound like thunder rolled across the chamber, sending dust and debris blowing past them.

This time, Randall wasn't blinded because he'd been looking the other way. But he still felt the heat of the explosion on his skin.

'No,' Oskar muttered. 'Veronica. *No.*'

It didn't make sense. They'd stolen the damn fancy-pants sniper rifle. So how could there be another explosion like that unless…?

Unless they had more than one of the damn things with them.

Randall resumed his march up the tunnel with renewed vigour. 'What did you say there?'

'Veronica.' Oskar's body shook like he was weeping. 'The sons of bitches done killed her.'

'Killed…?' Randall tried to process this. 'Wait a minute. Those things are unkillable.'

'Yeah, well,' said Oskar, 'I guess maybe we were wrong about that.'

'What about the other one?'

'Betty's fine,' said Oskar. 'I pulled her back. I...I don't want them to get her.'

Randall was vaguely aware of Oskar pushing something into his pocket, but he didn't stop to ask what he was doing. They were two-thirds of the way back up the tunnel now: nearly a home run.

Blast it, why was the last stretch always the hardest?

Somehow, though, they made it. Randall glanced back, and saw torchlight flickering at the base of the tunnel.

'Come *on,* you asshole,' said Randall, his legs stiff and feeling like rods of burning iron. He gulped at the damp, warm air and kept going, practically dragging Oskar across the glade to where they'd hidden their own truck back amongst the trees.

Randall said a silent prayer to the gods of hiding stuff when he saw the truck was still right where he'd left it. He laid Oskar down on the grass next to it just long enough to yank the side-door open and load Oskar into the passenger seat. His heart plummeted at the sight of him in the moonlight: his friend was breathing, but only just.

Randall got him strapped in, then closed the door and ran around the other side of the truck, getting in behind the wheel. 'That'll show those assholes, huh?' he said, but Oskar, slumped beside him, said nothing.

Something terrible was worming its way into Randall's thoughts, but he ignored it. His hand shook as he punched the ignition, but the engine caught immediately and he backed them out of there fast.

The truck was one of the multi-environment jobs the Authority liked to use, with big fat tyres in front and caterpillar tracks in the back—way more practical for this kind of terrain even than the one Merritt had been using. 'Hey,' said Randall, 'what he said about them closing down the Pathfinder Project. You think it's true?'

No answer. 'I mean, I'd like to think it's bullshit, except I can't think of one damn reason for him to make up a story like that.' He reached out and patted Oskar on his shoulder. 'Hey, don't you worry. We'll be back home in no time.'

He drove fast, not wanting to give one of Merritt's men long enough to blow them halfway to heaven with one of the atomic rifles. Randall talked the whole trip back to the transfer stage without getting any kind of response. From time to time he beat the dashboard with his fist, driving the truck so hard he nearly wrecked it a couple of times.

Then he saw it: the transfer stage, next to the ruins of an ancient flying machine made out of some kind of plastic or resin that didn't rust or fall apart. He drove the truck up onto the stage's platform, then jumped out and got the transfer process started.

He hurried back over next to the truck and waited next to it as Alternate Delta Twenty-Five faded from sight and another transfer hangar, back on Alternate Alpha One, materialised in its place. He pulled the truck's passenger-side door open and got Oskar in a fireman's carry before running down the transfer stage's ramp.

'Emergency!' he yelled, seeing Fred Danks, one of Major Howes men, at the stage controls.

After that, things got hazy. They took Oskar away on a stretcher, and he heard someone say they were going to medevac Oskar back to the Authority's alternate. Randall wanted to go with him but they wouldn't let him.

'Hey,' said Danks, holding him back as Oskar was stretchered

42

onto a transfer stage and zapped to a waiting ambulance a universe away. 'You need to be in the clinic. You look like you're about to keel right over.'

'I'm fine,' said Randall, even though he knew he wasn't. But he let Danks and a couple of others lead him out into the sunlight and into a jeep. They drove him to the island's solitary clinic and a doctor, a young Brazilian guy, looked him over.

Then he remembered Oskar had shoved something into his pocket. He reached in and fished it out: the control bracelet for the Chimeras.

# Kip

*University of New Mexico Hospital, Authority Home
Alternate*

'I see you're keeping yourself busy,' Kip said from the open
door.

Katya looked up from her wheelchair and smiled with
pleasure when she saw him. 'Oh, no more than usual,' she
said, dropping a notebook back onto her lap. 'You just caught
me in time.'

Kip saw several more notebooks scattered across the top of
the private room's bed where Katya could reach them easily.
He also noted copies of confidential reports piled on a bedside
table, and a stack of reference books on the room's single chair.
A small wheeled suitcase sat next to the door.

'You're going somewhere?' he asked, nodding at the suitcase.

'As a matter of fact, I just signed my release form,' she said.
'I just have to wait until there's someone available to wheel
me out of here.'

'So...you're all right? They told me downstairs they were
treating you for concussion.'

'*Suspected* concussion,' she corrected him. 'That's why they kept me in for a second night.' She rapped her knuckles on the thick plaster cast immobilising her right leg from the thigh down to the ankle. 'I was lucky. It could have been very much worse.'

'Indeed.' Kip had spent much of that morning reading the preliminary casualty reports from the Old Horse Springs facility. There had been six fatalities and nearly three times that number injured. Many, like Katya, had suffered nothing more than concussions and broken bones. Others had more life-changing injuries. Even so, she was right about one thing: she had been lucky. Given the severity of the accident, the cost to human life could have been much higher.

He stepped back towards the door and spoke briefly to the secret service agent standing guard in the corridor outside. 'I want you to make sure we're undisturbed.'

The agent nodded. 'Sir.'

Kip closed the door, shutting off the noise of a busy hospital. He stepped up towards the single visitor's chair and indicated the pile of reference books. 'If I may...?'

'Oh!' said Katya. 'Of course.'

Kip swept the books up, carefully placing them on the bed along with everything else.

'Here,' he said, taking a seat and opening a briefcase he had brought with him. He took out an envelope and passed it to her. 'It's for you.'

She slid a card out of the envelope and opened it, then laughed with delight. 'A *get well* card!' She looked over at him, her smile broader than ever. 'How wonderful.'

'Everyone we could find on the island you might possibly know signed it,' said Kip, putting the briefcase on the floor.

'All of the Pathfinders I could track down, plus most of the science staff you worked with when you were still stationed there.'

'This is delightful,' she said with sincerity, 'and so very kind.'

'They're treating you well?'

'I feel like an honoured guest.' Her smile became a touch uneasy. 'To be honest, after what happened, I thought they might throw me in a dungeon…'

He shook his head firmly. 'That's not going to happen.' Not that there weren't some in Washington who were willing to do exactly that. The cost of rebuilding even part of the Old Horse Springs Exotic Materials Research Facility was certain to be prohibitively expensive. It had taken some deft manoeuvring by both Kip and Senator Bramnik to keep the wolves at bay in the wake of the disaster.

'And Damian…?' she asked. 'After they dug me out of the rubble, I kept asking about him. Nobody would tell me anything.'

'He's alive,' Kip reassured her. He hesitated before continuing. 'But he got hurt worse than you did.'

Her expression stiffened, and she suddenly looked much older than her years. 'How badly?'

Kip sighed. 'My understanding is that he's still in intensive care.' He watched her face crumple. 'The same girder that landed on your leg crushed part of his ribcage. I talked to the doctors. They say he's lucky to be alive, despite a punctured lung, but it's likely he'll spend the rest of his days in a wheelchair.'

'Thank you for telling me,' she said haltingly. 'I just…' her voice trailed off.

Kip nodded at the notebook open on her lap, hoping to

distract her from morbid thoughts. 'Shouldn't you be resting, rather than working?'

She breathed deeply and nodded. 'Probably, yes.' She placed one hand on the notebook. 'I understand enough about these things to know that someone in your government will attempt to apportion blame for this incident. Naturally, I also wanted very much to know what went wrong.' She held his gaze. 'And I already have an excellent idea what it is.'

'Already?' Kip couldn't hide his surprise. He had been told by onsite investigators it might be weeks, if not months, before they had any idea what triggered the containment failure.

'I wasn't sure whether or not to talk to you about this,' Katya continued. 'But I don't know anyone apart from yourself who could possibly explain to me why someone might choose to interfere with the due running of the facility. Under the circumstances, I'm delighted that you came to visit.'

Kip glanced automatically over at the door, but of course no one was listening in. Or at least he hoped they weren't: there was always the risk that the secret service agent standing guard owed his allegiance to the same people as Merritt. 'Your English is as excellent as ever, Miss Orlova, but I'm not sure what you mean.'

'Records have been falsified,' she told him flatly. 'I don't see how I could put it any more plainly. Here.' She grabbed hold of a set of print-outs bound in a cardboard cover and passed it to him. Kip flipped through the pages, finding they mostly contained cost and safety analyses along with tables of figures.

'I have a reputation amongst my associates for being quite...wearing,' said Katya. 'They complain that I am not good at delegating. But I have made it a point of honour to be involved in every step of the design, construction and operation of the facility. That way, I can make sure that the process of creating and storing exotic matter, as well as building transfer stages, is as smooth, efficient and safe as possible. Every time a problem arises, I have been able to trace it either to someone failing to do their job properly or someone making a mistake. But this is different.'

Kip handed her back the bound pages. 'It's all a little over my head, I'm afraid.'

'It may seem complex,' said Katya, 'but it's actually quite simple. Some of the exotic matter we created is missing.'

Kip kept his expression as placid as possible, but all he could think of was the strange weapon Randall Pimms had just brought back from Delta Twenty-Five. 'What about margins of error? Misreporting?'

She shook her head. 'I can prove that *someone* extracted a quantity of exotic matter—specifically, antimatter—from the containment systems and placed it into portable magnetic units designed to keep it stable over long distances. Those units are missing from our inventory.'

Kip licked suddenly dry lips. 'How much is missing, exactly?'

She shrugged. 'A few thousandths of a gram, but more than enough to cause a great deal of damage were it mishandled.'

'I understand.' Kip didn't need any specialist scientific insight to know that just half a gram of antimatter could trigger a detonation on the scale of a medium-sized atomic bomb.

'I'm glad that you do,' she said, her expression increasingly grim. 'Whoever stole it didn't carry out the proper safety checks before they departed.'

'And that's what caused the explosion?'

'I am quite certain, yes.'

Kip glanced again towards the door, then reached down and again opened his briefcase. He extracted a photograph and passed it over to Katya.

'It's a picture of a rifle,' she said, studying the photograph with some bemusement. 'Although it's quite an odd-looking one.' She looked up at him. 'Why are you showing me this?'

'Two days ago, Randall and Oskar intercepted an unauthorised expedition to Delta Twenty-Five—the same alternate where you once discovered a working Hypersphere.'

Her eyes grew round. 'Please tell me they were not looking for other Hyperspheres.'

'I'm afraid they very much were, by their own admission, according to Randall Pimms. They used that same rifle to blow a hole in a door located in the lower caverns thirty kilometres from Site A.'

She frowned. 'My understanding is that those doors are impassable.'

'Based on Randall's observations, a single bullet from that rifle was enough to punch a hole through one of those doors.'

She shook her head. 'No single bullet could—' Her eyes narrowed. '*Chert vozmi*,' she muttered.

'Excuse me?'

'This casing around the barrel…it could be some form of coiled magnet.' She glanced at him with a frightened expression. 'You have this rifle?'

'Yes. Back on Alternate Alpha Zero.'

'You must be extraordinarily careful with it,' she insisted. 'In fact, I recommend you get rid of it. Program a stage to null coordinates and cast it into the void.'

'You're saying it's dangerous. We'd guessed as much.'

'Does it have an internal magazine? Were there any cartridges loaded in it?'

Kip nodded. 'Just two. We've never seen anything like them. They're certainly not conventional firearms cartridges by any means.'

She seemed to shrink a little in her wheelchair, as if suddenly ageing before Kip's eyes. 'If I were to make a wild guess, I would say that the rifle has been modified to fire bullets laced with antimatter.'

'Is that possible?'

'I would imagine the antimatter itself would be held in place inside the shell of each bullet by tiny but powerful magnets. The propellant, I imagine, would be conventional.' She stared off into space, clearly thinking hard. 'The amount of antimatter in each would be minuscule, but...' she shrugged.

'But still enough to blow a hole in a door we hadn't previously been able to so much as scratch.'

'Quite so, yes. These people—who are they?'

'This has to remain between us,' said Kip, his voice low. His gaze drifted towards the door, and back to Katya.

Katya, born to a lifetime of imprisonment and skulduggery, understood immediately. 'Of course,' she said, so quietly Kip almost couldn't hear her.

Kip moved his chair closer to hers. 'You're aware there are forces within the Authority that would like to experiment on a functioning Hypersphere, if one can be found. No expedition to find another one has ever been legally sanctioned.'

'But someone went ahead anyway?'

He grimaced. 'So it appears.'

'I received many requests to supply small quantities of exotic matter to your military for "research purposes". I refused them all.' She sighed. 'I see now I was naïve to think that might be the end of the matter. Now tell me more about this illegal expedition.'

Kip filled her in on the details. 'My God,' she said. 'Oskar...I'm so sorry. I didn't know him well, but he was a good man.'

'We've all been hit hard by his loss,' said Kip.

'And Randall? How is he coping? You should check him for radiation exposure. An antimatter explosion releases an intense burst of gamma radiation in its first moments.'

'We already checked him over at the clinic,' said Kip. 'It looks like he had a mild dose of radiation, but he'll live.' *At least for now*, he didn't add. There was no way to be sure the Pathfinder wouldn't have serious health problems further down the road.

'And what was on the other side of the door?' asked Katya.

'More machines,' Kip explained. 'But no Hyperspheres—at least not yet.'

'Are you *sure*?'

'Very.'

Katya made a disgusted sound. 'I'm sending in more teams to carry out a thorough search,' he reassured her. 'If they find any such thing, they're under orders to destroy them immediately.'

'And Merritt? What's happened to him?'

'He hasn't been back to the island since the incident, nor do I expect to see him again. For the moment I've decided to do without a second-in-command.'

She gripped the wheels of her chair, her knuckles white. 'Even so, we should be deeply concerned.' She swallowed, and he could see she was choosing her words carefully. 'If there are elements within your government actively looking for Hyperspheres—'

'The Authority is facing enormous challenges, as I'm sure you're aware.'

'*Challenges?*' she spat, her voice rising. 'How many dead worlds do you people have to see before you understand the same thing could happen to you?'

Kip's mouth worked. 'I'm not your enemy, Katya.'

'Then who is?' she demanded. 'They brought me here, to your Washington, when they granted me asylum. But do you know what I remember the most? Looking out of a car window and seeing people with their heads bent and shoulders hunched against freezing winds in the middle of August.' She made a disgusted sound. 'Even then, I gather, much of the population had already fled south.' Her eyes narrowed. 'I heard a rumour they are about to evacuate New York. Is it true?'

Kip swallowed. 'I'm afraid so, yes.' Tent-cities had been prepared in several of the southernmost States. Mexico had been reinforcing its borders with the US, fearing another influx of refugees.

'The truth is,' she continued, acid in her voice, 'there are people in your government who would rather see their citizens starve or freeze to death in their millions than let slip one iota of their power and wealth. I'm sure a Hypersphere must seem very enticing to such people—never mind what happens to those who get left behind.'

'I can't argue with your logic,' said Kip. 'But in the meantime we need to focus on repairing the facility or we won't have any hope of saving more than a few thousand.'

She fixed her gaze on him. 'It can't be done.'

He blinked at her. 'Surely—?'

'The damage is too great. Highly sensitive systems were

damaged by the radiation released during the explosion. Repairing them would take years.'

'Oh.' Kip smoothed his hands across his knees and got ready to stand, except all the strength seemed to have gone out of his legs. 'Then I suppose we have to consider more drastic plans,' he said weakly. 'There was talk of a lottery—'

She put up a hand. 'I may have a solution.'

Kip watched as Katya picked up a file marked CONFIDEN-TIAL and leafed through it. 'Under the circumstances,' she explained, unable to hide her eagerness, 'I thought we should explore radically different approaches to the problem.' She tapped a finger on a page. 'These are summary reports on alternates previously explored by the Pathfinders.' She passed the file over to him. 'Take a look at this one in particular.'

He studied the page. 'Alternate Gamma Three?'

Katya nodded. 'It was first explored and catalogued five years ago.'

Kip paged back to the introduction and summary. Gamma Three was a Category 2 NTPD—"NTPD" standing for "Near Total Planetary Destruction." A high-energy particle accelerator on that alternate had somehow punched a hole through the space-time continuum, creating a bottomless pit into which the planet's entire atmosphere had drained within days. All that remained was a barren, airless ruin.

He glanced back up at Katya. 'How does this solve anything?'

'The report suggests the pit was somehow created by a physics experiment on that alternate. Their civilisation, while roughly contiguous to your own in its politics, was nonethe-less several decades more advanced in its science. They had learned how to create and isolate significant quantities of exotic matter.'

He passed her back the file and she flipped to another page before returning it to him. This time, he saw a photograph of a factory-like building set amidst grey and black devastation. 'I believe that building may have served as a storage facility for exotic matter,' she explained with barely-concealed excitement. 'My guess is they were close to developing their own transfer stage technology. But instead of creating a solid link to a parallel universe, they instead created a one-ended wormhole.'

'Where is this building, exactly?' he asked. 'I mean, its location on their Earth.'

'Seventy-five miles south of the Tunguska region,' she replied. 'Not too far from the mouth of the pit itself.'

He rubbed his hands over his cheeks, wondering if he dared hope she might be on to something. 'What else does the report say about this…storage facility?'

'Nothing,' said Katya. 'I've read the full report as well. None of you could have identified its purpose before I was around to tell you. Now, there are other pictures in the report that suggest backup power systems may still be running inside the building—most likely radioisotopic thermoelectric generators similar to the ones we use to store our own EM.'

'But you can't be certain if we went there we'd find any kind of exotic material, or in the quantities we need.'

'If their containment systems had failed,' said Katya, a gleam in her eye, 'the building and everything around it would have been blown to atoms.' She shrugged. 'And of course I could be wrong and there's nothing there. But we have to at least look.' She sat back, looking exhausted. 'I wish I'd thought of this years ago. It would have saved us a great deal of trouble.'

'So just to be clear,' said Kip, 'if we find EM there in the right quantities, we'll be able to fuel our new transfer stages?'

She nodded. 'Undoubtedly. *If* it's there.'

Kip stood at last. Katya's excitement had proven infectious. 'I'd like to take those documents with me, if I may. I need to show them to some people.'

'By all means,' she said. 'Although I would be grateful if a second copy might be made for me.'

'Of course,' he said, adrenaline flushing his skin pink. *My God*, he thought, *I only came here to offer my condolences, and she's sending me away with a whole new plan for action*!

If only the idiots who didn't trust her solely because of her accent could have been here. But by God, he'd make sure they knew soon enough.

'So are we going to do it?' she asked as he headed for the door. 'Are we going to Gamma Three?'

He stopped, his hand on the door-handle. 'Consider it a foregone conclusion.'

# Rozalia

Rozalia and her team were most of the way back to the transfer stage when they ran straight into a King Crawler. They split up, running in different directions through the city ruins, before finding their way separately to the stage. Splitting up gave each of them a far better chance at outrunning or outwitting the beast.

Rozalia supposed she ought to be flattered the damn thing chose to come after her rather than any of the others.

She stopped with her hands on her knees, sucking down air and watching her sweat drip onto the dusty rubble underfoot. The transfer stage was handily located inside the ruins of a defensive tower that stood taller than almost anything else around it; all she had to do was look up and see it rising over the ruins to know which way she had to go. The tower in turn formed part of a long, crumbling wall long since traversed by the beasts that were now the dominant species on this alternate.

She couldn't see the King Crawler, but she could sure as hell

56

hear it. It let loose a roar that echoed through the ruins like thunder. She looked around and finally caught sight of it at her two o'clock. It emerged from the shadow of a collapsed tower block, thumping along the shattered remains of a broad street. Its four stubby legs could carry it along a lot faster than a human being could run. Its long, spade-shaped head swung from side to side, its tongue tasting the air as it hunted for her.

Then it turned in her direction.

She shrank back into the shadows of a stub of wall before it could see her, her heart feeling like it was trying to punch its way out of her rib cage. She glanced the other way, towards the tower about sixty metres distant: there was nothing between her and it but pulverised concrete and brick, and no place to hide. If she broke out into the open and ran for it, the King Crawler would catch her with ease.

But if she stayed where she was and it found her...

She chanced a peek out from cover and saw the beast still standing where it had been, its patterned flanks rising and falling with every breath. This particular King Crawler was a little smaller than the average, being about the size of a school bus. It had multi-coloured chitinous skin and a mouth that bristled with huge, flat teeth like spades. Rozalia had seen video of one of the beasts digging through concrete before tunnelling through the soil beneath at phenomenal speed.

The King Crawler's tongue flicked in and out. Then it began to move towards her.

Rozalia's muscles tensed in readiness.

All of a sudden the King Crawler again came to a halt, opening its mouth and chewing at the rubble underfoot. She watched with a mixture of awe and horror as it rapidly dug a pit in the ground before pulling itself down inside it. In less than a minute, it had disappeared entirely from sight.

The ground beneath her feet rumbled and shook as the creature passed somewhere beneath her. The thought it might emerge directly beneath her galvanised Rozalia into action, and she ran as hard as she could towards the tower.

*I'm getting too old for this*, she thought. There was a touch of stiffness in her lower spine, and recently she'd been getting more tired and less able to exert herself.

Not to mention opportunities to get out in the field were increasingly rare. How often had she been on missions in the last year? Twice, including this trip. The longer they all sat around the island with nothing to do, the duller their instincts became.

She ran past the remains of tanks and whole blocks that had been razed in a last-ditch attempt to keep the Crawlers at bay.

She saw Jerry in the doorway of the tower, beckoning to her. The ground still rumbled beneath her, as if the creature were keeping pace with her, and she remembered the creatures were supposedly able to follow a person by the sound and pressure of their footsteps.

Which meant, she realised, the King Crawler was heading for the tower as well.

She wanted to yell a warning, but her lungs already felt fit to burst. Despite her terror, the closer she drew to the tower the more she could see that Jerry was holding himself stiffly, his jaw clenched as if he was holding down his temper.

She guessed that he and Chloe had been arguing. *Again.* Whatever the hell it was going on between the two of them, she wished—really, really wished—they'd damn well sort it out. Life was hard enough without having to deal with their bickering.

She reached the door and collapsed onto the cool concrete floor inside. 'The stage,' she managed to gasp. 'Power it up. The Crawler is right behind me.'

Chloe hurried to her side, but she came to a halt as the floor beneath them began to shake. It occurred to Rozalia it was probably too late already.

Then the rumbling faded; the King Crawler had passed them by—for the moment.

'Let's get out of here before it heads back this way,' said Yuichi. Rozalia could see him out of the corner of her eye; he sat crosslegged next to a temporary transfer stage, a laptop balanced on his crossed legs, his long grey hair tucked untidily behind his ears.

'It felt like you were out there for ages,' said Chloe. 'Which way did you go?'

'I don't know,' said Rozalia, seeing the way she angled her body so she didn't have to look at Jerry. Rozalia looked past her and gave Jerry a meaningful look, but his only response was a small shrug. 'All I know is I saw that damn thing come tearing up out of the ground and I ran like hell.'

Chloe nodded. 'I never want to be that close to one of those critters again.'

'I've been closer,' said Yuichi, his gaze still locked on his laptop.

Rozalia stood back up and looked over at him. 'What about the reactors?'

'It's a wash.' He looked up at her. 'They weren't where we thought they were going to be.'

'Guess that's it,' said Jerry, still keeping an eye out through the door for any signs of movement. 'No pocket fusion generators for us.'

'Doesn't mean we shouldn't still keep looking,' said Rozalia. 'Especially given how long they're saying it'll take to rebuild Katya's facility.'

Yuichi closed his laptop and got back up. 'Two years, just to get back up to where things were before the accident. That's what I heard.'

'I heard it could be up to five years,' said Chloe.

The ground rumbled again, although more faintly this time. They all looked towards the door and the ruins beyond, and heard a drawn-out animal shriek echoing from somewhere far away.

'Time to go,' said Yuichi, stepping inside the circle formed by the stage-components.

\* \* \*

A little while later, the four of them materialised on one of two transfer stages housed within the transfer hangar on Alpha Zero's Easter Island. Rozalia glanced towards the second stage and saw a truck manoeuvring down the ramp and guessed it had materialised just moments before they had.

'Is that a water-truck?' asked Chloe, looking towards the vehicle.

'It is,' said Yuichi. 'Guess we're having problems with the local supply again.'

They made their way down the ramp of their own stage and dropped their heavy backpacks on the ground. Yuichi and Chloe got into conversation with a soldier manning the stage controls.

Rozalia took hold of Jerry's arm and led him a short distance away from everyone else. 'Spill,' she said, turning to face him.

'Doesn't take a genius to see you and Chloe have been biting each other's heads off again. What started it this time?'

Jerry's face crumpled. 'I wish I could tell you. She bickers at me, I argue back. I don't even really know what about. I spent the last three nights sleeping on our couch.' He looked at her with a pained expression. 'Could you *please* talk to her again?'

Rozalia raised her eyebrows, hands on hips. 'Do you remember what happened the last time I talked to her and she found out it was because you asked me to do it?'

He winced. 'I guess.' He sighed. 'The whole thing is…exhausting.'

Rozalia was pretty exhausted herself, and now here she was trying to sort out someone else's problems—again.

*Look after yourself first*, she pictured Nadia saying, *before you start worrying about anyone else*.

'Maybe she's worried about you,' said Rozalia. 'I mean, after what happened to Oskar, we're all on edge.' She reached out and touched his elbow. 'Have you thought about just *asking* her what's got her so worked up?'

Jerry looked at Rozalia like it was the dumbest thing she could have said. 'Of course I have. See how far it got me?'

She laughed, low and derisive. 'So what's your thinking in all this, exactly? You think because I'm a girl she'll open up to me?'

Jerry's face coloured very slightly. 'Well, yeah.'

'I swear, there are times when you show all the emotional *nous* of a kid on his first day in kindergarten.' She slapped him on the shoulder and gave him a look of sympathy. 'My best advice,' she said, 'is to give her some time until she's ready to talk. And when she is, *you* need to talk to her, not me or anyone else.'

Jerry's face grew red and he mumbled something under his breath. Rozalia turned away and went to join the other two Pathfinders, who had in turn been joined by Kip.

'Glad to see you're back in one piece,' the Director said to Rozalia. 'Chloe was just giving me a quick rundown of how things went.'

Rozalia shook her head. 'Not so good, I'm afraid.'

'It was a long shot anyway,' Kip conceded with a shrug. He favoured her with a brief smile. 'Now, I know you're just back, but there's been some new developments we need to talk about.'

'What kind of developments?' asked Yuichi.

'I've asked the other Pathfinders to join me for a briefing,' Kip explained, 'now that you're back. They're waiting for you across the compound.'

Rozalia gave him a quizzical look. 'Why such short notice? The way I've been hearing it we're on the verge of being retired, and now we're getting sent back out already?'

'This might be the most important thing I've asked any of you to do,' Kip said, his tone serious. He gestured towards the hangar entrance, seeing the surprised looks on their faces. 'Get yourselves freshened up first and I'll expect you all in Debriefing Room Six in fifteen minutes.'

\* \* \*

Rozalia had a quick shower and a change of clothes in the hangar's ready room, then joined Chloe and Yuichi as they made their way to a prefab building on the other side of the island's military compound. The sky above Rano Kau was dark and heavy with storm clouds, and a stiff, cool wind caught at their hair as they walked.

Nadia was already in the debriefing room, as were Selwyn and Winifred, perched on cheap fold-down seats arranged around a table. A dust-laden lectern stood in one corner next to a steel trolley that bore a projector. A projection screen had been rolled down. There was no sign of Randall.

'So what's this about?' Winifred was asking as Rozalia walked in. 'I had one of the Major's men at my front door telling me I had to come here pronto.'

Selwyn shrugged. 'Same here,' he said. 'Hardly finished my bloody coffee before one of them had me in the back of his jeep.'

'Don't complain,' said Rozalia, finding somewhere to sit amongst the rest of them. 'It's not like we've been over-whelmed with work for a while now.'

Selwyn grunted an acknowledgement. 'True. I must have read every paperback on this island at least twice in the past six months.'

'Amen to that,' muttered Winifred. She looked around. 'Has anyone heard how Randall's doing?'

'Holed up in his place listening to country records,' said Jerry. 'I went round to talk to him, but he wasn't exactly talkative.'

'Those two were like peanut butter and bread,' said Nadia. 'Couldn't hardly separate the one from the other.'

'The reason I ask,' said Winifred, 'is we need to talk about a wake.'

'What about bringing another Oskar back?' asked Selwyn. 'Has there been talk about that?'

'I'm afraid that isn't going to happen,' said Kip, walking in and pulling the door shut against a sudden squall of wind. He placed a briefcase next to the projector.

Selwyn looked confused. 'Why not?'

'Because we're excess to purposes.' Nadia's voice was flat, her gaze directed at Kip. 'Right?'

Kip's face flushed red. 'That's hardly true.'

'Yeah?' said Yuichi, arms folded. 'I heard what Randall told you when he got back from dee-two-five. How that Merritt guy said we were going to get shut down within weeks.'

Kip looked at him sharply. 'Preston Merritt is no longer part of the Pathfinder Project, as I'm sure you're all aware by now.'

'So he was lying when he said that?' asked Yuichi.

'You know,' said Kip, 'I remember a time when you people were less than thrilled about having to investigate all these alternate universes for us. What changed?'

Jerry shrugged. 'Everything. Nothing. Back then we didn't know what you wanted from us and now we do. We just want to know what's going to happen to us *now*.'

Kip sighed and stepped over to the projector. 'I'm aware you've all been under-utilised as of late, but you're not quite ready for retirement yet.'

'Before we start,' asked Nadia, leaning forward on her chair, 'how about telling us what the situation is right now with the water supply? I saw water trucks coming out of the hangar, and there's another storm on the horizon.'

'As a matter of fact,' said Kip, 'I meant to talk about that as well. There'll be another curfew when the storm hits, most probably tonight, if not sooner. You know the drill: don't go outside without protection from the rain. You don't want to end up in the clinic.'

Selwyn nodded. 'I heard about those soldiers who got caught out.'

'Yes.' Kip nodded his head gravely. 'We can ride a toxic storm out, of course. We've done it enough times in the recent past. But I don't know how long we can keep shipping water in from the Authority. It's getting harder to justify keeping operations running on this alternate now we have an entire unpopulated world in Nova Terra.'

'But if we have to move from here,' said Yuichi, 'how do we maintain our independence?'

'Strictly speaking,' said Kip, 'we've never been "independent". It's just that we were something of a side-show for a long time. Now with Katya, well…' He shrugged. 'These days we're centre-stage because of her. And that's bringing changes.' He cast a brief look around them. '*Good* changes.' He gestured to the projector. 'Now, if I may?'

He waited until several moments of silence had passed before hooking the projector up to a wire that led to an external generator. 'You all know about the disaster at the Old Horse Springs EM facility,' he continued as he worked. 'It's going to take years to rebuild it, if at all.'

'"If at all?"' Nadia echoed.

Kip finished fiddling about with the projector and switched it on, shining a square of white light onto the drop-down screen. He glanced towards the door as if concerned someone might be standing there listening. 'Look,' he said in reply to Nadia, 'the fact is there probably won't *be* an Authority in another five years.'

Nadia stared at him. 'What exactly do you mean?'

'I mean the collapse of the mean global temperature on my alternate is increasing,' Kip explained. 'Without a clear and workable plan for evacuation to Nova Terra, we can expect the total breakdown of society in the very near future—and that's the optimistic view. The failure of the Old Horse Springs Facility makes it inevitable.'

'That's just the US,' said Chloe. 'What about the rest of your alternate?'

'In all cases,' said Kip, 'the prognosis is far worse. And that brings me to your mission—I'm sending you to retrieve exotic matter.'

Yuichi sat up, suddenly alert. 'You've found a source?'

'On an alternate named Gamma Three. You were first on the ground there a few years back, Yuichi, if I recall.' He looked around at the rest of them. 'We didn't know it was there until Katya looked through some old files. Now, I want a team of four of you to transfer over there, the same number as last time. But there are risks involved, so I need the rest of you to pay attention in case you're needed for backup.'

The door opened just then and Katya hobbled in on a pair of crutches. Next to her was a supplies officer named Riggs, guiding her in by her elbow.

'Thank you, David,' Katya said to Riggs. 'I can take it from here.'

Riggs nodded and left. Nadia and Rozalia stood and helped Katya into a seat.

'You're just in time, Miss Orlova,' Kip said to her.

'It's good to have you back in one piece,' said Yuichi. 'We were all worried about you.'

'Thank you,' said Katya, leaning her crutches against the side of the table before taking a quick glance around at the rest of them. 'I got your card. It was delightful.'

'I think we should get straight down to things,' Kip said to her.

'I agree,' she said. 'Before we start, however, I have a small request.' She looked around at them. 'Some of you remember Damian Kuzakova, who was in charge of the Soviet scientific delegation some years ago when I first came to this alternate and this island. Damian was hurt much more badly than I in the accident at the Old Horse Springs facility. He would appreciate visitors should any of you have the opportunity. I fear he may have to remain in hospital for some considerable time.'

'Of course,' said Nadia. The others nodded.

Katya nodded in turn to Kip. 'The slide projector, please?'

'Here,' he said, passing her the projector's remote. Katya clicked it and a broken landscape appeared on the screen. The picture had been taken from what appeared to be the slope of a mountain or hill, and showed the jagged remains of buildings spread out beneath a starless sky.

'What's the catalogue title for this one?' Nadia asked Kip.

'Category 2 NTPD.'

'Self-inflicted?' asked Rozalia.

Katya nodded. 'You can see from the sharpness of the picture that Gamma Three lacks any breathable air or indeed any atmosphere of any kind. It was drained out through this.'

The picture changed, showing a round black flat circle that cut through part of a hill. It was hard to judge its scale unless you looked at the surrounding terrain, in which case it revealed itself to be perhaps fifteen or twenty kilometres in diameter.

In fact, it wasn't a circle, Rozalia realised, but a pit—a huge one. She glanced over at Nadia and saw that her face had grown marginally paler.

'A physics experiment involving exotic forms of matter resulted in the creation of a one-ended wormhole,' Katya explained. 'You're looking at its mouth. The far end of the wormhole has been receding from the surface of Gamma Three at the speed of light for nearly a quarter of a century.'

'I'm still amazed by it,' said Yuichi with a half-grin on his face. 'Imagine—a hole twenty-five light-years deep, and getting deeper with every passing second.'

'Gives me the heebie-jeebies,' said Nadia with a shiver.

Selwyn shook his head, apparently baffled. 'I don't get it. The Earth is what—thirteen thousand kilometres across? So how can a pit be deeper than the planet is wide?'

'Because the nature of a wormhole is that it extends outside of the physical boundaries of the universe that births it,' Yuichi explained. 'It's a little like how the transfer stages work, except the wormhole in that case is open at both ends and very, very short.'

Selwyn's face took on a look of horror. 'So how do we know the same thing that happened to Gamma Three couldn't also happen to Katya's facility? Or one of our transfer stages?'

'I believe the people responsible for generating that bottomless pit made certain fundamental errors of judgement,' Katya replied. She clicked the remote again and more pictures appeared on the screen, this time showing different views of a single building standing alone amidst a flat and devastated landscape. 'A few of you explored this structure when you were sent there. I'm quite certain it's an EM containment facility, although you wouldn't have realised its significance at the time. Their EM—most likely antimatter—fuelled the creation of that wormhole, and that same exotic matter can allow our transfer stages to establish stable connections between alternate Earths.' She shifted in her chair so she could again look around at all of them. 'If I'm right, what you find there could more than make up for the damage to my facility. It could help save tens of millions, if not hundreds of millions, of lives.'

'Well, that sounds easy,' said Nadia. 'We go there, bring the EM back, and all our problems are solved.'

'*If* I'm right,' warned Katya. 'Otherwise we're right back where we started.'

'When do we go?' asked Yuichi.

'I scheduled a transfer slot for tomorrow morning,' said Kip. 'Nadia, Chloe, Jerry—I'd like the three of you to join Yuichi on this one. You're all the best qualified.'

They each nodded their agreement.

'Excellent,' said Kip, opening his briefcase. He pulled out a handful of documents with "TOP SECRET" stamped on each and passed them out to each of the Pathfinders. 'I want you all to get yourself acquainted or re-acquainted with everything known about Gamma Three by tomorrow morning.'

'I guess we ought to talk this over,' said Chloe, turning to the three other Pathfinders scheduled to travel to Gamma Three. 'How about now? We could get some breakfast over at Yuichi's and go over the details.' She nodded to Rozalia. 'Want to tag along? You've still got a thousand-yard stare after nearly getting munched by that lizard back there.'

'I guess,' said Rozalia. She and the other Pathfinders headed outside, and she noticed the air tasted damper than when she had gone in.

'It's going to rain later,' said Chloe gloomily, gazing up at the grey skies. 'I never thought I'd be afraid of rain. How many curfews is that we've had in just the last six months? Twelve?'

'More like sixteen,' said Yuichi. 'It's some kind of miracle we've lasted on this island as long as we have. Merritt might be a murderous son of a bitch, but I can't help thinking he was right about us needing to abandon it altogether.'

'And go where?' asked Rozalia. 'Nova Terra?'

'It's not like we didn't make our own plans,' said Chloe, her voice low. 'The question is do we light out now, or later?'

Rozalia looked at Chloe and wondered if this was, indeed, the time to light out. For years now, she and the other Pathfinders had been secretly stockpiling supplies on a relatively low-risk alternate with the intention of using it as a bolt-hole should the need arise. From the moment Katya Orlova had joined the Pathfinder Project, the Pathfinders themselves had become yesterday's heroes—and she wasn't sure she wanted to stick around long enough to find out just what plans the Authority might have for them once they decided they really were excess to requirements.

A silence fell over the group as they trudged across the grass towards a car pool next to the compound gates. 'I don't think there's any hurry,' Rozalia said at last. 'Or at least, nothing's going to happen without Kip warning us first. Besides, we've got this mission to do. We can talk again after it's over.'

They reached the car pool and the rest of them piled into jeeps. Rozalia hesitated, then turned to Nadia. 'I need some space after that damn thing tried to eat me,' she said. 'Like maybe taking a ride on the bike.'

Nadia looked towards the horizon. 'You know, that storm's probably going to hit in just the next couple of hours. Remember what happened to Major Howes' guys. One of them died, Roz.'

'I've faced a lot worse than toxic rain,' said Rozalia. 'And I'll go nuts if I'm stuck in that house for too long. I know how to take care of myself, honey.'

Nadia pulled her close. The others had already piled into jeeps and driven off through the compound gates and back towards town. 'I don't need you,' said Nadia, 'any crazier than you already are. At least wait until tomorrow morning. Maybe the storm'll be over by then.'

Rozalia grinned and touched Nadia's lips with her own. 'Then I guess I can wait if I have to.'

# II

# Raggedy Men

# Rozalia

*Easter Island, Alternate Alpha Zero*

The storm came rolling over the island just after midmorning, blanketing the town like a dark grey curtain drawn across the sky. The rain continued on through the evening, and Rozalia spent much of the day reading while Nadia busied herself in the kitchen. Lightning flashed and the old wooden house they shared creaked and moaned like an old man with aching limbs.

There had been a storm the night Rozalia and Nadia's world ended. Rozalia had been aboard a research submersible two kilometres beneath the surface of the Pacific, and six hundred kilometres east of the New Zealand coast. By the time they surfaced, she and the two oceanographers who had also been aboard found themselves in a world changed beyond recognition.

It was a long time before they learned that a white dwarf star a hundred and fifty light-years from Earth, called HR8210, had turned supernova. The burst of radiation generated by the nova had been powerful enough to burn away much of the ozone layer and kill the plankton thriving in the uppermost layers of the ocean in less than a day.

The result was a slow, creeping apocalypse. In the absence of oceanic plankton, the food chain faltered, then began a gradual collapse—much as it had for different reasons on Alternate Alpha Zero. Millions who had escaped radiation poisoning were subsequently killed by the deadly super-storms that erupted worldwide in the weeks following the gamma burster. Then came a series of desperate wars over dwindling food supplies that took care of nearly everyone else.

Somewhere in all of that, Rozalia had managed to track down Nadia, who had been on holiday caving in the Adirondacks at the time the burster struck. One of Nadia's holiday companions, a biologist, understood better than most the severity of what had happened, and persuaded her and the others with them to remain in the mountains. By the time Rozalia finally returned home to the States, more than two years had passed, and another six months went by before she reached the mountain chalet where she and Nadia had previously spent many summers.

Rozalia had made her way out of the forest and across the glade in which the chalet sat. She ran for cover when someone pushed a shotgun out of a window and shouted a challenge. Another moment passed before Rozalia recognised the voice as Nadia's.

By then, the biologist had died of a fever, and the others had either been killed raiding the nearby towns or gone in search of their own families and loved ones. None of them ever returned.

Several more years went by before the two women concluded there very well might be no one else left alive in the whole world but them. And before they could even come to terms with that, the Pathfinders had come and taken the pair of them away to a new universe and a whole new life.

* * *

'Maybe you could stop off at the fishing hut,' Nadia yelled from the kitchen when Rozalia got dressed early the next morning. 'I'm pretty sure I left a half-bottle of tequila there.'

Rozalia stopped, one leg halfway into a pair of jeans. Through a window, sunlight glistened on wet grass. 'Why?' she shouted through the bedroom door. 'Don't we have enough functioning alcoholics on this island already?'

Nadia stepped through, wiping damp hands on her own jeans. 'No, we definitely don't,' she said. 'A girl needs a hobby.'

Rozalia raised an eyebrow. 'I thought *I* was your hobby.'

Nadia laughed and went back through. Rozalia heard the clank of wet dishes. 'I just don't want to waste it, is all. It's not like we're going to go fishing any time soon.'

Rozalia pulled the jeans the rest of the way over her hips and went through to the kitchen. 'You're the one I'm worried about,' she said. 'I'm not the one going to some airless ruin with a giant hole in it.'

Nadia grinned, then poured coffee into a thermos before screwing the top on and passing it to Rozalia. 'Remember that time we were stuck in the middle of the Atlantic, except it was frozen solid? That was worse.'

Rozalia nodded and coughed into her hand, then coughed again.

'I really wish you'd go and have that cough checked out,' Nadia said with a look of concern. 'I swear it's getting worse.'

Rozalia cleared her throat and unscrewed the thermos, taking a sip of the coffee before screwing it shut again. 'You're like a mother hen, woman.'

Nadia grinned and gave her a kiss on the cheek. 'Careful as you go. I'd rather be the one taking the bike out for a ride, believe me.'

* * *

Rozalia wheeled her Honda four-stroke out of the garage. The weather was clear and the sky blue and streaked with faint high clouds. The roofs of the neighbouring houses were still shiny from last night's rain. It seemed the storm was over, but she erred on the side of caution regardless, packing a spare hazmat suit in a pannier.

She straddled the bike, kicked the starter, and felt it grumble into life. Just the purr of the engine was enough to loosen up her insides a little.

She rode down brick roads lined with palm trees and low, one-storey buildings with corrugated iron roofs rusting from long neglect. The storm had scattered debris and bits of palm frond all across the roads and even knocked down a couple of the larger trees, most of which would likely be left where they were.

The fishing hut lay on the south-east coast of the island, less than fifteen minutes drive from town. She decided to take the long route around the island so she could approach the hut from the north.

Easter Island had a roughly triangular shape, with its one small town, Hanga Roa, near the southernmost tip. She followed the coast road as far north as she could. The island was small enough you could drive all the way around it in no more than three or four hours assuming you were taking your time.

The storm had left the air pleasantly cool, although grey clouds still edged the horizon. Out of habit, she counted *Moai* as she passed them, their long, semi-comical faces gazing down at her with typical disapproval.

On her way back south she felt drops of rain. The sky had grown darker, the wind picking up. She stopped immediately and pulled on her hazmat suit just in time before the clouds opened. She wheeled the bike up next to a palm tree, which offered at least a little shelter. She kept her head down and waited it out.

The rain passed after another twenty minutes. Rozalia kept the hazmat suit on in case it started raining again. Before long she came over a low rise and saw the fishing hut off in the distance. If the rain did come down, she'd at least be able to take shelter there.

She braked suddenly, seeing a crowd of people standing huddled around the door of the hut. She was still far away enough that none of them looked her way. The wind was blowing towards her, so more than likely they wouldn't be able to hear the Honda's engine until she got much closer.

Something didn't feel right. Her heart picked up its pace and she felt a tightness in her chest and shoulders. And if there was one thing Rozalia had learned from visiting more than a hundred post-apocalyptic alternate Earths, it was to trust her instincts.

She turned the engine off and quickly wheeled the Honda back over the low rise in the road. She lowered it carefully on its side before reaching into another of the panniers, digging around until her hand closed around a pair of binoculars.

Rozalia moved towards the side of the road and peered at the hut through the binoculars. They were all men, their clothes ragged as hell. They all had a gaunt, starved look to them.

Whoever they were, they definitely weren't soldiers, and they sure as hell weren't part of the Authority's civilian staff. Her instincts had been right.

She watched as more of the strange men emerged from inside the hut. She soon counted eighteen in all. *Must have been pretty crowded if all of them were in there*, she thought. Most likely they had taken shelter from the rain. Now she had time to study them, she could see that a number of them were dressed in dark suits beneath heavy mismatched coats and different-coloured rain-slickers, like they'd raided a jumble-sale. Their hair was unkempt, their chins heavy with beard, and most carried a rifle slung over the shoulder. A few looked seriously ill, so incapable of standing their compatriots had to help them stand up.

Chances were the ones who were ill had been caught out in the rain. But there still remained the question of who the hell they all were.

The wind carried their voices towards her. By the sounds of it, several of them were arguing.

She moved away from her bike, crawling through the grass at the side of the road until she got a little bit closer to the hut. When she looked back through the binoculars, she saw that one of them carried a heavy-looking sack filled with what looked to her eye like the components of a portable transfer stage. He was talking to another, slightly older-looking figure who looked strangely familiar. Indeed, he looked not unlike-

Rozalia nearly dropped the binoculars. She held them steady

with both hands, the breath rattling in her throat. She had to be mistaken.

*Had* to.

Years before, back when the Authority had retrieved her and Nadia from their own alternate, they had soon discovered they were not the *first* Nadia and Rozalia to be so rescued: another Nadia and another Rozalia, from an alternate with a history nearly identical to their own, had lived and died as Pathfinders before them. Their deaths had in part been due to a rogue Authority agent named Harden Greenbrooke.

Jerry had once given them both a thick folder of documents and photographs that told the story of that other Nadia and Rozalia's lives on this very island. Nothing, Rozalia had quickly discovered, twisted up your head like seeing another version of yourself leading a life you had no memory of. She recalled that a photograph of Greenbrooke had been inside that folder.

One of those strange, gaunt men gathered around the fishing hut bore a remarkable resemblance to Greenbrooke. Except, of course, that Greenbrooke was supposed to be dead.

But then, so were she and Nadia.

The men moved in a huddle away from the road and towards the island's interior. Small as Easter Island was, it didn't lack for places to hide.

Before long, they had vanished from sight past the low curve of a hill. From the hurried way they moved and looked around themselves, it was obvious they were afraid of being seen.

Rozalia stood back up and hurried over to the Honda. She wheeled it up next to the hut and took a look inside. It had been trashed; shattered dishes had been swept into a corner. Almost as bad was the awful stink, and she guessed that the men had spent the night crammed together inside the hut to avoid the rain.

She searched through cupboards and on shelves and soon found that all the fishing lines and tackle were gone. They'd even taken Nadia's tequila, along with anything else that might be remotely usable or edible.

'Okay,' she said aloud. 'Something really, really weird is going on.'

There was still a little drinking water left, though, in a canister. She drained it to slake a sudden thirst, then closed and locked the door of the hut.

Something else drew her attention: bundles of dark rags around the rear of the hut. She hadn't noticed them before, perhaps, she thought, because they were obscured by shadows.

She stepped closer and stared, seeing milky white skin amidst the rags. They were bodies.

By the looks of things—and no way in Hell was she getting close enough to be certain—five or six of the strange invaders had died and their bodies left piled up next to the hut.

The likeliest explanation she could come up with was that they had succumbed to the worst effects of the toxic rain. It had already killed one of Major Howes' soldiers, after all, and judging by the half-starved look of the raggedy-men it would hardly be a wonder if their immune systems were ill-equipped to deal with water-borne toxins.

She got back on her bike and drove fast in the direction of town. The air was feeling warmer as the day moved towards afternoon, but something cold and unpleasant had wormed its way deep into her bones.

* * *

Barely twenty minutes later Rozalia pulled up outside the house she shared with Nadia and ran through to the bedroom where an old file cabinet stood in one corner. She dug through prior mission summaries and reports until she found a yellow cardboard folder, flipping rapidly through its pages and feeling her throat grow tight at the numerous photographs of another Rozalia and another Nadia.

At last she came to a set of laminated photographs mounted on card that showed the two women along with the rest of the Pathfinders. They stood in a gaggle before one of the island's towering *Moai*. Judging by the camouflage gear they all wore, it had been taken during a training exercise.

She touched the photograph, tracing the long, dimpled scar on that other Rozalia's cheek. Then she glanced towards the mirror on the bedroom dresser, seeing her own, unblemished cheek.

Harden Greenbrooke stood at the back of the group, talking to Kip back in the days when Kip had still only been second-in-command to then-Director Bramnik. The Greenbrooke in the photograph looked well-fed compared to the man she'd seen, but they were, undoubtedly, the same man.

Or rather, she thought, a different *version* of the same man…from another alternate.

She pressed one hand against her belly, feeling her guts twist up. She forced herself to breathe steadily, then walked back outside. It had started to rain again. Technically, outside of an emergency or essential duties, she was expected to stay indoors once home until the rain stopped.

This definitely qualified as an emergency. She got her hazmat suit back out and pulled it on before again mounting her bike. As she drove away, she wondered just what Kip would say once he learned they'd been invaded by a parallel universe.

# Kip

'We still don't know where Merritt's disappeared to,' Major Howes admitted. 'The only thing we can say with any certainty is that he didn't transfer back here after the incident on Delta Twenty-Five.'

Kip stared out the window of his office as the Major spoke. The buildings across the road glistened with fresh rain, but at least it had stopped for the moment. A figure strode by—one of Howes' men, his features obscured by the partly transparent hood of a hazmat suit.

Even now, Kip still found it hard to believe something so entirely innocuous as rain could be life-threatening. He would have preferred that no one venture outside at all, so long as there was any risk whatsoever of contamination, but the bureaucratic and day-to-day functions of the island still had to be carried out.

'And what does Washington say?' he asked, turning back to face the Major. Howes also wore a hazmat suit, but with the hood unzipped and tucked under one arm.

'They deny all knowledge.'

*Of course they do,* thought Kip. Merritt had by now surely slunk back into the grey murk of the Authority's intelligence community, especially now that Randall was in a position to testify to what he and Oskar had seen.

Randall sat on a wooden chair near the door and behind the Major, a faraway look on his face as he played with the intricate-looking bracelet on his left wrist. 'Randall,' Kip asked him. Did Merritt say anything about where he might be going after he left Delta Twenty-Five?'

No answer. Randall's lips twitched, the tips of his fingers moving back and forth across the face of the bracelet.

'*Randall,*' Kip said again, stepping up close to the Pathfinder.

Randall blinked and looked around at Kip and the Major as if he'd entirely forgotten they were there. Kip repeated his question.

'Nope,' said Randall. 'He didn't say anything about that.' He looked from one to the other. 'So that's it? The son of a bitch gets away with what he did?'

Kip smoothed one hand over his face. 'I don't like it any more than you do.'

'He *murdered* my best friend,' said Randall, his voice rising. 'I just want to get my hands on the little fuck and…' he formed claws out of his hands as he spoke, then squeezed them into fists.

The Major gave Kip a look. 'I was given to understand you want to send an expedition back to Delta Twenty-Five.'

Randall looked at Kip in surprise. 'What for?'

'We still need to explore the rest of those lower chambers,' Kip said to Randall, 'and make certain there's no more Hyperspheres down there.' Kip indicated the Major with his chin. 'Just sending you and Oskar last time was a mistake. This time you're going with the Major and every man he can spare from the island. You're going to scour those chambers. And if by any chance you *do* trip across any Hyperspheres, your job is to destroy them on sight.'

'Yeah.' Randall nodded, his expression once more sliding off into the distance. 'Sounds good.'

Howes appeared to hesitate a moment before he next spoke. 'Is this an *official* expedition, Director, or...?'

'I would prefer it remain off the record,' Kip replied carefully. 'It's better that way, don't you think?'

'I do, sir,' Howes replied. 'And my men? What should I tell them?'

*Nothing* would have been Kip's preferred answer. Howes had long since proven himself to be a man Kip could trust, but certain of the soldiers under his command could well be another matter. There was no telling whom some of them might report to back on the Authority's home alternate, and Kip was rapidly learning that being in a position of power necessitated a somewhat paranoid outlook.

'Tell them you're searching for evidence of wrongdoing,' he said after a pause.

Randall shrugged. 'Guess it beats sitting around drinking all day,' he said in a quiet voice.

'I want to be clear,' said the Major, 'that if we run across any other illegal expeditions on that alternate I don't intend to engage with them.' He nodded at the modified rifle that now sat on Kip's desk. 'Not if they're going to be armed with something like *that*. What are we even going to do with it? You can't just leave it lying around here where anyone could find it.'

'Take it,' said Kip. 'Put it in the compound armoury until I *do* figure out what to do with it.'

The Major picked the rifle up with exceeding care. 'I'll brief my men,' he said, 'and get them ready for transfer as soon as possible. You can rely on me, sir.'

'Of course,' said Kip. 'It goes without saying.'

The Major turned to Randall, who still sat hunched on his chair, his expression morose. 'I could use your insight during the briefing, Mr Pimms.' He nodded to the door. 'If you'd care to join me?'

'Sure.' Randall stood slowly and carefully.

Kip put out a hand as the Major pulled the door open, as if something else had occurred to him at the last moment. 'Actually, Major,' he said, 'there's a matter I'd like to discuss with you, if I may.'

Randall looked between the two men from beneath a furrowed brow. 'I'll go ahead,' he said, pulling the door shut after him. After another minute, Kip saw him through the window, stepping out onto the street, still zipping a hazmat suit up over his own clothes.

'He's having a hard time,' said the Major, watching him go.

'You'd think a man who'd seen a whole world die could cope with the death of just one individual,' said Kip.

'Unless you've known that individual for a particularly long time,' the Major pointed out.

'Of course.' Kip shook his head. 'According to Randall's report, while he and Oskar were captured, Merritt claimed the Pathfinder Project was facing imminent closure. You were back home recently—did you hear anything?'

Howes sighed. 'There are rumours—bar-room talk, but nothing remotely official.'

'Nothing official, *yet*,' suggested Kip.

'Sir…there are rumours, and then there are rumours. In Washington, depending on who's saying them, some can carry more weight than a presidential directive.'

'So you think Merritt was telling the truth?'

'I can't see any reason not to.'

Kip felt as if he'd grown suddenly heavier and sat carefully on the edge of his desk. 'I suppose I should have seen this coming.'

'Sir,' said Howes, 'perhaps it's for the best. Yesterday, I had to write a letter to the family of the man who died from being caught in the rain. And I'm almost certainly going to be writing more of those letters before this week is out. Maintaining a base on this alternate makes less and less sense now we have Terra Nova.'

'It's the Pathfinders I'm concerned about,' said Kip. 'We haven't made any contingency plans regarding them whatso-ever.'

Howes shrugged. 'They'll be evacuated to Terra Nova, along with everyone else when the time comes.'

'I suppose.' Somehow, Kip didn't think it was going to be quite as easy as all that.

Howes cleared his throat. 'You know, sir, you might not have to worry about them as much as you think.'

Kip frowned. 'I'm not sure what you mean.'

Howes glanced towards the door, then stepped a little closer to the Director, as if sharing a confidence. 'I've been aware that some of our supplies have been going missing for some years now,' he said in a low voice. 'I can't say for certain who's been taking them, but I have a pretty good idea.'

Kip gazed at him through narrowed eyes. 'Are you talking

about the Pathfinders? How much, exactly?'

'A lot.' Howes paused. 'Enough to set up in some remote part of Terra Nova, if they wanted to. Or even some other alternate entirely, if they had the coordinates.'

'Well.' Kip blinked owlishly.

'They're not the only ones,' Howes continued. 'I've heard of people charged with preparing Terra Nova for the mass evacuation disappearing into the woods over there, loaded up with heavy backpacks and never coming back.'

'I see,' said Kip. He'd been to Terra Nova a handful of times: it was an untrammelled wilderness of an alternate. A man could easily lose himself in vast forests that spread unchecked across an Earth that had never known men.

'Now, back home they don't like to talk about it too much,' Major Howes continued. 'But the fact is Washington doesn't have nearly as great a hold over us as they did before we had Nova Terra. And now we have the means to find other viable—'

Just then the door opened. Borawicz, Kip's aide-de-camp, stood there with a sheaf of papers under one arm regarding them both carefully. Kip felt a sudden flash of guilt and wondered if the man had been listening.

'Sir.' Borawicz nodded to Kip. 'I just got handed the latest toxicity reports. Do you want to see them now, or…?'

'Of course.' Kip took the papers from Borawicz and he departed. Outside, he heard the sound of an engine drawing closer and glanced towards the window. A harried-looking Rozalia Ludke, wearing a hazmat suit, dismounted a motorbike before stepping up to the front entrance of Government House. He could hear her talking to Borawicz.

Kip stepped past Howes and into the corridor outside his

office. Borawicz was arguing with the Pathfinder, telling her she couldn't just walk in without an appointment.

'It's all right, Borawicz,' said Kip, and the aide-de-camp fell silent. He nodded to Rozalia as she unzipped the hood of her hazmat suit, tucking it under one arm. 'You look like you're in an all-fired hurry. What is it?'

'We need to talk,' she said, her voice urgent. 'Right now.'

Kip motioned to her to follow him into his office. Once inside, she nodded to Howes, who regarded her with apparent bemusement.

'What is it, Roz?'

'I saw something,' she replied immediately, a wild look in her eyes. 'Up north.'

'Up north,' Kip repeated. 'When?'

'This morning.' She took a deep breath. 'I'd taken the bike out for a run and—'

Kip put up a hand. 'It's been raining heavily all morning, Miss Ludke. There's a reason for the curfews and restrictions. It's far too dangerous to be—'

Rozalia made a disparaging sound. 'The number of post-apocalyptic alternates I've visited, and you think I don't know how to look after myself? Listen to me—I saw Agent Greenbrooke. He's *still alive.*'

'Agent—' Kip caught himself. 'Did you say Greenbrooke?'

She nodded rapidly. 'I got caught in the rain and figured I could take shelter at the fishing hut. When I got there, I saw them.'

A look passed between Kip and the Major, who stood behind and slightly to one side of the Pathfinder. 'You got caught in the rain?'

Rozalia pushed both hands through her hair. 'Look, I know

this sounds nuts, but I saw Greenbrooke, *alive*, along with more than a dozen others. They were all ragged, all skinny like they'd been starving. And then I realised what was happening. We're being invaded, Kip—from *another alternate*.'

Kip touched Rozalia's elbow and gave her what he hoped was a reassuring look. 'Wait one moment,' he said.

Kip stepped back out of his office and approached Borawicz at his post. 'Call the clinic,' he told the aide-de-camp in a half-whisper, 'and ask Doctor Rodriguez to come here. Tell him we may have another patient for him. Bring him into my office and do whatever he tells you.'

Borawicz's eyes widened slightly. 'Sir,' he said, and reached for a telephone mounted on the wall just inside the front entrance of Government House.

Kip returned to his office, carefully closing the door after him. 'How long were you out in that rain?' he asked her.

'I—' she paused, her skin flushing. 'What are you saying, that I was *seeing* things? I had my hazmat suit on!'

'Did you actually *speak* to Greenbrooke?' asked Howes.

'No, I only saw them from a distance.' She clenched her fists. 'Kip, listen to me. I'm telling you the truth.' She stabbed a finger towards the window. 'If you don't believe me, go see for yourself!'

'I want you to understand I'm not doubting you,' said Kip. 'When you saw these men,' asked Howes, 'was it before or after it started raining?'

Something like fear spread across Rozalia's face and she started backing away from the two men and towards the door. 'Listen, Kip,' she said, putting up both hands as if to ward them off, 'whatever you're thinking, it's wrong. Look—maybe I could have found a better way to put it, but—'

She looked around, startled, as the door behind her banged open. Rodriguez stepped into the office, accompanied by Borawicz. There were dark circles under the doctor's eyes; he'd spent most of the night dealing with patients who needed to be kept under constant sedation. The office felt suddenly much too small and crowded with all five of them in there.

'Oh, for God's sake,' Rozalia shouted. 'I'm not *delusional.* I see weirder stuff pretty much every time I step on a transfer stage. I—hey. Hey!'

'I'm sorry, Miss Ludke,' said Rodriguez as he and Borawicz grabbed hold of her by either arm. 'This is for your own safety.'

'Let *go* of me!' she shouted. She looked at Kip with pleading eyes. 'For God's sake, Kip, what are you—?'

Kip moved out of the way as the two men fought to man-handle her out through the door. She kicked out, knocking a standing lamp over, still struggling like a wildcat. '*Fuck* you, Mayer!' she shouted at Kip. 'You are *so* going to regret this!'

Rodriguez pressed something against her shoulder and within seconds Rozalia became limp, her head rolling forward and her voice becoming a half-coherent mumble.

Kip watched from the window of his office as Rozalia was half-carried away. He walked back over to his desk and sank into his chair.

'Tell me I've done the right thing,' he asked, looking at Howes.

'You know,' said Howes, 'one of my men currently under Doctor Rodriguez's care apparently got it into his head to try and swim to the Chilean mainland.'

Kip frowned. 'But that's—?'

'All of three thousand miles away.' Howes favoured him with a grim smile. 'We were lucky we got a boat out to him before he drowned. He acted like setting out to swim to the nearest continent was the most reasonable thing in the world to do. You did the right thing, Director Mayer.'

# Nadia

Upon arriving at the compound earlier that same morning, Nadia, along with Yuichi, Chloe and Jerry, got to work prepping for the mission to Gamma Three.

A robot had already been zapped over to that alternate: its job was to check the terrain was safe enough to transfer across. The Pathfinders meanwhile put on lightweight pressure suits with heavy air tanks and took turns checking each other to make sure everything that needed to be was sealed or plugged in the right way. Finally, at 0900 hours Alpha Zero time, they boarded a vacuum-adapted EV truck and drove it onto a transfer stage.

The stage powered up, and the transfer hangar, along with Alternate Alpha Zero, vanished. Nadia experienced a familiar rush of vertigo, there and gone in a flash, and then they were on Gamma Three.

Nadia looked out through the windscreen at a perfectly black sky above an expanse of broken tarmac. External pressure readouts showed there was vacuum outside the

95

truck. Her gaze was drawn to a metal sign on top of a concrete post, lettered in Cyrillic. Thanks to her long-departed grandmother, Nadia knew just enough Russian to understand they were in a car park on the outskirts of what had once, apparently, been an industrial estate.

Compared to most post-apocalyptic alternates she'd visited, Gamma Three had clearly been through some spectacularly rough times. Pancaked cars and vans lay crumpled up against the side of a nearby building. Everything above the first floor of the building was gone, presumably torn away during the maelstrom caused by the sudden appearance of the wormhole.

Opposite the car park, a dome-shaped monitoring station with a rigid interior frame stood between concrete pillars that supported a concrete canopy extending out above the front entrance of a second building. The dome, which could be entered through a zippered outer airlock that gave it the appearance of a futuristic igloo, was several metres in diameter, easily big enough to fit all of them inside.

Nadia was about to ask Yuichi why the dome had been placed beneath a concrete canopy when she worked out the answer. Without any atmosphere to stop them, micro-meteorites could easily puncture the station's thin outer shell, making it impossible to pressurise and, hence, useless for return expeditions. Placing it under cover reduced the chances of it being damaged.

'Helmets on, everyone,' said Nadia. 'It's quicker just to depressurise the truck than cycle us out of the airlock one after another.'

They put their helmets on, then waited as a hidden pump sucked the air out of the truck. 'Comms check,' Yuichi said over his radio. His voice sounded loud enough inside Nadia's helmet to make her wince and she dialled down the sound levels. 'Everyone receiving?'

Nadia grunted a reply. Chloe and Jerry both confirmed they could hear him and vice-versa.

'Good,' said Yuichi. 'First one who makes a crack about this place having no atmosphere loses their oxygen privileges.'

Chloe made an irritated sound. 'You tell that same joke *every* time.'

Jerry was first out of the truck. He unloaded a trolley stacked with equipment and got to work setting up a temporary return stage—a circle of miniaturised field-pillars spaced evenly around the truck. Nadia meanwhile lifted spare air-tanks onto a second trolley and wheeled it next to the monitoring station. Yuichi and Chloe worked together to attach the tanks to nozzles protruding from the dome. Within minutes the dome had been fully re-pressurised and proved to be lacking any holes whatsoever. They then took turns cycling through its single tiny airlock before taking their helmets off.

Chloe headed immediately for a heavy-looking insulated crate sitting in one corner of the dome. She opened it up and lifted out a rugged-looking laptop computer, placing it on one of several tin trestle tables left behind by the previous expedition. Once the computer had booted up, she tapped at its keyboard for several minutes.

'I hate alternates like this,' said Jerry, placing his helmet on the floor of the dome. He looked flushed and pink.

Yuichi chuckled. 'Then you're in the wrong business.'

'NTPD's, I mean,' Jerry explained. 'At least if there's plague or an ice age or the animals start attacking everyone then some people have at least *some* chance of surviving.' He shivered. 'But there's no chance of surviving what happened here—none whatsoever.'

'Something's weird,' said Chloe, staring at the laptop screen, her expression intent. She erected a second table in the centre of the dome, then rummaged through a backpack she'd brought with her from the truck. She pulled out a rolled-up map and spread it out on the second table. When Nadia went over to see what it was, she saw detailed drawings of hills and roads. The top left of the map, however, showed nothing but a wide black curve entirely lacking in detail.

'This,' said Chloe, tapping a gloved finger on the map as the others surrounded her, 'is the terrain immediately north of us and extending towards the EM storage facility we're headed for.' She moved her finger closer to the top of the map. 'The facility itself is located here, on the outskirts of a settlement seventy-five kilometres south-west of the Tunguska forest. It lies directly between us and the wormhole itself.'

Jerry looked over her shoulder. 'And where are we, exactly?'

'Here.' Chloe moved her finger again, until it was close to the bottom right corner of the map. 'A road leads from here directly to the facility.'

Nadia raised her eyebrows. 'Why not just transfer over to some point closer to the facility, so we don't have to drive all that way?'

'The terrain gets more and more impassable the closer you get to the edge of the wormhole,' Yuichi explained. 'It's all torn up and covered in wreckage from when the wormhole first appeared. We spent most of the last expedition just trying to find a clear path to it.'

Jerry gave Chloe a concerned look. 'You said there was something weird?'

'The previous expedition placed monitoring equipment at

different distances from the wormhole.' She nodded at the computer she'd pulled from a crate. 'The idea was to keep an eye on it and see if there were any changes over time.'

'And?'

'This map,' she said, 'shows the terrain surrounding the wormhole as it was when the last expedition was here. But when I asked the computer for updates, it gave me new measurements suggesting the nearest edge of the pit is forty kilometres from here, instead of seventy-five.'

Yuichi frowned. 'So we made a mistake with our measurements. Or the computer's futzed.'

'Or,' said Chloe, 'the pit got bigger between now and when you were last here.' She gave him a significant look. 'Maybe a *lot* bigger.'

Jerry looked between them. 'Is that possible?'

Yuichi shrugged. 'Who knows? The only way to be sure is go and look at the damn thing.'

'Now, the measurements *could* be wrong,' Chloe conceded. 'But the safest thing is to assume they're correct.' She looked around them all. 'If they are correct, the wormhole's already thirty metres wider than it was just a month ago, and more than thirty *kilometres* wider than when we first sent an expedition here. That means it's been slowly getting bigger over time.'

Yuichi rubbed at his chin, clearly bemused. 'Makes you wonder how big it'll get.'

Jerry, Nadia noted, at least had the grace to look utterly horrified. 'Just to clarify things,' she asked Chloe, 'how far has the edge of the pit grown in relation to the facility we're here to find?'

Chloe sucked air through her teeth. 'Honestly, judging by

what the monitoring equipment is saying, I think there's a pretty good chance the whole thing's already gone tumbling into that hole.'

Jerry stared at her. 'So our mission's a wash before we even got *started*?'

'Doesn't mean we don't still have to take a look,' Nadia said levelly.

\* \* \*

The four of them re-boarded the truck. Rather than spend the entire journey trapped in their suits, they re-pressurised the vehicle so they could at least remove their helmets and gloves.

It didn't take Yuichi long to relocate the road that would take them to the EM facility—assuming, as Chloe had said, it hadn't fallen over the edge of the expanding wormhole. Somehow, Jerry and Chloe managed to bicker the whole damn way. Nadia couldn't even begin to imagine where they found the energy.

Fortunately, the truck was more than capable of traversing the roughest terrain. In reality it was closer to a mobile lab, designed for long-range reconnaissance in hostile environments. Even better, it was over nine metres in length, which meant that while Jerry and Chloe argued over what sounded to Nadia like literally nothing, the rest of them could stay up front where Yuichi was driving. Out through the windscreen, Nadia saw tangled and uprooted trees, smashed buildings, and tumbled and ruined vehicles piled up against each other in great droves of steel and glass.

Since Yuichi had been key to mapping the route to the edge of the wormhole on the previous expedition, he took the wheel, Chloe's copy of the map spread out on the dashboard next to him. Nadia watched him, hunkered low over the wheel, eyes fixed on the horizon. From time to time he swore and muttered, usually when he had to navigate past some particularly tricky obstacle.

At one point they drove through the petrified remains of a forest. The great storm that had followed the appearance of the wormhole had ripped most of the trees from the ground, although a few had somehow managed to cling on by their roots and escape being sucked into the wormhole. Yuichi drove over or around their remains, the truck shaking and rattling and bouncing on its heavy suspension.

Nadia found herself wondering what it must have been like on the day the wormhole formed. She imagined a vortex, a single massive cyclone tens of kilometres across, snatching planes from the sky and ripping any building more than a storey in height loose from its foundations. That anyone could actually have got close enough to the vortex to see it without being instantly killed struck her as unlikely.

After a while, Jerry left Chloe to get on with the job of checking the spare oxygen tanks and other essential equipment and came up front to talk to the rest of them.

Nadia cast a significant look down the other end of the truck at Chloe, then moved her gaze back to Jerry. He lifted his shoulders and dropped them heavily.

'I'd offer to speak with her,' said Nadia, 'but I'm really not any good at that kind of thing.'

Jerry slumped onto one of the truck's passenger seats, just behind Yuichi. 'Maybe don't do that,' he said in a quiet voice.

Yuichi glanced back at him and raised his eyebrows. 'Spill.'

Jerry shook his head. 'I'd rather not—'

'We've had to put up with the pair of you acting like teenagers for weeks now,' said Yuichi, his irritation showing. 'So will you *please*—'

'She's been talking about whether we need to take a break for a while,' said Jerry.

Yuichi returned his attention to the way ahead. 'Maybe that's not a bad idea. Give her time to cogitate her way through whatever's in her head.' His voice still had a soft Californian hilt, even after all these years. 'Maybe she's getting sick of being a Pathfinder.' He shifted in his seat and glanced back at them both. 'Fact is, none of us are getting any younger.'

'Maybe you're right,' said Jerry. He looked over at Nadia, his gaze narrowing suddenly. 'You okay? You're looking a little pale there.'

Nadia shook her head. 'It's nothing.'

'I seem to recall she's not too keen on heights,' said Yuichi. 'I suppose the idea of a bottomless pit isn't too appealing, right, Nads?'

Nadia glowered at the back of his head. 'Why the hell would you think I'm afraid of heights?'

'Like the time I saw you standing on a ladder trying to change a lightbulb? You were sweating like you were hanging off a ledge halfway up the Matterhorn.'

She scowled. 'Bullshit.'

'He's got a point,' said Jerry. 'I definitely remember one time on Beta Nineteen you wouldn't come near a cliff-edge while the rest of us were looking over it. You looked the same then—sort of pasty and twitchy.'

'It's just…' Nadia shook her head, unable to find the words.

'Hey,' said Yuichi, pointing ahead. 'Check this out.'

Jerry leaned forward, peering past Yuichi's shoulder. 'What?'

'Ground's angling downwards the closer we get to the wormhole,' Yuichi explained. 'I remember noticing the same thing last time I was here. The terrain surrounding the edge had caved in, creating a circular concavity around the mouth of the wormhole.'

Nadia tried to see where he was pointing, but mostly all she saw were murky black and grey shapes rolling past them on either side. 'In fact,' Yuichi continued, 'I think that's the wormhole boundary over yonder.' He twisted in his seat, peering down the far end of the truck. 'You were on the money, Chloe. The sucker's way bigger than it was before.'

Chloe came up front, squeezing roughly past Jerry. She peered out through the windscreen. 'Just *look* at that,' she said. 'Isn't it the damnedest-looking thing?'

Past the truck's headlights, the ground sloped downwards for several kilometres before coming to an abrupt end. A brilliantly clear full moon illuminated a grid of roads that terminated at the pit's edge. Nadia saw the ruins of what might once have been a village just a hundred metres ahead, judging by what might have been the spire of a church.

Something about the sight of that clean black edge twisted her gut, as if it were in some way intrinsically offensive. The more she looked at it, the more her skin became clammy and sticky, her heart pressing hard up against the roof of her chest.

'How far to the facility?' she asked, her voice hoarse.

Yuichi glanced at the dashboard map. 'Fifteen kilometres.'

'That far?' asked Jerry.

'If the route I mapped last time hadn't disappeared into that damn hole,' Yuichi replied, 'we could probably get there a lot sooner. But we're going to have to follow the curve of the pit for a while before we can find out if the facility is even still there.'

Nadia saw Chloe looking at her with a worried expression. 'You okay there, Nads?'

Nadia somehow summoned up the will to keep her voice from trembling. 'I'm fine.'

It seemed hardly possible, but as they drove away from the ruined village the terrain became even more rugged and difficult to traverse. Nadia found her mind wandering, and pictured the truck sliding out of control towards the edge of the pit and tumbling into unending darkness...

She pushed the thought down hard. The pit's edge briefly vanished from sight as Yuichi guided the truck past the remains of a jetliner that had come to rest against a stub of wall.

A faint tremor rolled up through the wheels of the truck.

'What the hell was that?' Nadia demanded, her voice pitched higher than usual.

'Seismic activity?' suggested Jerry.

Chloe laughed. 'In *Siberia?*'

'Slippage, I think,' Yuichi said over his shoulder. 'If the pit is growing incrementally, year on year, then it stands to reason that soil and rock are going to crumble off the edge pretty much continuously. If the chunks are big enough, that'd probably trigger tremors.'

Forty minutes later, Yuichi once again pulled to a halt. He hooked an arm over the back of his seat and turned to address them all. 'This is as far as we can take the truck—we're going to have to walk the rest of the way. The good news is, it's just a couple of kilometres.'

'Hey,' said Nadia. She felt curiously light-headed. 'You used robots to map out the facility on the last expedition, right?'

Yuichi nodded. 'Why not send *them* to retrieve the EM, instead of us?'

He got up and stretched, then patted her on the shoulder. 'Our objective's too valuable to leave to machines, don't you think?'

They got busy re-securing their helmets and gloves, then waited as Yuichi depressurised the truck. Just before she headed out through the open airlock, Nadia saw the look of sympathy on Chloe's face and felt a sudden spurt of anger. She turned away from the others before they could see her furious expression.

*Fuck the pit.* Somehow, thinking of it as alive helped, making it into something she could defeat. *Fuck it and its inky, abyssal depths.* They were all survivors of the worst a multitude of alternate realities could throw at them. What was some stupid hole in the ground next to *that*?

She got to work helping Jerry lift some of the oxygen tanks down from the truck and onto a trolley, then helped him push it as they all followed Yuichi past the twisted remains of an electricity pylon. Beyond the pylon, the ground sloped downwards at an increasingly sharp angle before ceasing to exist altogether. The thudding in Nadia's chest grew until it boomed like a great bell. Any last shred of bravado she still clung to fled at the sight of that terrible blackness barely a few dozen metres from where they stood. The moon had risen, revealing faint striations in the far wall of the pit, kilometres distant.

She barely suppressed a whimper when another tremor passed through the ground.

'Maybe let's not get too close,' said Yuichi.

They retreated further from the edge. Nadia looked along

105

the curve of the pit in time to see the remains of a building crumble into dust as the rock and soil supporting it gave way. The moonlight sparkled on bits of glass mixed in with lumps of concrete and brick as they began their long, slow tumble into eternity.

'Okay, I admit it,' Chloe said over their shared comms. 'This place gives me the heebie-jeebies.'

'I could never work out the physics of the thing,' said Yuichi.

Nadia looked at his bespectacled face, visible through the face plate of his pressure suit. 'Huh?'

'It's a wormhole,' he said, 'but the dimensions are weird. It should look like a black sphere, any way you approach it. Instead, it looks like an actual hole in the ground. But the *really* weird thing,' he added, 'is that it appears to have internal gravity consistent with the local topography.'

'In English,' said Jerry.

'If something goes over the edge of the pit, it falls, just as if it were under the influence of the Earth's gravity. But there's nothing down there except empty space. Nothing to pull anything down.'

'I don't think the Earth's gravity just cuts off at the pit's edge, Yuichi,' said Chloe.

'It must cut off eventually, though,' Yuichi mused. 'I'd guess there's enough gravity at the mouth of the pit to accelerate any object falling into it in a generally downwards trajectory. And by the time the gravitational field stops having an influence, there's nothing to stop that object falling at the same speed and direction forever.'

'Do we even know yet if the facility is still here?' asked Jerry.

'I think I see it,' said Chloe. She raised one gloved hand and pointed at a cluster of shapes a little further along the pit's edge. 'See that building teetering right on the edge? I hate to say it, but I think that's where we're headed.'

Nadia saw a blocky concrete and brick shell sitting atop a spur of rock and dirt overhanging the pit's edge. By the looks of it, part of the building had already toppled into the darkness.

'We'd have to be insane to even attempt to enter that building,' Jerry protested. 'Look at it! The whole thing looks like it's ready to collapse over the edge.'

'We didn't come all this way just to turn back now,' Yuichi said drily.

'Even so,' said Jerry, 'it looks pretty risky.'

'I'm not expecting anyone to do anything that feels like it's taking too big a risk,' said Yuichi. He turned towards Nadia. 'Nads, if you'd rather hang back, then I'd quite understand—'

'Let's just get it over with,' Nadia snapped before Yuichi could finish his sentence. She took the lead, walking parallel to the edge of the pit without waiting to see if they followed. 'And don't ask me something like that again.'

Nobody said anything more, and when Nadia glanced back a while later she saw all of them following in her wake, Jerry and Yuichi guiding the trolley over the rough terrain.

\* \* \*

They felt two more tremors over the half hour it took them to walk the rest of the way to the EM facility. It looked like it had been cut in half; girders and chunks of concrete overhung the very edge of the abyss.

They found a door on the side of the building furthest from the pit's edge. Stepping inside, they unclipped torches from their belts and played them around what appeared to be a foyer.

They stepped through a door that led into a tiled corridor, the far end of which yawned open. The part of the building it originally led to had long since gone tumbling over the edge. Yuichi, who seemed to know where he was going, guided them around a corner and along a branching corridor that was much shorter, terminating at a stairwell leading downwards.

Yuichi shone his torch into the darkness below to confirm the lower floors were still there, and still, so far as any of them could see, accessible.

'You have to be fucking kidding me,' said Jerry, his voice flat. 'You want to go down *there*?'

'That's where the main storage area was,' said Yuichi. 'It had to be below ground in case of a containment failure. The surrounding rock would have absorbed the worst of an explosion.'

'There *is* no surrounding rock,' said Jerry. 'At least, not any more.'

'From what I saw out there,' said Yuichi, 'the spur of rock this building is sitting on has to be a good sixty or seventy metres deep. I agree it's a long way from ideal, but as long as it holds and we're in and out of here quickly, I think we can do this.'

'I don't know,' said Chloe, her voice full of uncertainty. 'Maybe Jerry's right. Maybe this *is* too dangerous.'

Yuichi paused and looked at them each in turn. 'Then let's make it a vote this time. Do we retreat, or do we go on? Raise your hand if you want to stay.'

Some seconds passed while they all looked at each other through the face plates of their helmets. Then Chloe hesitantly raised her hand, followed by Yuichi. Jerry muttered something under his breath, then followed suit.

They all looked surprised when Nadia also put a hand in the air, her expression defiant.

Yuichi nodded and dropped his hand back down. 'Then we're agreed: we keep going. Two of us can go down first. Nadia, you stay up here and monitor our progress in case there's any problems. Me and Chloe will—'

'I'll go down with you,' Nadia said firmly. 'Chloe can monitor things from up here.'

'Nadia—' Yuichi started to say, a warning in his voice.

'I don't mind,' Chloe interrupted. 'Really.'

Yuichi looked at her like he was about to say something, then didn't. He pointed his torch at Nadia and she saw the resigned look on his face. 'Then I guess it's you and me, Nads. Jerry, I'd like at least one of us outside the building—just in case.' He looked back at Nadia. 'I want you to stay put until I reach the first landing, then follow me down once I give the signal. Clear?'

She nodded. 'Clear.'

\* \* \*

Once Yuichi reached the next-down landing and confirmed it was safe, Nadia joined him. She waited there while he progressed to the sub-basement, then followed him down once he gave another all-clear.

Her heartbeat had smoothed out a little, although her skin still prickled with nervous energy. The shadows surrounding them were hard black in the vacuum.

Nadia's torch showed concrete walls, painted green. Yuichi

shone his torch ahead of them, revealing a basement area.

'Doing all right?' Yuichi asked over the radio as he panned the torch. His own voice sounded shaky.

She shrugged inside her suit, then remembered he couldn't see it. 'Fine, under the circumstances.'

They walked forward, their boots stirring up ancient dust. The basement was filled with shrouded equipment of indeterminate purpose. Two doorways were set into the left and right walls, leading into what looked like anterooms. Each of them was illuminated from the inside by a faint blue light that unnerved Nadia, as if it were some supernatural manifestation.

'What is that?' she asked, pointing towards one of the anterooms with her torch.

'That's where the EM storage units are,' Yuichi explained. 'If there's still light showing, that means the dedicated generators are still running.' He grinned from inside his helmet with apparent satisfaction. 'Let's take a look.'

She followed him into the room on the right. Dials and screens covered one wall. It was strange to see something still powered and active amidst so much silent desolation.

Yuichi pointed at what looked to her like suitcase handles embedded into a wall. There were six altogether, arranged vertically one above the other. Each handle was attached to a flat plate of steel with a readout screen.

'Bingo,' said Yuichi. 'I'm starting to think this'll be easier than we thought.' He motioned to Nadia. 'Bring your torch here.'

Nadia shone her torch onto a wall-mounted keyboard while Yuichi tapped at it. He used a stylus gripped in one thick-fingered glove, pecking out one letter at a time.

In response, a screen flickered into life, and text began to flow down it.

A fresh tremor shook the ground beneath them just then. They both stood stock-still until it had passed, then looked at each other.

'Thought we were done for there,' said Yuichi with a shaky laugh. 'Okay. Now, each of these containers should be equipped with a dedicated radioisotopic battery to keep it running for a day or so after we remove it from the main power supply. So long as we don't take too much time to get them to a power supply, the EM matter inside them should remain stable.'

'What happens if it doesn't?'

He gave her a sickly grin from inside his helmet. 'At least it'll be quick.'

'How many containers are there?' asked Chloe, who had been listening in over the radio.

'Six in the room we're in,' Yuichi radioed back. 'There's two containment rooms and it looks like both are still powered.' He tapped at a dulled light next to one of the drawer-handles. 'From what I can tell most of the containers are empty, though.'

'How come?' asked Nadia.

'At a guess, it probably all got used up in the experiments that caused that wormhole to form.' He turned and looked back the way they'd come. 'There might be more in the other room. We should take a look.'

'How many of the portable units are active in the room where you are?' asked Chloe.

'Three,' Yuichi replied.

'Is that enough EM for Katya's purposes?'

'Based on my understanding,' said Yuichi, 'and the notes she gave me, it should be just about right.'

'Then just get those three and get out, is my best advice. We're pushing our luck the longer we stay here.'

'I'm with Chloe,' said Nadia.

Yuichi shrugged and turned his attention to one of the still-lit panels. 'Okay,' he said, reaching towards the controls. 'Moment of truth time.'

He pressed a sequence of switches and one of the drawers automatically slid out from the wall. Yuichi took hold of its handle with both hands and started to pull. After several long seconds, and with no small amount of effort, he had managed to drag the long steel box most of the way free of its slot.

'Give me a hand,' he said, his voice strained. 'Damn thing's heavy as hell.'

Nadia got hold of the other end of the containment unit with her thick gloved fingers and helped him slide it the rest of the way out before carefully lowering it to the floor. It was shockingly heavy.

'Christ,' said Nadia, straightening again. 'This is going to do hell to my back.'

'That's another tremor,' said Chloe, in the same instant that a hard vibration rolled through the floor beneath them. 'How many of those units have you got so far?'

'Just one,' said Nadia.

'Then maybe that's enough,' said Chloe, sounding agitated. 'We should cut and run while we still c—'

'No,' said Nadia, surprising herself. 'We get all three.'

'It's too dangerous,' Chloe insisted. 'Yuichi, tell her.'

'I think Nadia's right,' said Yuichi.

Chloe cursed under her breath. 'Jerry?'

'Don't ask me,' he said over the radio. 'I'm not the one down there risking my life.'

'I'm okay with retrieving all of them if we can,' said Yuichi. 'Because if we don't, several billion people are a long way up shit creek.'

'Then it's settled,' said Nadia.

\* \* \*

In the end, Chloe had to come down and help Nadia carry the first two containment units back up the steps, one after the other. Once each unit was up top, Chloe and Jerry got to work dragging it to a relatively safe distance from the facility before loading it onto the same trolley they'd used to carry extra tanks of air. Nadia listened to their muffled curses and grunts as they worked.

'Last one,' said Yuichi, when Nadia went back down to join him. He paused as another tremor shook the walls. 'Hey, does that feel stronger than the last one?'

'Please let's just get the hell out of here, okay?' Chloe said over the radio.

'Amen,' said Nadia, grunting as she lifted one end of the last containment unit. Together, she and Yuichi carried it back through to the stairs.

Just then, Nadia saw what looked like fresh bootprints in the dust. They led into the left-side containment room, the one they hadn't been in. The bootprints were well-defined, as if someone had walked there only moments before.

'Hey,' Nadia grunted. 'Did you go into that other room?'

'Nope,' Yuichi replied. 'When would I have done that?'

Was it possible, she wondered, that the prints had been left there by the previous expedition? With no air to disturb them in the long decades since the wormhole had sucked up all of this alternate's atmosphere, they could easily look as fresh as the day they were laid down.

Then again, months or years of constant tremors would have long since wiped them out of existence. And they did look *awfully* fresh...

They hauled the unit down the corridor, Yuichi walking backwards and facing towards Nadia, who gripped the other end in her gloves. Once they reached the lowermost step of the stairs, they stopped to catch their breath.

'All good?' Yuichi gasped over the radio.

'Listen to you wheezing,' said Nadia. 'You sound like a goat in heat.'

He chuckled quietly. 'I smell worse. Why did you ask me if I'd been in the other room?'

'I thought I saw something.' She straightened, her back stiff from effort.

Light shone from above as Chloe made her way down to join them. 'Last one?' she asked over the radio.

'Looks like it,' Yuichi replied. He looked at Nadia. 'Ready?'

'One second.' Nadia walked towards the left-side containment room.

'Hey,' said Yuichi, his tone sharp. 'What are you doing?'

'I just want to check something out,' Nadia replied. 'I swear I won't be a moment.'

'No, Nadia,' said Jerry, listening in over the shared comms. 'We need to leave *now*. I saw a big collapse further along the rim of the pit just a couple of seconds ago. A pile of dirt the size of a hill went sliding over the edge.'

Nadia ignored him for the moment, standing at the entrance to the left-most containment room and shining her torch on what were, indeed, bootprints.

Which meant, impossible as it seemed, that they weren't alone.

She turned and swung her torch towards the main part of the basement and its dust-shrouded shapes, suddenly unsettled. Was it possible someone on this alternate had survived the wormhole event? If so, what were they doing here, in a building perhaps seconds from plummeting into a bottomless abyss?

'*Nadia!*'

She ignored Chloe's cry, stepping towards a sheet and flicking it aside to reveal a server unit, quiescent and dark. The room was filled with computer equipment, all of it hidden beneath heavy shrouds. There were plenty of places a person could hide—assuming they had a reason to do so.

The worst tremor by far rolled through the floor of the basement and Nadia's heart almost seized up. *Screw this*, she decided. Whatever was going on here, it wasn't worth her life. The building could take its secrets with it.

'I'm coming,' she said over the radio, and hurried back towards the stairwell. The others had already gone up.

Just as Nadia started to climb the stairs, the rumbling grew worse. Her centre of gravity shifted, and she felt herself tip backwards. The concrete steps warped and shattered beneath her boots. She landed back on the floor of the basement, only to find it had been transformed into a slope. She scrabbled for purchase, but found none. Chunks of concrete and brick went thundering past her and she instinctively threw her arms over her helmet to try and protect it.

As if from very far away, she heard someone shouting her name over the radio.

For the briefest moment Nadia was in free-fall. Then she slammed into something with sufficient force that it knocked the wind out of her lungs. Dust and rubble went rushing over and past her, but soon abated.

Her hands grasped something solid. She held on tightly, her breath coming in short, panicked gasps. She could feel nothing to either side of her. She crouched low, terrified of losing her grip.

At least her air supply seemed to be holding steady. She knew she should feel for rips or tears, but she couldn't bring herself to lift a hand.

*I should be dead*, she thought. *Or falling.* But she was neither.

She forced herself to slow her breathing and look around. The dust had cleared enough by now that she could see she was balanced atop a girder protruding from a wall of rock and earth.

Then she looked down and saw nothing beneath the girder but darkness and the promise of an unending drop into eternity.

# Kip

The first hint Kip had that something was wrong came in the form of a terrible stench. He sat up in the darkness and fumbled for the watch he kept on his dresser. It was just after midnight.

Only then did he become aware of a silhouetted figure standing at the open door of his bedroom.

'Who the hell are—?'

'Get up,' said the figure, moving closer. The moonlight coming through the window revealed a man in his late twenties, his face gaunt to the point of being skeletal. He wore a torn and stained shirt beneath a heavy parka and heavily patched combat trousers. His hair was buzzed unevenly, his gaze feverish and fanatical.

It took Kip a moment to identify the small enamel badge pinned to the intruder's parka. It signified that the wearer was a member of the Patriot Agency—formerly a division of the Authority's security services, until its rapid dissolution following a major scandal. Then his gaze moved to the rifle

117

clutched in the young man's hands.

'I said *get up*,' the man snarled, pushing the barrel of his rifle towards Kip's head.

'Okay, okay.' Kip did as he was told, pushing his blankets aside and standing in his T-shirt and shorts. The awful stench came off the young man in waves. 'At least tell me who you are?'

'Questions later.' Unfathomable rage burned in the young man's eyes as Kip pulled on a pair of pants. Something made him reluctant to ask questions.

Once Kip was dressed, the intruder motioned at the doorway with the barrel of his rifle. 'Outside.'

Then it hit him: the intruder could only be one of the soldiers who had fallen prey to environmental toxins. Clearly he had escaped the clinic and was acting out some deluded fantasy. But that didn't explain the man's starved appearance, or the awful stench.

'*Now.*' The man reached forward and grabbed hold of Kip's arm, tugging him towards the door. Kip allowed himself to be pushed and prodded down the steps, past several office doors and out into the cool evening air. It had at least stopped raining.

Kip heard shots from the direction of the compound, mixed with the sound of revving engines and occasional shouts. His fear deepened, and he watched in growing alarm as a jeep pulled up next to Government House with another starved-looking young man behind the wheel. A third intruder sat beside the driver; he had a rifle aimed at two of Kip's civilian staff, who sat side by side in the rear of the jeep. They, too, looked like they had been snatched from their beds.

One of the two prisoners, a young man named Dean, stared

at Kip with wide and frightened eyes. He was clad only in dark blue pyjamas. 'Sir?' he asked. 'What's going on? I keep asking them, but they won't—'

The intruder who had woken Kip pulled him towards the jeep. The Director was forced into the back next to Dean and a secretary whose name was either Marjorie or Margaret—he couldn't recall which.

The jeep took off towards the compound with a screech, the cold night air whipping against Kip's skin where it was exposed.

At least, he thought, it wasn't raining.

\* \* \*

They drove past the runway, and past a cluster of new buildings that had, until recently, been Katya Orlova's primary research facility. They soon passed through the gates of the island's military compound. Kip saw some of the Major's men kneeling in the dirt with their hands clasped on their heads. More starved and gaunt young men with rifles stood watch over them.

'Sir?' Dean asked Kip. 'What's going on—are we being invaded?'

Kip stared at him, thunderstruck. *Invaded*. The very notion was preposterous. Invaded? By whom—the Russians? It hardly seemed likely.

'I'm sure I'll get to the bottom of it soon enough,' Kip replied. He managed to sound reassuring despite the cool sweat that clung to his skin. 'Try not to worry.'

Neither Dean nor the woman beside him looked remotely convinced. But before Kip could say anything more, the jeep came to an abrupt halt outside the transfer hangar. Two more of the invaders stood outside its doors, holding rifles. They came forward and ordered Dean and the girl out of the jeep. The driver, meanwhile, took Kip by the arm and led him inside the hangar.

'Where are you taking those two?' Kip demanded. 'Who are you? Do you even realise how much trouble you're in—'

His voice faltered when he saw Langward Greenbrooke standing just inside the entrance of the hangar. Like the rest, he cradled a rifle in his arms.

'Mr Mayer,' said Greenbrooke, coming closer. His clothes were as ragged and worn as those of his presumed compatriots, and his face and cheeks were equally drained of fat. Something bright and, thought Kip, not entirely sane burned in the hollows of his eyes. 'Do you know who I am?'

'Agent Greenbrooke,' said Kip. The words came out in a half-mumble. 'How did you survive?'

Greenbrooke regarded him quizzically. 'Am I dead in your alternate?'

*Your alternate.* Kip felt his legs sag beneath him. 'You're not from here.'

Greenbrooke allowed himself a small, feral smile. 'No, I'm not. I need your cooperation, Mr Mayer. I knew another you, back where I come from. A very diligent man. A very *practical* man, who I think understood the necessity of cooperation when faced with overwhelming odds.'

'What do you want?'

The hardness around Greenbrooke's eyes softened fractionally. 'Very good, Mr Mayer. Who's in charge here?'

'I am.'

'So you're a Project Director now.' Kip nodded. 'I see. What

I want is safe passage. Me and my men want to go home. But there's something we need first.'

While Greenbrooke spoke, Kip caught something out of the corner of his eye. Two more of the ragged-looking men were fussing over a burlap sack, peeling it down the sides of a tall metal drum with a console on its upper surface. Then his eyes widened, recognising it for what it was.

Greenbrooke turned to follow Kip's stare. 'Something that interests you?'

Kip struggled to form his next words. 'That's a SADM. A backpack nuke.' He moved his gaze back to meet Greenbrooke's, a cold chill gripping his innards. 'What are you going to do with it?'

Greenbrooke grabbed hold of Kip's arm and drew him further away from the nuke. Kip was all too aware of the devastating use such devices had been put to back in the 1980s, in the closing days of World War Three. They allowed for pinpoint targeting of strategic targets—sometimes military, and sometimes civilian targets such as runways and bridges. They were firecrackers next to most missile-borne nukes, but they were nonetheless terrifyingly effective, with a yield somewhere in the region of one to two kilotons.

'None of your business,' said Greenbrooke, his mouth locked in a snarl. 'I need your supplies of antidote for the neuro-alvarium virus.'

'The—' Something cold raced down Kip's spine. 'The bee-brain virus? Why do you need the antidote for that?'

'Tell me where the supplies are,' Greenbrooke insisted, 'or we start shooting your people one by one.'

'All right,' Kip said hastily, his voice shaking. 'I can do that.'

Greenbrooke dragged Kip towards the entrance. 'Show me.

Now.'

Kip led him across the compound and towards the research huts, which stood together in a cluster apart from the rest of the compound. On the way there, he saw that the doors to the barracks stood wide open: by the looks of it, Major Howes' men had literally been caught napping. But then again, on an alternate empty of all other human life, what was there to guard against?

*Except*, he thought sourly, *for invaders from an alternate Authority. That* no one had planned for.

Then it hit him: Rozalia had warned them, and he had dismissed her as insane or ill or both. That her story had sounded like an elaborate fantasy made no difference: she had done her job while he, by contrast, had entirely failed. And to make matters even worse Major Howes, along with the remainder of the island's military forces, was off on a mission to Delta Twenty-Five.

Kip led Greenbrooke inside a hut. A large sign on the door proclaimed WARNING—CONTAGIOUS MATERIALS. AUTHORISED PERSONNEL ONLY PAST THIS POINT.

Greenbrooke flicked on a light switch, revealing low wooden tables and cupboards rising to the ceiling. An airlock-like entry system built into an interior wall gave access to a second room for the handling of dangerous biological materials.

'Here,' said Kip, hunkering down and opening a cupboard close to the ground.

Greenbrooke eased him aside and lifted out a tray of steel bottles, placing it on a table. 'I need hypodermics as well, Director Mayer.'

'Of course,' said Kip, pulling open another drawer and lifting out a box of sharps. He hesitated for a moment, then asked: 'I'm assuming our histories are very similar.'

Greenbrooke nodded, and from the way the flesh sagged on his face, Kip wondered how many days the man had gone without sleep. 'I don't claim to understand these things very well,' said Greenbrooke, 'but my understanding is that the event braids for our worlds diverged only very recently.'

'I see.' He paused a moment, then asked: 'why did you come here, Langward?'

'Because back where I come from,' Greenbrooke replied, 'the whole world is a tomb.'

Kip looked at the bottles of serum, thinking hard. In his own timeline, Casey Vishnevsky had kidnapped Greenbrooke before deliberately infecting him with the bee-brain virus. Vishnevsky had intended to transfer the infected Greenbrooke over to the Authority, with the specific intention of dooming everyone on that alternate. If not for the quick thinking of Jerry Beche, he might have succeeded.

'If you or your people are infected,' Kip said quietly, 'my own people are going to need the serum as well.'

Greenbrooke gestured at the bottles. 'Is this all you have?'

'On this island? Yes.'

'But back home? On your Authority's alternate?'

'I believe there are more stocks there, yes. The serum wasn't developed here.' Kip hesitated a moment, then asked: 'If you need our help, why not just ask for it? Why come charging in here and kill good men in cold blood?'

'Is that what you'd have done?'

'Yes.'

Greenbrooke smiled gently, as if Kip had proven some point. 'You know what happens when a bunch of men in filthy rags turn up on a closely related alternate, infected with a terrible disease and desperate for help? Instead of offering salvation, they try extraordinarily hard to murder you.'

'You mean—?'

'We already tried "just" asking for help, Director Mayer.'

'Am I to understand,' asked Kip, 'that this isn't the first alternate version of the Pathfinder Project you've visited?'

'We've been to a number of them actually,' Greenbrooke confirmed. 'All but one had been decimated by the bee-brain virus. We thought we'd found salvation on that alternate; instead they tried to slaughter us.' His expression became bleak. 'We're all that's left out of more than a hundred.'

*Jesus.* Something cold slithered down the back of Kip's throat and wrapped itself around his heart and lungs. 'You must be aware it isn't enough just to inject yourself with the serum once. It takes repeated treatments, over a period of weeks. But if you're staying here—'

'We're not staying here,' said Greenbrooke.

Kip's brows knitted in a frown. 'Then…?'

'Those buildings next to the runway,' Greenbrooke asked instead. 'There was nothing like them on *our* alternate, or any of the others we visited. What are they for?'

Kip hesitated, but saw no immediate benefit in lying. 'They're an experimental facility.'

'What kind of experiments?'

'For building transfer stages.' An idea came to Kip just then. 'If you want to find your way to some alternate where you'll be safe, I'm more than happy to help—'

'Did you say *building* transfer stages?' Greenbrooke regarded him with outright amazement. 'Do you mean to tell me you actually figured out how the things work?'

124

'Yes,' Kip said after a brief pause. 'We...worked it out.'

'And you can program them? Travel to non-apocalyptic alternates?'

'Yes.' Kip was careful not to mention Katya's involvement: the last thing he wanted to do was draw this man's attention to her, and not just because she was their most valuable asset. 'You know,' he added, 'we could help you find a safe alternate—one you'd have all to yourselves. One where humans never evolved, say.'

Greenbrooke regarded him carefully. 'You could really do that?'

'Of course,' said Kip. 'We could start straight away. In fact—'

'Not just yet,' said Greenbrooke, stepping back and taking a firmer grip on his rifle. There was a speculative look on his face, such that Kip could almost see wheels upon wheels turning and calculating deep inside his head: the mark, thought Kip, of a man born to skulduggery. 'Pick up the tray,' Greenbrooke added, opening the door with one hand. 'And take the box of sharps as well. We're done here.'

# Rozalia

Rozalia was back in the dying forest, her rifle propped up on a boulder. She peered down the grassy slope at the roof of the chalet that had been her and Nadia's home for going on five years.

Nadia crouched next to her, a heavy satchel in her hands. Rozalia glanced over and saw the satchel was crammed with grenades they'd filched from an abandoned army base a few months back.

A man came around the side of the chalet, darting his head around. He held a rifle loosely in one hand.

'There you are, you son of a bitch,' Rozalia muttered. She leaned into the rifle and took aim.

Nadia put out a hand to stop her. 'Hold your fire. We still don't know how many of them there are—there's no point starting a fight if we wind up outgunned.'

Rozalia scowled at her. 'I got a good enough look. There's two, maybe three of them at most.'

Upon their return from yet another failed scavenging

126

expedition the previous morning, they had been confronted by the unexpected sight of a truck parked next to their chalet. It had been more than a year and a half since they'd found any evidence that anyone, anywhere might still be alive apart from the two of them.

Surviving this long had taught both Rozalia and Nadia to be cautious. The men had been stealing food and supplies out of their chalet and loading it into a truck when Nadia appeared, alone, at the end of the trail leading towards the building.

They had acted friendly at first, only opening fire on Nadia once she got within twenty metres. Rozalia, who'd remained in hiding behind the stump of a tree lower down the hill, provided covering fire long enough for Nadia to scramble to safety.

Even so, a bullet had grazed Nadia's thigh. She wouldn't be doing much walking for a while.

They retreated to a cave higher up the slope where they'd previously stashed emergency supplies in case of precisely such an attack. They spent the night monitoring the chalet from above, listening as its new occupiers hollered and whooped. It sounded like they were digging deep into the stockpiles Nadia and Rozalia had built up since the gamma-ray burster.

The forest was silent around them, the grass threadbare and largely dead. The birds and insects were gone, and the only things still thriving were lichens and mushrooms. Around the mouth of the cave, grey-barked trees that no longer produced leaves shook listlessly in the wind.

The men reappeared the next morning, carrying the rest of their supplies out to their truck.

'They're getting ready to go,' said Nadia, lifting herself up slightly.

Rozalia heard the truck's engine start. One of them was guarding the truck, keeping a watchful eye on the dead forest around him. He didn't spend too much time looking upslope, however.

'I'll go now,' said Rozalia, crawling out from the cave entrance. 'You sure you can cover me from here?'

Nadia nodded, her expression intent. 'Just go. I'll see you on the flip-side.'

How Rozalia hated that phrase; hated how it sounded like Nadia thought one or both of them was going to die.

She made her way down the slope, hunkered down low. She moved slowly, so the bag of grenades slung over her shoulder didn't make too much noise. She dropped down against a tree trunk just a couple of metres from the truck and waited until the rest of them had come out and climbed inside it. Before too long the truck engine grumbled into life.

'Okay,' said a man's voice from inside the cabin of the truck. 'Let's roll.'

*Good idea*, thought Rozalia, pulling the pin from a grenade and tossing it under the truck.

The explosion lifted the whole vehicle up off the ground before dropping it back down on its side. A man who had been riding in the back staggered away from the blazing wreck, his shirt on fire.

Rozalia heard the whine of a shot in almost the same instant that the man collapsed, oily smoke drifting up from his still-burning clothes. The smell of cooking meat triggered a powerful hunger response in Rozalia's stomach.

Nobody moved. She turned and looked back up at the dense forest reaching to the top of the slope behind her and waved.

128

Then she focused her attention once more on the truck.

She edged closer to the blazing wreck, hunger taking a firmer grip on her. Hell, it wouldn't be the first time; and more than likely, they'd lost a good chunk of their carefully hoarded supplies. The least the assholes could do was give up their flesh and blood so she and Nadia could—

She stopped, and gazed down at the face of the dead man. There was something familiar about it.

A name came to her then: Greenbrooke.

His eyes blinked open, and he looked up at her.

Rozalia woke with a gasp. Overhead strip lights burned into her eyes. She squeezed them shut, seeing blue and red afterimages float against the darkness.

The last thing she remembered, she'd made her way to Kip's office. She'd been telling him about...

*Greenbrooke.*

It all came back in a rush.

She had to warn the others—

She tried to sit up, only to discover her wrists were secured to the rails of a hospital bed by thick leather straps. She let out a panicked gasp and lifted her head a little. From what she could see, they'd taken all her clothes and replaced them with surgical scrubs.

She was in a ward. Moonlight spilled in through a window at the far end. It took another moment before she realised it must be the ward in the island's single clinic.

Three of the five other beds she could see were also occupied, by men she didn't recognise. Judging by their military-looking haircuts, they were Major Howes' men, the same ones who'd got caught in the rain.

They, like her, were secured to rails running along each

side of their beds by tough-looking restraints. Two of the men appeared to be asleep, but a third sat up suddenly before staring at Rozalia with haunted eyes. He mumbled something incomprehensible, his skin slick with sweat. His eyes rolled in his head as if in the grip of some terrible vision.

Then his eyes more clearly focused on her, and he began to shout incoherently.

Moments later, a harried-looking medic with olive skin came bustling in and headed straight for the soldier. The soldier reacted by trying to twist out of reach of the medic, his voice reaching new heights of volume. The medic pushed a needle into the man's shoulder, and within seconds he had slumped back down.

'Excuse me,' said Rozalia, her voice cracking slightly. She recognised him now as the same man who had stuck a needle in her back in Kip's office. 'Could you please tell me what's going on?'

The medic turned to stare at her. 'You sound a lot more lucid than these other guys.'

'I don't know why I'm here,' she said. 'I was talking to Kip—I mean, Director Mayer. I tried to warn him.'

The medic's expression became wary. 'Warn him of what?'

'That there's…'

She faltered. Kip had not only failed to believe her story, he'd clearly taken it as evidence she'd been exposed to toxic rain.

She tried a different tack. 'Did you run blood tests on those guys?'

'Sure.'

'And on me as well?' she asked.

'Yes.' He hesitated for a moment. 'Although I'm still waiting on the results.'

Of course he was: most likely the samples had been transferred over to the Authority for an analysis, meaning God only knew how long it would take them to figure out she was entirely sane. 'Look—you said it yourself. I'm *way* more lucid than any of those guys, right?'

'Yes, but you were exhibiting irrational behaviour and—'

She bit back a laugh. 'What's your name?'

'Sam Rodriguez.'

She nodded. 'I'm guessing you just rotated through here, right, Sam? How long's it been?'

He looked like he was having an internal debate about whether or not they should even be having this conversation. 'Two months,' he said at last.

'Okay, Sam,' she said. 'Here's the thing: Kip's not a fucking doctor. *You* are.' She worked hard to keep from sounding strident. 'If you won't let me go, then at least get someone to come here and talk to me. If not Kip, go and find one of the other Pathfinders. You know by now where they all hang out, right?'

'I'm afraid I can't—'

He paused at a loud bang from somewhere outside. While it didn't sound close, it sounded an awful lot like a gunshot.

Rozalia thought of men in tattered rags, carrying rifles as they sneaked across the island under cover of darkness.

Then came a second gunshot, and a distant cry of pain. Rozalia heard the angry whine of tyres skidding on concrete.

This time, it took considerably more effort to keep her voice calm. 'You heard those gunshots just now, didn't you?' Sam nodded. 'Here's what I want you to do: there's a gun locker downstairs in the ground floor admin office. The key to the

131

locker is in the second drawer of the desk. Got that?'

He gave her a strange look. 'Yeah.'

'Good,' she said. 'Head downstairs and open the locker and bring up whatever's in there, plus some ammunition. You don't have to give it to me if you don't want to, but we need to be able to defend ourselves. And I ask you—use your judgement to figure out whether or not I'm suffering from the same thing as *those* guys and *goddamn untie me.*'

She watched as indecision warred across the medic's face. Then, to her immense relief, he stepped around the side of the bed and freed one of her wrists.

She groaned with relief. 'Now the other one.'

She heard more gunshots—closer this time. Rodriguez's eyes grew wide with alarm.

'I'd better go,' he said. 'You know how to use a gun?'

'For God's sake, of course I do!'

'I'll just be a second,' he said, hurrying out the door and leaving her there with one hand still secured to the bed.

*Oh damn you, you stupid kid.* She bit the words back. But as long as he got some kind of weapon and brought it back upstairs they should—

Another two shots rang out, sounding very, very close, and then silence.

Rozalia bit back a string of expletives. It was better, she thought, to be angry than scared. Even so, her heart fluttered inside her chest like a caged bird.

The noise had been sufficient to rouse the rest of her fellow patients from their drug-induced sleep. One lifted his head and cried out, then fell back down, his chest falling and rising with worrying rapidity.

Rozalia heard footsteps coming up the stairs, slow and

careful. Much too careful, she thought, to be Rodriguez.

Rozalia pushed her free hand back inside the opened restraint and lay back, letting her mouth droop open a little. She closed her eyes to narrow slits.

The footsteps came to a halt at the entrance to the ward and she heard the sound of a gun being reloaded. She watched through slitted eyes as one of the raggedy-men she had seen the previous morning stepped further into the ward, peering around. By now her heart was pounding so hard she was surprised the whole bed didn't shake from it.

'What the hell?' he muttered to himself.

He didn't even look at Rozalia. Instead he moved past her, stopping at the foot of the bed holding one of the soldiers. She watched as he prodded the prone man in the chest with the butt of his rifle; the soldier twisted in his restraints, whining and growling like an animal.

The raggedy man swore under his breath, then turned and walked back over to Rozalia's bed.

This time, Rozalia kept her eyes shut. She didn't need to see him to know he was standing over her; he stank of sweat and terror and long days and nights clad in the same rotting rags. It took all her strength not to twist her head around and bury her face in her pillow to try and block out the awful stench.

The inside of her eyelids darkened slightly, and she guessed he was leaning over her. Her free hand bunched into a fist.

She heard him move away again, and she allowed herself to breathe out, just a little. She opened her eyes a fraction and saw him poke at the loosened restraint around one wrist.

The strap flopped open, and his eyes grew wide.

Rozalia didn't allow herself the luxury of thought. She sat up as far as she could go with her left wrist still secured to the opposite bed rail and grabbed hold of the stock of the raggedly man's rifle with her right. She pulled hard, trying to wrench it from his grasp, but he held on despite being taken by surprise.

Rozalia brought her right leg up between them and shoved the raggedy man in the chest. He went sprawling onto the floor, leaving her still grasping his rifle with one hand.

There wasn't time to try and loosen her left hand. She lifted the rifle up and turned it one-handed until the barrel was pointing away from her. She pushed her fingers through the trigger guard and managed to get the butt of the rifle against her shoulder. It was awkward as all hell, but she was having to improvise.

The raggedy man clambered back onto his feet, cursing and snarling. He saw Rozalia, his eyes growing wide with horror in the fraction of a second before she unloaded the rifle at him.

The recoil just about ripped the rifle from her grasp, but the bullet caught him square in the chest, flopping him back onto the floor. It felt like a miracle that she'd managed to hit him at all.

Rozalia listened to her own panicked breathing and waited to see if he got up again. He didn't.

*Time to get the hell out of here.* She scrunched her legs underneath her so she could sit upright and work at undoing the strap around her left wrist. If the raggedy man's friends weren't nearby, she was pretty sure they would be before long.

Rozalia hurried downstairs, nearly stumbling over Rodriguez's body, sprawled in the downstairs office. A semi-automatic handgun lay in his outstretched hand. Across the office, the gun locker stood open. It was empty: she didn't even see so much as a spare magazine for the handgun.

Rozalia pried the handgun from Rodriguez's fingers and muttered an apology before checking it had a magazine inserted in its grip. Then she ran outside.

She looked around, seeing several more raggedy-men at the far end of the street. They were clearly headed in the direction of the clinic. One of them let out a shout and she ran around the back of the building, jumping over a rotting fence separating the clinic from a neighbouring property and running across its overgrown yard. She made her way down a narrow alley and onto an adjacent street.

She heard an engine approaching and hunkered low in the doorway of an abandoned house. An open-top troop transport rolled past, and she saw Selwyn sitting in the back, along with several of Howes' soldiers and a couple of civilian staffers, all of them guarded by one of the raggedy men. From the way they were all sitting hunched forward, she guessed their wrists had been cuffed behind their backs.

They were being invaded, she thought, by dead men.

* * *

Over the next couple of hours, Rozalia learned enough to confirm for herself that things were just about as bad as they could be. All of the raggedy-men were well-armed, and it was starting to look like they'd taken complete control of the island. They were mostly concentrated in a couple of places. About a dozen of them remained in the compound. That made sense, because that was where the transfer hangar was located. A few others stood guard outside the hotel-bar that was Yuichi's domain. From a hidden vantage point, she watched as prisoners were either led inside the hotel, or taken back out of it.

She began to get a sense of what was happening. They were picking up people from all across town and putting some of them in the Mauna Loa hotel. Then other raggedy-men would transport these prisoners to the compound in twos and threes.

In the distance, the transfer hangar flashed with light at regular intervals for several hours. Clearly they were sending people somewhere, but where—and why? There was no way she could get to the people inside the Mauna Loa that she could see: there were at least four raggedy-men there at all times, two standing guard out front, with one inside and the fourth stationed around the back of the building as well. All of them appeared to be well-armed.

After a while, it grew dark and the hangar ceased to flash with light. The more she saw, the more sure she was that she remained the only one as yet uncaptured, and the more convinced she felt that her first priority should be to discover the identity of these invaders and what they wanted.

She needed to find out exactly where these people had come from, and if they were using the transfer hangar so much, there was a good chance they were travelling back to their own alternate as well.

She made her way across the deserted runway that lay roughly halfway between the compound and the town. She kept away from the roads, and when she approached Katya's old research facility, she heard the sounds of activity from within. One of the raggedy men stood outside one of its buildings, a rifle over one shoulder.

She ducked her head lower and moved quickly away from the facility. The facility contained its own, separate transfer stage, and she'd thought she might be able to use it. By the looks of it, that wasn't going to be possible.

Once she was within sight of the compound she ducked across the road and made her way down to the shore. She hurried along the pebbled beach, seeing the dark bulk of the transfer hangar rising above her to her left. The moon came out from behind clouds and she ducked low, although it was unlikely any of the raggedy-men would have seen her coming this way.

Once she was around the back of the transfer hangar, she pulled herself back up a low embankment and crept to one corner of the building. For the first time in hours, the compound was quiet and still.

It was clear that Greenbrooke and his men came from some parallel version of the Pathfinder Project, but some part of her, even after all these years of exploring exotic parallel universes, rebelled against the idea. It had been hard enough accepting that the multiverse was big enough to contain more than one Rozalia Ludke. That it might also contain a multitude of Easter Islands and an equal plethora of Pathfinders—possibly an infinite number of them—just made her want to curl into a ball and take a long, long nap.

She crept towards the rear entrance to the hangar and edged it open, peering inside. There was no sign of movement.

She slipped inside, taking cover behind a canvas-covered truck that had been parked next to one of the transfer stages until she was sure she was alone. Then she stepped past the truck and headed for the nearest set of stage controls.

She called up the most recent coordinates that had been programmed into the stage. Each set of numbers and letters, sometimes hundreds of characters long, specified the $n$-spatial coordinates for a different alternate universe. Rozalia had been a Pathfinder long enough she could, by now, recognise the most frequently used coordinates by their first dozen or so characters.

The most recently used set of coordinates, however, were unfamiliar to her, yet they had been used more than a dozen times over the past twelve hours—often enough that someone, presumably one of the raggedy-men, had made it the default destination.

Either the raggedy-men were sending a lot of prisoners to that address—or it was where they had come from. If she knew where that was, maybe she could figure out what they wanted.

Then again, her first duty should be to get to the Authority and warn them. She stood there undecided, then heard voices from somewhere outside.

That decided it: reprogramming the stage to take her to the Authority would take too long, and put her at risk of being caught. It would be quicker and easier simply to visit whatever alternate had been set as the default.

Rozalia touched a button on the console, then ran up and onto the stage. She had just reached the top of the ramp when light filled the hangar and carried her away to an unknowable destination.

# III

# The Other Selwyn

# Nadia

Most likely, thought Nadia, there were a lot worse ways to die than falling into a bottomless pit and waiting for the air in your suit to slowly run out. But at that precise moment, balancing precariously on a steel girder with nothing beneath her but a drop into eternity, almost any other way of meeting her maker seemed preferable.

'So I got to thinking,' Yuichi continued, his voice crackling over the radio as he shoved rubble out of the way, 'about collective nouns. Like, what's the collective noun for a bunch of people who're all the last man and woman on Earth?'

'Surely if by definition you're the only one of something, you can't have a collective noun, can you?' asked Chloe, breathing hard as she worked.

'Just hurry up,' said Nadia, her voice trembling. They were both trying to keep her mind off things by acting like this was just a regular working day. She wanted to scream at them that it wasn't helping.

Yuichi muttered a profanity under his breath. 'Sorry,' he

said. 'Ankle hurts like hell.'

'Take it easy,' Chloe told him over the radio. He'd sprained his ankle during the collapse, but he'd insisted on doing his part to try and dig down to her. 'And conserve your energy, Nadia,' Chloe added. 'We're almost there.'

*Liar.* She didn't see how a dozen people could dig through a whole building turned to rubble before her air ran out. Even so, Nadia focused on her breathing, holding the air in her lungs for long seconds before letting it out. After a minute or two, the thumping of her heart grew a little less frenetic.

She lifted her head and peered up through her suit's visor at the ceiling of the basement—or what was left of it—several metres above where she crouched on the girder. The broken edge of the basement floor was just out of reach. She'd looked around for some way to climb back up, but there were no foot or handholds to be had. A tangle of cables that emerged from a pipe embedded in the concrete floor, and which she might have been able to grasp in order to pull herself back up, remained tantalisingly out of reach.

A slight vibration rolled through the girder, and Nadia stiffened. Then it faded, and she remembered how to breathe.

She looked down without meaning to. That was bad: looking down meant thinking about what it might be like to fall for ever and ever…

She decided to put her mind to the question of the boot-prints instead. And who might have made them.

'The bootprints,' she announced. 'We have to figure them out.'

Yuichi chuckled nervously under his breath. 'Once again, Nadia, there's no one else here but us.'

'I wasn't seeing things!' she snapped. 'We took the containment units from the storage room on the right side of the basement. None of us went into the storage room on the left. Or is one of you lying?'

Chloe groaned. 'Oh, come *on*.'

'How about you, Yuichi?' Nadia demanded.

'I think I'd have remembered if I had,' he replied somewhat tersely.

'Well, neither did I,' said Nadia. 'Which begs the question, who *did* make those prints?'

'This is crazy talk, Nads,' said Chloe.

'No crazier than *us* being here,' Nadia snapped.

There was a short pause before Chloe replied. 'Let's just focus on getting you out of this fix,' she said. 'You'll be back drinking gut-rot in the Mauna Loa in no time at all.'

'Hey guys?' It was Jerry, calling over the radio on the general channel, his voice choppy with static. 'I think we, uh, have a problem.'

Something in Nadia's chest became icy cold.

'What kind of problem?' asked Yuichi, sounding weary.

'I can't get back home.'

'What are you talking about?' Chloe demanded over the same shared link. 'You mean the transfer stage won't work?'

Jerry had volunteered to make his way back to the transfer stage, using one of a pair of lightweight electric scooters mounted on the EV truck's rear rack. The plan was for him to transfer back to the island so he could rustle up the equipment and volunteers to rescue Nadia.

'The stage works fine,' said Jerry. 'But something's blocking the transfer from the other side. It just powers down after a couple of seconds. All the diagnostics tell me there's nothing wrong with it.'

'I seem to recall the stages having inbuilt locking systems to take them offline in emergencies,' said Nadia. 'Could be something like that.'

'Sure, maybe,' said Yuichi, 'but what could possibly constitute such an emergency?'

'Is there any way to trigger an override if something *is* blocking the transfer from back home?'

'Not from this side, no,' said Yuichi.

'Then we have a serious problem,' said Chloe. 'Our air isn't going to last forever. And as far as I know, you need high-level authorisation codes before you can trigger an emergency shutdown. The only people with those codes are Kip and Major Howes.'

The girder vibrated gently beneath Nadia and she froze until it had passed. A few fragments of rubble and plaster went sailing past her on their own long journey into infinity. She cautiously adjusted her crouching position to try and relieve the growing ache in her muscles. It seemed the tremors were coming more frequently.

The others had gone silent. She guessed they had all switched over to a shared private channel so they could discuss things they'd rather she didn't hear—such as the increasingly slim likelihood of her being rescued.

She was quite certain that she was going to die, and the longer she clung to her girder, the more she felt she was putting the lives of the others at risk. Really, the best thing she could do was to let herself fall so they could retrieve some other Nadia from the multiverse to take her place.

Instead she clung on, hating herself for it. When it came to heights, she had no greater fear.

How she wanted to be with Rozalia in that moment.

*Click, click.* 'So, uh, Nadia,' said Yuichi, 'we've been doing some thinking. Jerry just figured out he can still connect with the transfer stage inside Katya's old research facility back on the island. He's going to transfer back there to get help for you and maybe find out what's gone wrong with the main stages while he's at it.'

'Probably some trainee stage operator screwed up the settings,' Jerry chipped in.

'Or maybe *you* screwed up,' said Chloe, her voice bitter. 'Ever consider that?'

'Christ,' Jerry snapped. '*Now* you're ragging on me? You know what, to hell with it. You want to quit on the relationship? *Fine.* I'll go first, how about that?'

'Jerry—' Chloe started to say.

'No, *you* listen,' he said, clearly on a roll. 'I am *sick* and *tired* of this constant bickering. I swear to God, there are days I'd rather stick my head in the mouth of one of those goddamn Chimeras than risk waking up to another morning of being told I'm a useless, good for nothing—'

'I can't keep doing this,' said Chloe, something in her voice cutting him off. Both seemed unaware that the others were still listening in appalled silence. 'This...*life*. How could you bring up a child knowing this is all there is for them?'

Nadia felt her eyes grow wide even as she clung to her girder. There was a long pause, Chloe's words hanging in the air like a sheet of glass in the instant before it shatters on concrete.

'What are you talking about?' asked Jerry, his voice thick with uncertainty.

'I'm *pregnant*,' Chloe wailed over the shared comms.

'Wow,' Nadia said into the silence that followed. '*Guys.* Let me be the first to congratulate you on your excellent timing.

Maybe we can throw a baby shower on top of a volcano next time, maybe?'

Neither Chloe nor Jerry answered. They had gone silent, having presumably switched over to their own private channel in order to bicker further.

'Okay,' Yuichi said heavily. 'That's going to take me a minute or two to process.'

There was a *click* after another minute, and Jerry came back online. 'Yeah, um. Sorry about that, guys, from both of us.'

'Yeah,' said Chloe, her voice small, like a child's. 'Sorry.'

'I'm going to transfer across now,' said Jerry. 'Uh, good luck, Nadia. By the time I get back here with the others, I figure you'll be long out of that hole in the ground.'

The truth was, they would never pull Nadia out of the pit. And Jerry would never again return to that alternate.

# Randall

'Well,' said Major Howes, after the ground had stopped rocking underfoot, 'if that doesn't make the place secure, nothing will.'

Randall stepped back from the building that housed one of the tunnels leading into the deep caverns as dust billowed up from its depths. The ground rumbled and shifted once again as another set of charges blew somewhere far below where they stood. Strange animals darted around the branches of the seaweed trees past the building entrance, frightened by all the noise and shaking. The moonlight gave the forest around them a sinister appearance, as if the trees were hulking beasts watching them silently.

'Good riddance,' said Fred Danks with a shiver. 'Those damn caverns gave me the creeps.'

While they'd been laying charges all through the underground vaults, Danks had looked about ready to jump out of his own skin. It wasn't just the darkness that made him nervous, Randall knew: it was the weird, alien quality of the silent machinery surrounding them, and the soft, otherworldly glow of the bacteria clinging to the roof of the caverns.

Randall waited until Danks looked his way, then tipped his torch up until it shone directly under his chin, turning his eyes into twin pools of black above an evil grin. 'Just imagine all the ghoulies and beasties that'll come crawling oot of the darkness now,' he said, 'just looking for a snack in a uniform.'

'Just so you know,' said Danks, his voice sour, 'I am not above giving a man a busted lip for trying to put the wind up me.'

Randall grinned. 'You know that's a man-eating tree you're standing under, right?'

Danks jerked violently away from the tree he'd been standing next to.

'Stop harassing my men,' Howes told Randall. 'I think we can count this expedition a success. Nobody's going back down into those caverns any time soon.'

'I'll just be glad never to see this alternate again,' said Randall, turning towards the EV truck parked close by.

* * *

There were six of them: Randall, Major Howes, three soldiers and a Lieutenant. They'd transferred over to Delta Twenty-Five at midday island-time and made their way to the caverns where Oskar had got himself killed, spending most of the day laying charges at various points. As soon as they'd boarded the truck, Randall had stretched out on one of the truck's rear seats and gone to sleep with his chin tucked into his chest.

'We're there,' Lieutenant Satsura called from up front, waking Randall. 'Homeward bound, boys.'

Randall rubbed his hands across his face then went up front

to peer out through the windscreen at Delta Twenty-Five's endlessly weird flora. Satsura guided the truck along a rutty path that led to a flat expanse of concrete on which stood several warehouses and a small hangar containing a single transfer stage.

The lieutenant guided the truck inside the hangar and up a ramp leading onto the transfer stage before finally hitting the brakes. Satsura then disembarked and walked back down the ramp in order to program the stage controls. Light surrounded the truck just as Satsura got back behind the wheel, and Randall experienced a fleeting yet very familiar sense of weightlessness. The light faded to reveal the transfer hangar back on Easter Island.

'Hey,' said Satsura, peering out through the windscreen. 'I've never seen that guy bef—'

The windscreen shattered before he could finish speaking. Satsura jerked hard, red blossoming on one of his arms. He made a sound like he'd been punched in the belly.

A second shot came through the windscreen, angled higher this time and punching a hole in the roof of the front cabin. 'Out!' bellowed a voice. 'All of you, hands in the air! Now!'

There were two of them outside, Randall saw: gaunt-looking men in dark, filthy-looking rags. From out of the corner of his eye he saw Howes reaching for his holstered pistol.

'Don't,' said Randall, putting a hand on the Major's arm. 'We don't know how many of them there are.'

Howes looked at him like he was insane. 'I only see two.'

Randall shook his head. 'Takes more than two to take over the island's hangar without starting a shooting match. Something's happened here while we've been away. Don't get yourself killed before we find out what it is.'

Howes nodded, his face pale. 'You'd better be right.'

The rear airlock door slammed open and a third man stepped inside, waving a rifle at them. He wasn't just gaunt, Randall saw: he looked half-starved. There was something wild and not entirely sane in his eyes, and his clothes were hardly more than patched-up rags. Randall's nose wrinkled. The stranger stank to high heaven.

'All of you, out!' the rifle-wielding stranger bellowed at them. 'Any one of you makes a move for a gun or anything else, you're all dead!'

They did as they were told, filing out of the truck, Satsura coming last and supported by Howes. As they exited, one of the two other men searched them and relieved them of their weapons.

By the time they were all outside the truck, yet more of the hostiles had entered the hangar, each as ragged as the next. More importantly, every last one of them was armed to the teeth. Randall stared around, seeing no sign of anyone he knew. Nothing but these strange, filthy, foul-smelling strangers.

'Take it easy,' Howes said to the nearest of them. 'I'm Major Howes. I'm in charge of military security here. Who the hell are you, and where are the rest of our people?'

Instead of answering, one of the ragged men pushed open the hangar doors, letting in sunlight. They had about them a look Randall recognised from a time when his life had been very different: the look of men who'd had the misfortune to outlive their entire world.

Randall, the Major and the rest of the soldiers were led out of the hangar and into the sunlight. Randall found himself thinking of hot griddled pancakes paired with one of Yuichi's more palatable beers, but he had a feeling he wasn't going to be having any late suppers any time soon.

Outside were yet more of the ragged hostiles. So far he'd counted nearly a dozen.

Then he took a closer look at one of them and nearly stumbled to a halt: the man was older than the rest, and was talking to two others. He had about him the manner of a man comfortable with authority.

*It can't be*, thought Randall.

One of their guards prodded him in the back with the barrel of his rifle. 'Keep moving!' the man shouted.

Randall was too stunned to do anything but let himself be pushed inside an empty storage shed along with Howes and his men. The door was bolted shut and locked from the outside.

Fred Danks immediately went to a window and peered through the glass. 'Just one guard out front, so far as I can tell,' he muttered. 'Couple more out front of the transfer hangar.'

'Did you see him?' Randall asked Howes. *'Did you see him?'*

'If you're talking about who I think you are,' said Howes, his voice soft and ponderous, 'then yes, I saw him.'

Danks glanced around at them in apparent confusion. 'See who?'

'Greenbrooke,' said Randall.

Danks looked at the Major with a quizzical expression. 'Before your time,' Howes told him.

'He's supposed to be dead,' Randall explained for Danks' benefit. 'I don't know who the rest of those guys with him are.'

'Either way,' said another of the soldiers, a Private Freitag, 'who is he?'

'You're not cleared to know,' the Major told him.

'Is it possible?' asked Randall. 'That he's…'

'Another Greenbrooke, from some other alternate?' Howes lifted his shoulders in an exhausted shrug. 'Unless that's his twin brother standing around out there, I'm damned if anything else makes sense. Plus, I'm pretty sure some of them were wearing Patriot pins.'

'Cleared or not,' Freitag muttered, 'nothing you're saying makes any damn sense.'

\* \* \*

What happened next didn't make much sense either.

They sat crammed into the tiny wooden hut for most of two hours. While they waited, they did the best they could for Lieutenant Satsura, improvising a tourniquet and putting pressure on the wound. When the door of the hut did finally crack open and they were led back outside, they found themselves under cover of two hostiles armed with assault rifles that had clearly been filched from the compound armoury.

This time, there was no sign of Greenbrooke. Randall peered at one of the hostiles, who appeared to be seriously ill. He sweated profusely, and the barrel of his rifle weaved somewhat in the cool night air, as if he were struggling to remain upright.

'Back into the hangar,' said another of the hostiles. 'Start moving.'

'Wait a minute,' Howes demanded. 'How about you at least tell us what—?'

The hostile lowered his weapon and fired into the ground

at Howes' feet. The Major stumbled back, cursing under his breath.

'Jesus!' Danks shouted. 'What the hell was that for?'

'Next one who talks, dies,' the invader hissed.

Nobody said anything after that. They were herded inside the hangar and onto the same transfer stage they'd arrived by. There was no sign of the truck they'd had with them the last time.

'Hey,' Randall yelled down at the hostile manning the stage's controls. 'Where in hell are you sending us?'

'Somewhere out of the way,' he replied.

That was the last Randall could say before the transfer-light filled the stage. Then he found himself looking at a different, smaller hangar he immediately recognised as the one back on Delta Twenty-Five.

'There's medical kits over there,' said Randall, indicating a set of steel drawers situated in one corner of the hangar. 'Might be fresh bandages there.'

Danks and Young went to investigate and found fresh gauze, which Howes used to replace the blood-soaked dressing on Satsura's arm. 'Why did they send us back *here*, of all places?' asked Freitag.

'I think it's just like they said,' Howes replied. 'They want us out of their way.'

'Except there's nothing to stop us transferring straight back there,' noted Danks.

'How's he doing?' Randall asked, nodding at Satsura.

'The bullet made a clean exit,' said Howes, standing back up. 'He's lost a little blood, but he'll be fine.'

'Could we do that?' asked Satsura, looking at Howes. 'Go back?'

'They took all our guns,' Howes reminded him. 'Even if we had them, we'd be sitting ducks the moment we materialised. No, our first duty is to get back to the Authority and raise the alarm.' He caught Freitag's eye. 'How about you get the stage set for transferring us back home, Private?'

Freitag headed for the stage controls. 'Getting help is one thing,' Randall said to the Major, 'but the rest of our people are still back there on that island and we have *no* idea what those assholes are going to do with them.'

'I didn't see anyone else,' said Howes. 'Could be they've dumped all our people on other alternates same as they did with us.'

'Maybe,' said Randall. 'If we knew what the hell they even wanted—'

The air above the transfer stage began to glow. Howes motioned to Satsura. 'Up on your feet, lieutenant. Time we went home and called the cavalry.'

'Sir,' said Freitag, 'I haven't powered the stage up yet.' He stared at the screen before him with uncertainty. 'I think they must be sending something else here from the island.'

Randall began to move towards the stage. 'Maybe they're sending over more hostages.'

The light reached its maximum brightness. Randall shielded his eyes with the back of one hand as he approached the stage. Two small, dark objects shimmered into existence at the same moment that the light faded, rolling across the stage before coming to a halt. Randall stared at them, transfixed, then turned and ran towards the hangar entrance.

'Get the hell out of here!' he screamed.

Major Howes grabbed hold of Satsura by his uninjured arm and ran towards the exit, dragging the lieutenant after him. Randall had a brief glimpse of Young and Danks staring towards the stage in stunned horror before they, too, turned to run outside.

Randall emerged into the sunlight, legs pumping, and heard a sound like a thousand hammers slamming a bass drum. At the same moment a brick wall crashed into him from behind, throwing him several metres through the air. He landed face-first and lay unmoving for several seconds, waiting for a red tide of pain to subside.

He rolled onto his back and managed to sit up, although it felt like he might have broken a rib or two. He turned his attention towards the hangar and saw its roof had collapsed, while black smoke billowed from out of its entrance. Freitag lay sprawled on the ground, unmoving. The others were struggling to their feet.

Randall stumbled over to Freitag's side. He lay sprawled on the ground, quite dead, and with a look of mild surprise on his face. A large piece of metal had embedded itself in his chest.

Howes came up beside Randall and looked down at Freitag. He made a disgusted sound and went to peer inside the hangar. He turned back after a moment, coughing hard from the smoke still billowing out.

'Damn stage is fucked,' he said, walking back over to join the rest of them. He put his hands on his knees and coughed harder.

'What the hell did they do that for?' asked Young. He brushed dirt off his trousers, his eyes wide and unblinking like he couldn't quite comprehend what had happened.

Howes coughed again, clearing his throat with some effort. 'They don't want us coming back. And they don't want any of us going for help either.'

Randall looked out at the jungle surrounding the plaza, thinking. 'Remember there's another stage half a day's drive from here,' he said. He pointed at an EV all-terrain mobile lab parked some distance away, next to one of the warehouses. 'And at least we've got that.'

The Major nodded. 'Good thinking.' He looked back over at Freitag. 'Danks, Young, find something to wrap him up in.' He looked at Randall. 'I want very badly to hurt those assholes, whoever or whatever the hell they are. But first we've got to think of somewhere to put Freitag until we can ship him home.'

'There's lab facilities over by the warehouses,' said Randall, 'but I don't think they've got a freezer or anything large enough to take him.' He found himself unconsciously playing with the bracelet Oskar had given him. 'For what it's worth, nothing here's going to try and eat him, not even the bugs. We're not compatible with the flora and fauna on this alternate. I wish I had better news, but the best thing we can probably do is just put him where we can find him.'

The Major sighed, massaging his brow for a moment. 'Fine. Then maybe let's take a look at that truck over there and see if it'll run.'

\* \* \*

As it turned out, the truck was fuelled and ready to go. In the meantime, Danks found a canvas tent in one of the lab buildings, and he and Young got to work wrapping Freitag up in the canvas before placing his body inside one of the warehouses. It was hardly dignified, but it was a temporary solution at least.

Danks followed Young and Satsura over to the truck where Howes and Randall were waiting. He cast a glance back at the warehouse where they'd temporarily laid Freitag to rest. 'It doesn't seem right,' he grumbled. 'I know we need to go get help, but I'd really like to lay my hands on the sons of bitches who did this.'

'All of you get in the truck,' said the Major. He looked at Randall, sitting with his back to one of the truck's wheels, the fingers of his right hand stroking the bracelet on his left while the others laid Freitag to temporary rest. 'You too, Pimms.'

'Hey,' said Randall, standing now. 'I, uh, got kind of an idea.'

'What kind of an idea?' asked Howes.

'Maybe Fred's got a point,' said Randall, nodding at Danks. 'I mean, we don't *all* need to go back to the Authority. Just one of us is enough to raise the alarm. That means the rest of us could reconnoitre back on the island.'

Major Howes gave him a withering look. 'And how exactly do you expect us to defend ourselves?'

Randall held up his left arm so the Major could clearly see the bracelet. 'We got this.'

Young snickered. 'Jewellery?'

'It's a communications device,' Randall corrected him. 'Oskar used it to control the Chimeras. One of them got killed at the same time he did, but the second Chimera is still right here on Delta Twenty-Five. And frankly, either one of the creatures is more effective than a whole nest of machine-guns.'

Howes stared at him, one hand on the rim of the truck's rear airlock door. 'Are you serious? You expect us to make use of one of those…monsters?'

'Oskar knew how to control them,' said Randall. 'You've seen him do it before.'

'Yes,' Howes replied with barely concealed impatience, 'but that doesn't mean *you* can.'

Randall shrugged. 'I've had some practice.'

Howes stepped back from the truck and walked over to him, hands on hips. 'How much practice, exactly? I seemed to have the impression you were shit-scared of them.'

'I am,' said Randall. 'I mean, I *was*,' he quickly corrected. 'See, I figure we could take the remaining Chimera back to the island and set it loose on the hostiles. I mean, sure, they're armed, but they wouldn't stand a chance against even just one of the creatures.'

Howes scratched behind one ear. 'Say I believed even for a second you really know how to control one of those things,' he said, his tone contemptuous. 'How do I know it won't attack our own people as well as the hostiles?'

'It won't,' said Randall, sounding more certain than he really felt.

'Where is the beast, anyway?' asked Danks.

Randall turned to him. 'It lives in a set of caverns separate from the ones we just blew up.' He tapped the bracelet. 'See, as long as I'm on this alternate and wearing this, I know exactly where Betty is.'

'Betty?' asked Danks. 'Who the hell is Betty?'

'It's what Oskar called the damn beast,' said Howes, regarding Randall with weary eyes. 'You'll do no such thing. I've seen just what a Chimera can do to a human body, and we've wasted too much time already.' He jerked a thumb at the truck. 'Everybody on board *now*.'

Randall watched the rest of them file on board, his frustration overflowing. 'Major, just what do you think is going to happen when you go running back to the Authority and ask

158

for help? They're going to blame *you*. Worse, it'll give them even more reason to shut the whole project down. I don't think you want that any more than I do.'

Howes' face turned red, and Randall wondered for a moment if he'd pushed things too far.

'Sir?' It was Satsura, standing at the truck door. 'I think Mister Pimms has a point. Our priority is to alert the people back home about what's going on, but it's going to make things go our way much more if we can be seen to be cleaning up our own mess.' He nodded at Randall with his chin. 'And I've seen what these Pathfinders can do. If he's willing to give it a shot, then I think the rest of us are willing to take our chances with the Chimera.'

The Major glared at Satsura, then shifted his gaze back to Randall. 'No bullshit, Randall. Can you control that thing as well as you seem to think you can?'

Randall forced down a grin. 'If anything goes wrong,' he said, 'I'll be the first one it kills. But it won't. Or, you can go back to the Authority and let someone else sort things out.'

Howes stuck a finger in Randall's face. 'The moment I think that animal is a danger to us,' he said, 'it's over. How do you want to do this?'

'I already called her to me,' said Randall. He nodded up at the truck. 'I figure if we get rolling now, she can rendezvous with us on our way to the other stage.'

# Kip

After Greenbrooke had finished with him, they locked Kip in a supplies hut with his hands manacled behind his back and a rope firmly secured around his ankles. He sat there alone in the darkness for what must have been a couple of hours before someone returned to fetch him.

It gave him too much time to think. Finding out you'd made a terrible mistake was one thing: discovering it by having a man in rags burst into your home and force you out of bed at gunpoint, however, took the experience to a whole new level.

As bad as it had been for him, he had no doubt it must be far worse for Katya Orlova. Of all the damnable luck! It was more than a little ironic that she should return to the island for the first time in months only to be captured by armed madmen. She'd spent too much of her life being imprisoned or interrogated only to have to live through the same thing again.

When the door opened, a young man with pale, narrow features and eyes that were rimmed with red kept his rifle aimed at Kip while a second invader untied his legs and ordered him outside.

It was a matter of debate which of the two men looked more ill, and for a moment Kip debated making a run for it. He was less sure, however, that he could outrun a bullet, let alone find someone in a position to remove his handcuffs. He had no choice but to allow them to guide him into the back of another jeep.

They drove him back out of the compound. At first he thought they were headed back towards the town, but instead they pulled up next to Katya's former research facility opposite the runway. Kip was then led inside an office where he found Greenbrooke waiting behind a desk he had commandeered.

The paler of Kip's two guards coughed abruptly, and Kip felt his skin crawl at the thought of being in the same room as him. Both men's skin was glossy and stretched-looking, more like tight-fitting masks than flesh and bone.

'I just finished interrogating the Orlova woman,' Greenbrooke said to Kip, tapping one of several thick folders scattered across the desk. 'How she came to be on this island makes for quite a story.'

Kip fought to control his emotions. 'What have you done with her?'

A small greasy smile worked its way onto Greenbrooke's face. 'Nothing she won't recover from.'

Kip took a step forward, and one of Greenbrooke's men hauled him back by the elbow. 'I assure you,' Kip seethed, 'that if you've harmed one hair on her head—!'

Greenbrooke put up a hand as if to mollify him. His manner was that of a man in complete control. 'She was entirely cooperative, once she understood we weren't willing to take 'no' for an answer.' He opened one of the folders and flicked through it, then looked back up at Kip, studying him at length. 'You're very protective of her, aren't you? I admit to being a little surprised, given she spied on your people on behalf of a foreign power.'

'Where is she?'

'She's safe.'

'I'd like to see her.'

Greenbrooke didn't reply. Instead he said: 'I can't tell you how amazed I was to discover not only that you weren't lying, but that Orlova was the one who taught you how to build transfer stages!' He chuckled with apparent incredulity. 'It changes everything, of course.'

Kip's heart sank. 'It does?'

'Originally, we planned to transfer over to Washington—*your* Washington, that is.'

'Then why come here?' asked Kip. 'Why not transfer straight there?'

'Because we knew the reception we'd get if we did.'

'I see. Whereas here on this island, we're comparatively easy pickings. Am I correct?'

'I'm sure you understand the principle of establishing a beach-head. Plus, we had to acquire more supplies of the serum, and quickly.'

Kip nodded. 'Then why the SADM?'

'Our original plan was to use it to blackmail your Authority into cooperating with us. If they tried anything, I'd blow all of us to atoms, including anyone and everything in the vicinity.'

'That sounds...' *Insane.* 'Risky.'

Greenbrooke favoured him with a fatalistic smile. 'That *was* the plan.' He dropped the folder he'd been holding back down on the desk. 'But then I discovered this facility connects to another, far larger facility on your Authority's alternate. That, Director Mayer, is our new destination.'

'Why?'

'There was an accident, was there not? It would explain why it's almost entirely deserted. Luckily for my men, since they met with minimal resistance when they transferred over to that other facility in just the last few hours. They've taken the SADM with them and planted it in a vulnerable location. If we're interfered with, we'll detonate the device and all your evacuation plans will be blown to kingdom come.'

Kip fought to keep the shock from his face, but judging by Greenbrooke's smirk it wasn't working. 'Who informed you about the accident? Katya?'

'Eventually. And just to be clear, Director Mayer, that facility is now under our control.'

Kip bit back sour bile, and when he next spoke, he kept his voice calm and steady. 'Remember I told you we can find you a safe alternate. Not some post-apocalyptic—someplace genuinely safe with no other people.' He forced himself not to look around at the two guards with their strangely misshapen heads. 'We can even send a few doctors with you to treat the worst cases.'

'Some untouched Eden?' asked Greenbrooke, his tone gently mocking.

Kip bristled. 'It's a serious offer, damn you!'

'And you can transfer us there right now?'

Kip licked his lips. 'Well, no…'

'In fact, according to Orlova, the process of locating any such untrammelled paradise could take months, if not years. Am I correct?'

Kip's shoulders slumped in defeat. 'Perhaps.'

'Even if what you were saying was true, the answer would still be no.'

Kip stared at him. 'But *why?*'

Something flared in Greenbrooke's eyes. He thumped the desk hard, sending some of the folders sliding onto the floor. 'We want to go *home*, Director Mayer. Or at least to some version of the home we knew. One with medical facilities and labs that can reproduce the serum in the quantities we need. A place where we can live like civilised human beings and not animals grubbing in the dirt.'

Greenbrooke pushed himself out of his chair and moved past Kip, pulling the door open. 'We'll transfer him now,' said Greenbrooke, and the two guards took Kip by his arms, yanking him around until he faced the door.

'Svenson,' said Greenbrooke, addressing one of the guards. 'You've been treated?'

'Sir.' Svenson nodded, his voice a bare croak. 'Both me and Ethan.'

'Good.' Greenbrooke glared at Kip. 'Bring him.'

Ethan and Svenson took hold of Kip by the shoulders, half-dragging him back outside the building. He was marched towards a steel and aluminium dome housing the first of Katya's experimental transfer stages. Inside, Greenbrooke programmed the coordinates himself before joining Kip and the two other men as the light crescendoed.

* * *

They materialised in a transfer hall in the heart of the main EM facility on the Authority's home alternate. It proved to be just as deserted as Greenbrooke had said. The last time Kip had been here, some weeks before, it had bustled with activity. This time, however, it had about it the air of a place abandoned for years rather than a few days.

Kip's gaze alighted upon what at first appeared to be half a dozen people lying sleeping in a huddle in one corner of the hall. Then he saw the traces of blood on the walls and floor and guessed they must have been murdered by Greenbrooke and his men. Some of the bodies were clad in the brown and orange colour-coded uniforms of special response engineers, emergency workers whose job was to take control of the facility in just such a crisis. His heart plummeted to think of anyone dying so senselessly.

'Sir?' said the one called Svenson.

'Put the Director with the others,' said Greenbrooke, leading the way down the stage ramp. They moved towards a row of electric carts parked at the entrance to a corridor that stretched into the distance. 'If anyone's looking for me, I'll be with Murchison in the control room.'

Greenbrooke boarded a cart and drove down the corridor and out of sight. Kip's two guards pushed him into the back of another cart. He looked over at the bodies of the emergency workers and felt anger flow thick and dark in his veins. Hard as it was to believe, this Greenbrooke was an even nastier piece of work than the one he'd known.

They got under way, at first following in Greenbrooke's wake, then taking a right turn. Svenson, in the front passenger seat, acted as navigator, consulting a pocket map designed for visitors.

'Greenbrooke is insane,' Kip said to the backs of the two men. His voice was loud over the soft electric hum of the cart.

'All of you need expert medical attention as soon as possible. I can make sure you get it.'

Svenson twisted around in his seat to regard him with bloodshot eyes. Kip wondered how long he had been infected with the bee-brain virus, and just how much time the man had left before he turned. 'I heard you say that before.'

'I didn't—'

'Not you,' said Svenson. 'Another you, but he said the exact same words. After that, they came for us with guns.'

Kip's heart beat loud in his ears. 'I swear I would never let that—'

'Fifteen hundred miles,' Svenson snarled, madness bubbling in the depths of his eyes. 'That's how far we had to drive when all this started. A thousand of us in a convoy across infected territory. Barely a hundred of us made it. We'd have given up after that if it hadn't been for Agent Greenbrooke. And then most of us were slaughtered when we thought we'd found someplace safe.'

'I understand,' said Kip, struggling to keep his voice even. 'But—'

'But that's just it,' Svenson snapped. 'You *can't* understand. But those people—the Pathfinders?—*they'd* get it. Go ask them what they'd do if they were in our shoes.'

'I swear to you I can help!'

The one called Ethan pulled the car to a sudden halt and dug around in a pocket before producing a handgun and pointing it at Kip's face, his features twisted with hatred. The hand holding the gun shook, and Kip wondered if he might pull the trigger without even meaning to.

'Shut up,' Ethan snarled. 'Shut up, or I will blow your fucking head off.'

'Ethan,' said Svenson. 'We have orders.'

Ethan didn't move or say anything at first, his eyes as wide and empty as a desert. 'Then he's your responsibility,' he muttered, lowering his weapon. 'Keep him quiet, or I'll shoot him and tell Greenbrooke he made a run for it.'

Kip sat back and said nothing. Ethan stuffed the handgun back in his pocket and then they were underway again. Another minute passed before Kip remembered how to breathe.

They made two more turns before entering a cargo elevator that carried them down to a place of bare concrete and strip lights that drew parallel bars of shadow and light on a dusty floor. The cart soon arrived at a dead-end corridor with rows of steel doors all marked STORAGE.

Svenson disembarked first, looking somehow even more ill than he had before they transferred over. He stood before one of the doors with his rifle pointed at it. Ethan took Kip by the shoulder and led him up to the door. He unlocked it and pushed Kip inside.

Jerry and Katya stared back at him with as much surprise as Kip felt seeing them. The door slammed shut behind him with a loud *clang*.

'My God,' said Kip, his voice shaking. 'You have *no* idea what—'

'Sssh,' said Katya. She hobbled past him, one leg still heavily bandaged, and pressed an ear to the door. Kip listened, hearing Ethan and Svenson's muffled voices. After a moment came the faint whine of the cart's motor. It soon faded into the distance.

Katya stepped back. 'I heard one of them say he's going to the control room.' She looked at Kip. 'How many of them were there?'

'Two.'

'Then that leaves only one to guard us,' said Jerry.

'We shouldn't talk too loudly,' said Katya in a low voice. 'If I can hear him, he can certainly hear us.'

'Just so you know,' said Kip, 'Greenbrooke was with me when they brought me over to the facility. I know he's headed for the control centre himself.'

Kip studied Katya as he spoke: he hadn't seen her since the briefing for the Gamma Three expedition. It felt like a year had passed since then. Her face was bruised, her features pinched and angry, and there was something in her eyes almost frightening in its intensity. He couldn't make up his mind if it was fury, or terror, or both. She held herself carefully, and he noticed that she no longer had her crutches. Even if they did find some way to escape, they'd have to carry her just about the whole way.

'At least one of the two men who brought me here is very sick,' Kip added. 'I don't think he's got long to go.'

'Long to go before *what?*' asked Jerry.

'It appears a number of them are infected with the neuro-alvarium virus,' he explained.

Jerry's eyes grew wide. 'The *bee-brain* virus?'

'What are you talking about?' asked Katya.

'It's a gene-engineered virus that wiped out an alternate we explored years ago,' Kip explained. 'It's imperative we stop them infecting my own.' He turned to Jerry. 'How did you get here? Last I knew, you were still on Gamma Three with Yuichi and the others.'

Jerry grimaced. 'The mission went badly *snafu* and I transferred home to get help.' He nodded at the storage room door. 'As soon as I showed up, I had a bunch of those guys sticking guns in my face. They tied me up and shoved me in a corner until a couple of hours ago. Then they brought both me and Katya here.'

'What do you mean "something went wrong?"'

'Nadia's in trouble,' Jerry explained. He quickly summarised everything he knew.

Kip took a moment to absorb the news. Bramnik, when he'd been Director, had seemed to take this kind of thing in his stride. 'And you?' he asked Katya. 'Greenbrooke told me that he questioned you.'

'He wanted to know everything about this facility. I…' She swallowed hard. 'He is not a pleasant man.'

'Kip?' asked Jerry, a pained look on his face. 'She told me about this guy Greenbrooke. The name's just a coincidence, right?'

Kip shook his head. 'I'm afraid not.'

'But that's impossible!'

'It's not,' Kip reminded him. 'You should know that by now.'

That took some explaining too. Jerry seemed to curl in on himself as Kip relayed everything he, in turn, had learned.

'Surely,' Katya said once he had finished, 'your government must have realised something is wrong by now?'

'I assume so. I think Greenbrooke must know that too. From what I gather, he and his men want to find some hiding place right here on my own alternate.'

'That's nuts,' said Jerry. 'The infection would spread and you'd have a lot more to worry about than just an impending ice age.'

'The things they've been through would drive anyone insane,' Kip agreed. 'Crazy or not, this version of Greenbrooke isn't a fool, or he never would have got this far.'

'All right,' said Jerry, standing and pacing around the small, confined space. 'We know what we're up against. So what do we do about it?'

'From inside a locked room with an armed guard outside?' Kip shook his head. 'Not a great deal.'

'So if they get away,' said Jerry, thinking the options through, 'they could infect this entire alternate. But if we stop them and Greenbrooke detonates that nuke you say he has, we lose this whole facility.'

'In turn dooming tens of millions to starve and freeze to death with no way to get to Nova Terra.' Kip shrugged, his voice fatalistic. 'Whichever way you look at it, the outcome's bleak.'

They all looked at each other for a long moment.

'That might not be the case,' said Katya, her voice tremulous.

Kip looked at her. 'I don't understand.'

She smoothed her hands on her thighs in a nervous gesture and swallowed visibly. 'I...may have a confession to make.'

Kip shared a look with Jerry, then returned his attention to her. 'What kind of confession?'

'There's...more than just this one facility, Director Mayer.'

'You mean the original facility, back on the island?'

'No.' Kip could see she was having a hard time meeting the eyes of either of them. 'I didn't expect to tell you about this for some years, but it seems that circumstances dictate otherwise. There is a second facility, on the same scale and identical to this one.'

Kip regarded her numbly. 'That's not possible,' he muttered. 'I think we'd have noticed.'

'Not if it had been constructed in Russia, you wouldn't.'

'What?'

'I have been in charge of the facility in which we are currently imprisoned for two years now,' Katya explained, her tone becoming defensive. 'It has been...difficult. The more I see, the more I understand there are many amongst your people, Director Mayer, who would willingly abandon their citizens to their deaths even while they escape to an unblemished paradise.'

'Am I hearing you right?' asked Jerry. He was clearly working hard to suppress a grin. 'The Russians built a whole other facility, just like this one? And we didn't even *know* about it?'

Kip's chest felt constricted, like he was having trouble breathing. 'If that's true,' he rasped, 'you've committed treason.'

'Really?' Katya's tone shifted from defensive to defiant. 'I am not a citizen of the Authority. Nor am I a citizen of the Soviet Union, as your government continues to insist. I have been given no guarantees of any kind regarding my welfare, once my usefulness is over. How, then, can I have committed treason?'

Kip fought for words. 'You can't just...hand state secrets over to other nations!'

'This is an international, not a national matter,' she said. 'You told me that yourself. There is no reason not to share this technology with the Soviets, with the Chinese, with everybody else *immediately*. And since *your* government persisted in delaying any decision on that matter, I took matters into my own hands.'

'Oh my God,' Kip muttered weakly.

'And there are others under construction right now,' Katya

added. 'In Shengen, West Africa, and Brazil. Do you see? If we lose this facility, it would be a blow, yes—but there are many other nations able to take up the slack.' When she next met Kip's eyes, her gaze was steady. 'So you see, there *is* a solution to our problem—if we can get out of here.'

# Rozalia

*Alternate Alpha Zero (non-local variant)*

The transfer stage hangar faded from around Rozalia—and then reappeared around her.

She blinked in confusion. Was it possible the transfer hadn't worked?

She looked again. While superficially identical, only one of the overhead lights was working, and it flickered spasmodically. Crates that hadn't been there a moment before were stacked everywhere, with the majority situated close to the bottom of the stage on which she stood.

It dawned on her that the transfer had worked, and that, incredible as it seemed, she was on some other version of Alpha Zero's Easter Island. The idea sent a chill through her. And judging by the numerous rolled-up sleeping bags and bits of camping gear that covered the floor, the hangar had until recently been doing double-time as someone's home, although it now appeared to be deserted.

She stepped hesitantly down the ramp. Her nostrils picked up the overpowering stink of too many unwashed bodies crammed together for too long. The worst of it came from a curtained-off area in one corner she darkly suspected functioned as a latrine.

A number of the crates had been torn open, and when she investigated she found they contained field-rations and bottles of water. She opened one of the bottles and drank thirstily. Then she tore open a pack of field-rations and gorged herself on protein bars and strips of dehydrated beef before hurrying towards the rear entrance. She was eager to be out of sight before someone found her there.

She stepped outside. The ocean, at least, looked much the same as it ever did. And the air tasted fresh and salty on her tongue. The moon occupied the same position in the night sky it had back where she'd come from.

She approached the nearest corner of the building and peered across the compound: in every possible way it appeared to be the same. Despite everything she had seen inside the hangar, some part of her still rebelled against the idea she was not on the alternate that had been her home for some years now.

There was, however, one major and noticeable difference: there were no lights. The compound back home was lit up twenty-four hours a day. The town, far off in the distance, was similarly dark. Of course, it *was* the middle of the night, but usually there'd be at least one person still burning the midnight oil.

The roiling in her guts told her there was something very, very wrong here.

She jerked her head around at the sound of a pebble skittering down the steep embankment just a few metres from where she stood, the same one she had climbed up after following the shoreline back home. She stepped back as a figure suddenly lunged into view, laboriously climbing up the grassy embankment.

The moonlight revealed something in the shape of a man, but with a head so swollen that the facial features were distorted into a grotesque mask. Once it was on level ground it came straight towards her, its mouth stretched unnaturally wide.

Rozalia reacted instinctively, pivoting on one hip and delivering a round kick to one of the creature's knees.

It collapsed onto one leg, and she got close enough to slam a fist into its skull—something she immediately regretted. It felt like punching rotten fruit. When the creature forcefully exhaled, the stench was far worse than anything inside the hangar.

It tried to struggle back upright, and she kicked it again, breathing as shallowly as possible to keep from puking. The creature gave up, crawling away from her before again stumbling upright. She saw it take a misstep, tumbling over the edge of the slope and back down to the shore below.

She stared down at the darkened shore, her heart thundering in her chest. *What the hell is a bee-brain doing here?*

She gazed fixedly at her hand—the one that had come into contact with the bee-brain. She needed to get hold of the antidote in case she was infected already. There was some back home on her own island—

—except it was currently under the control of people who had escaped from *this* alternate. Even if she headed straight home, there were no guarantees she'd be able to locate supplies of the antidote without risking capture.

Which also meant she had anywhere from twenty-four

hours to a week before the virus—assuming she had been infected—became too advanced for the antidote to make any difference. That left her at least a few hours in which to take a look around and find out what had happened here...even if she was already pretty sure just what that was.

She made her way along the side of the hangar towards its front, scanning the surrounding darkness with even greater care. She saw someone had locked the big sliding doors of the hangar with a chain and padlock. Rotting bodies lay here and there across the compound.

She caught movement out of the corner of one eye and turned to see several more bee-brains emerge from the shadows near the fence that ran around the compound. Rozalia then tried to go back the way she'd come only to find yet more had appeared behind her, blocking her retreat.

Her throat became suddenly dry. They must, she thought, have climbed up from the beach. It had been a mistake to assume there was only one of them down there.

Yet more appeared, pushing through a part of the compound fence that looked like it had been trampled flat. She took out the handgun she'd taken from the clinic and aimed at the nearest of the bee-brains.

She pulled the trigger and it jammed.

'Oh, shit,' she said, very softly.

She pressed on the magazine to make sure it was home and checked that a round was chambered. It was: she worked the slide and tried to fire again, but it still didn't work. She found herself wondering just how long it had been sitting, forgotten, in its cabinet.

The bee-brains were much closer now, surrounding her in a loose ring. Rozalia's breath became ragged, and she gripped the gun like a club. She could try running, but by now there were just too damn many of them...

She heard a sound that was at once both familiar and terrifying: a metallic *shnick-shnack* that poured ice-water into her veins.

Then came another sound, like a ton of concrete being dropped onto sheets of metal, and the head of the bee-brain nearest to her exploded like an overripe melon. It collapsed soundlessly, and she noticed that it had been wearing the uniform of a transfer stage technician.

A new figure emerged from the shadows, wielding a pump-action shotgun. The figure worked the pump, ejecting the spent shell and firing again, killing another of the bee-brains.

*Shnick-shnack.* The figure, still shrouded in darkness, worked the pump once more and fired again. Another bee-brain went down. And another. And another.

Rozalia had frozen in a half-crouch, afraid whoever it was might mistake her for another bee-brain in the darkness, but then she realised that a path had been cleared in front of her all the way to the far side of the compound.

The figure ejected a final spent shell and hurried towards her, revealing itself, to her astonishment, to be Selwyn. He carried a heavy rucksack on his back, a pair of binoculars dangling around his neck.

It was immediately evident this Selwyn was quite different from *her* Selwyn. This one was older-looking, more...weary.

'This way!' he shouted, grabbing her by the wrist and dragging her after him.

Given the circumstances, it seemed wise not to resist.

They ran across the compound and past the remaining bee-brains. The older, scragglier Selwyn pulled her inside a storage shed, slamming the door shut and bolting it. The shed was windowless, and when he reached up to turn on an overhead light she was momentarily blinded.

He dropped his rucksack on the floor and cracked the shotgun open, feeding more shells into it. She noticed a pair of heavy bolt-cutters secured to the back of the rucksack with bungee cords. He closed the shotgun and held it with the barrel pointing down at the ground, staring at her in utter disbelief.

'Now I know I'm losing my mind,' he said matter-of-factly. 'I saw you die.'

Rozalia slid down to the floor with her back against a wall and stared up at him. 'As you can see,' she assured him, her voice shaking only slightly, 'I'm very much alive.'

'Yes, but I—' he halted mid-sentence, and looked down at the shotgun still gripped in one hand, as if remembering something.

She wondered if he'd been about to say *I killed you myself.*

'Just tell me what happened,' she said. 'Assume I don't know anything.'

His eyes were wide and haunted. 'You're not from here.'

'No,' she said. 'I'm not. Is it just the island?'

He looked at her with momentary confusion. 'You mean the bee-brains?' She nodded. 'No, my girl, it's everywhere, I'm sorry to say.'

'The Authority...?'

'Gone,' he said. 'It started there, then came here with the first wave of refugees.' He slumped down across from her, his gaze still fixed on her like he couldn't be sure she was real. 'If this means I'm mad,' he muttered, 'it's not as awful as I thought it might be.'

'You're not mad,' she assured him. At least now she understood what Greenbrooke had been fleeing. 'Are we safe in here?'

He shrugged. 'They're in no hurry, if that's what you mean.' He licked lips that looked cracked and filthy. 'Where did you—?'

'Please,' she said, interrupting him. 'First just explain to me how it started.'

'And then you'll tell me where you came from?'

She nodded.

He settled back and stared up at the ceiling. 'Casey Vishnevsky is the one responsible. He had some insane vendetta against the Authority, so he set out to destroy them. By the time we realised what he'd done, he'd already fled to some post-apocalyptic alternate. We never found him.' His eyes grew wide and he dropped his head back down to look at her. 'Is there a Vishnevsky where you come from?'

'We killed him,' Rozalia replied, 'before he could do the same thing to us.'

'Ah.' Not-Selwyn's brow furrowed in thought. 'I suppose that's where our histories forked.'

'Does the name Greenbrooke mean anything to you?'

'Yes.'

'Well, him and a bunch of his cronies just turned up on *our* alternate looking for a fight and took us by surprise. I came here hoping I could figure out what he wanted.'

'So that explains it,' he muttered.

'Explains what?'

'The transfer hangar—Greenbrooke and his men were living in there for weeks. I couldn't get near enough the place to see what they were up to. There were always one or two of them

179

up on the roof of the hangar, and they'd pick off anyone who got too close, human or bee-brain.'

'There's no one in there now.'

'I saw they'd pulled the snipers from the roof,' he said with some excitement. 'That was yesterday evening. I've been watching them, you see—from what I could hear, they've been running both stages day and night for weeks. I figured they were looking for some alternate to escape to, but I never imagined…' he broke off and shook his head.

'Selwyn,' she asked, 'how many of them are infected?'

'Some, if not most,' Selwyn replied. 'We had serum, but it got used up by the first wave of refugees.'

'We have serum,' said Rozalia. 'Is it possible that's what they want?'

'Maybe.' He shrugged. 'If it is, it's too late for them. They've been exposed to it for too long.' He glanced down at his shotgun. 'I suppose you've given me even more reason to finish what I came here to do.'

'Which is?'

'Destroy the hangar. Greenbrooke and his men killed a lot of good people when they took over here—people who were also trying to figure a way out of this mess. Now they've left the hangar unguarded, I want to make sure they can never use it again.'

Rozalia shifted closer to him. She put her hand over his, where it rested on his knee. 'Selwyn—what happened to the other Pathfinders?'

He smiled sadly. 'I'm the last of us, Rosie my girl—in this universe, at any rate.' His expression turned fierce. 'Listen to me—when you get back there, you have to kill Greenbrooke and all of his men. You can't risk the same thing happening there too. They don't care about anything or anyone that gets in their way.'

She stood. 'I didn't know what I'd find when I got here, but I never thought…'

'I know.' He stood as well.

She looked at him with grim determination. 'I need to get back home.'

From outside came a metallic clattering, and the sound of many feet tramping across the ground. Selwyn opened the door a crack and looked outside, then stepped back, nodding at Rozalia to take a look.

She peered outside. A stream of bee-brains were making their way across the compound, moving in the direction of town. Some wore the rags of civilian clothes, while others wore the tattered remains of military uniforms. They were dragging along pieces of junk, bound, no doubt, for some proto-hive they were in the process of building.

'What was your plan, exactly?' she asked him, pulling the door shut again.

Selwyn picked up the rucksack and opened it, angling it so she could see inside. 'There's enough industrial gelignite in here to put the Pyramids into orbit. That'll put paid to the transfer stages.'

'Jesus,' she muttered. 'What about you, Selwyn? Where are *you* going to escape to?'

He closed the rucksack, pulling it back on before favouring her with a tight smile. 'It'll be a lot harder to avoid them in the day,' he said. 'And dawn isn't far away. So let's do this now.' He nodded at the handgun she had pushed back into her waistband. 'Why didn't you use that?'

'It jammed.'

He pulled another handgun from his belt and handed it to her. 'A shotgun would be better, but between the two of us, we should be able to clear a path back to the hangar.' He snatched up a box of shells that had been sitting near the door, shoved them into a pocket of his khaki trousers and reached for the door-handle. 'Ready?'

Rozalia nodded. He carefully pushed the door open and took another look outside. 'Even more of the blighters than before,' he said over his shoulder. 'But we can't sit here all night, can we?'

'No, we can't.' Her body thrummed with nervous energy.

'Then let's make haste,' he said, slamming the door wide and stepping into the night.

She followed in his wake, and saw the nearest dozen or so of the creatures lurch towards them. Selwyn fired at one and it collapsed, half of its pulpy head sheared away.

Rozalia did the same. Fortunately, the majority of the bee-brains were locked into their path towards town, and they were soon able to reach the hangar's locked doors.

'Take this and reload,' said Selwyn, handing her the shotgun and the box of shells. 'This is going to take a minute.'

Rozalia took the shotgun and cracked it open, feeding in more shells, her back to the hangar doors. She cut down four more bee-brains that came staggering towards them, including one that got close enough to almost reach out to her. Next to her, Selwyn swore and muttered as he worked to sever the chain holding the doors shut with the bolt-cutters.

The chain rattled as it fell away and Selwyn slid one of the doors open. 'Inside!' he shouted.

Rozalia shot two more, then ran inside the hangar, helping Selwyn slide it shut once more. He slammed the inside bolt and the doors shivered under the pressure of bodies pressing up against it from the outside.

'That won't hold them for long,' said Rozalia, panic edging her voice.

'It doesn't need to,' Selwyn replied. 'Get the stage powered up.'

She nodded and ran over to the same stage by which she'd arrived, programming it for a return journey.

While she worked, Selwyn tore open his rucksack and pulled out bundles of explosive daisy-chained together with wire. He set a detonator next to the opposite stage and fiddled with it for a moment: Rozalia guessed he was setting a timer. Then he stood up and placed more explosives around the base of the stage she had just programmed.

Rozalia finished programming the stage and quickly ascended its ramp, pale lightning throbbing at the tips of its field-pillars. She heard the sound of splintering wood and saw the hangar doors bow inward.

'Selwyn!' she shouted. 'They're coming!'

'I'm nearly done,' he yelled back, still tinkering with something.

'I don't think you need to worry about blowing this place up,' she said. 'Those things are going to tear it apart.'

'Better safe than sorry.'

The light above her head grew stronger. 'For God's sake, Selwyn, get up here!'

He laughed softly and made his way over to the controls for her stage. 'I don't think so.'

'What?' She stared at him in horror. 'You'd be safe back on my alternate. You're not making any sense!'

'I'll die whether I'm here or there, Roz,' he said, his voice calm. As he spoke, he shrugged off his heavy jacket and rolled up a sleeve. She saw the black and red buboes marking his skin from the wrist all the way up to the shoulder.

'You're infected,' she said, her voice numb.

'I'm glad fate allowed me this last chance to talk to you, Rosie. But if you don't mind, I think it's best if I stay where I am.'

She tried to find something meaningful she could say, but the words wouldn't come. 'I'm sorry,' was all she could manage.

'On the contrary,' he replied, 'I take great comfort from the knowledge that the multiverse is full to the brim with uncountable Selwyn Rudd's. Where I fall, long may they continue.'

'I'll tell him about you,' she said as the light grew towards its peak. 'The Selwyn I know.'

'Tell him he's a drunken sot,' he replied, 'and that Gwendolyn Bennings of Hatcher and Hatcher Ironmongers, Cardiff, is still the finest sight that ever passed before his eyes.'

The hangar doors burst open, and a great swarm of bee-brains came pouring in. Selwyn turned, shotgun raised to his shoulder, and fired shot after shot into them as they swarmed around him.

The transfer-light washed over Rozalia. She screamed, thinking for a moment she had been caught in the detonation. But when her vision cleared, revealing her own transfer hangar, deserted in the middle of the night, she collapsed onto the stage, gasping and sobbing.

*Get moving*, she told herself, stumbling upright and making her way back down the ramp and towards the rear exit. She stepped out into moonlight and cautiously made her way along the side of the hangar to its front, déjà vu prickling at her senses. She ducked low when a jeep, carrying several raggedy-men, drove past.

She doubled back and made her way down to the beach. The moon was behind clouds, so she could hardly see a thing. Her imagination conjured a thousand hands grasping for her from out of the darkness.

An idea came to her. Instead of heading south towards town, she turned north, her destination the fishing hut where she had first seen the raggedy-men.

# Randall

'Hey, Danks! I said pass me the damn *wrench*!'

'Sorry,' said Fred Danks, who stood with his back pressed up against the side of the truck. He reached down into the open toolbox beside him, picking out a wrench and passing it to Private Young without once taking his eyes off the huge Chimera prowling across the grass just metres from where he stood. Young, who had made the request, snatched the wrench from Danks before squirming back underneath the EV truck.

'Can you keep it quiet?' Randall muttered from where he crouched on the ground several metres away, his attention fixed on the Chimera. 'I'm *trying* to *concentrate* here.'

Betty moved in slow circles, sniffing the air in a way that might have been cat-like, if a cat weighed one and a half tons and resembled the nightmare marriage of a dragon and a spiked mace.

'Beats me how you can stand even having that thing anywhere near you,' said Danks, his voice rasping slightly. He

186

stood with his rifle held close against his chest, his eyes wide and round and filled with abject terror, despite Randall's assurances that the Chimera would do him no harm unless he ordered it to.

Randall paused and turned to look at Danks with undisguised irritation. Then he slipped the bracelet off his wrist and held it out to him. 'I need to concentrate. Either shut up so I can figure out how to do this properly, or *you* can take charge of the damn thing.'

Danks made a disgusted sound and looked away.

Young squirmed his way back out from underneath the truck. 'Looks like something got damaged when we came down that slope above the river.'

'Think you can fix it?' asked Danks.

'Sure,' said Young, wiping sweat from his brow. It was the middle of the night back on the island, but here on Delta Twenty-Five, it was around midday and the sun beat down on them without mercy. 'Just have to cannibalise a couple of bits and pieces from another part of the truck.' He shrugged. 'Done it before.'

Randall moved away from the truck and closer to a copse of trees with something that looked remarkably similar to popcorn growing on their branches. Delta Twenty-Five was an alternate Earth, the same as every other he had visited, but on this one evolution had taken such a wildly divergent and—in Randall's opinion—deeply fucked-up path that it was sometimes easier to pretend it was an entirely *different* planet.

It occurred to Randall that maybe it wasn't such a bad thing the truck had broken down. He needed the time to work on figuring out how best to control Betty, who still prowled nearby. She'd come bounding out of the undergrowth to meet them less than half an hour after he'd called her to him.

He slipped the bracelet back onto his wrist and immediately felt the connection with the strange beast re-establish itself. Betty responded to his thoughts, but it took time, as Oskar had once explained, to train yourself to get the exact results you wanted.

To his surprise, however, Randall had discovered he was something of a natural. Certainly he was progressing far more quickly than he had expected, and possibly faster than Oskar.

He touched the bracelet with two fingers and felt the beast respond immediately, stretching its head upwards and opening its mouth to reveal long, wicked-looking fangs that gleamed in the midday sun like burnished steel.

*Deep breaths*, Oskar had told Randall more than once. *You gotta clear your mind. Let it come to you.*

Randall did just that, and the bracelet responded with a tingling sensation against his fingertips. Weird, indecipherable text flickered in his mind's eye, and suddenly it was as if he could see himself and Betty from above. He could even sense some of her thoughts, such as they were.

He moved his fingers and focused on an image in his mind. The Chimera responded by rolling onto its back.

Randall grinned with unabashed delight. He'd never imagined this would be nearly as much fun as it was turning out to be.

# IV

# The Long Fall

# Nadia

'How about a Cataclysm of Pathfinders?' suggested Nadia, shifting her grip on the girder yet again. She'd long since lost track of just how long she had been kneeling there. Hours, certainly.

'Doesn't work,' said Yuichi, the strain in his voice audible. Both he and Chloe had been working for the better part of an hour to clear more rubble from the stairwell, and it was taking its toll on them—especially Yuichi. 'Same reason as before: "Pathfinders" is what the Authority call us. It doesn't really say what we *are*.'

'Okay,' said Nadia. 'So how about a cataclysm of, of…'

'A survival,' said Yuichi.

'A survival of what? Survivors?'

'See?' said Yuichi. 'It isn't easy to find the right words.'

'Hey,' Chloe snapped. 'Quit wasting time and help me get this damn boulder out of the way. And please, Nadia, focus on conserving your air!'

A deep ache had spread across Nadia's ribs and shoulders.

She and Yuichi had both learned the hard way what happened when you told Chloe to take it easier what with her being pregnant and all.

'We're getting closer,' said Yuichi. 'Just a few more big rocks to get out of the way and—'

'My arms and legs are getting really numb,' said Nadia.

'Breathe shallow,' said Yuichi. 'I'll even stand you a drink when we head back home. I just brewed a nice fresh batch of porter beer.'

She laughed weakly. 'Are you trying to *make* me let go?'

Chloe laughed too, but it sounded halfway to a sob.

*You like acting tough*, Rozalia sometimes told Nadia. *But sometimes I wish you'd just admit it when you're scared.*

That would be about now, but Rozalia wasn't there to tell. Nadia glanced at her suit's oxygen readings: if they didn't get her out in the next fifty minutes, she'd be out of air.

She had already decided she would hold on to the girder for as long as possible once her air ran out. The last thing she wanted was to be conscious when she started a fall that would never end.

The radio clicked, indicating that Yuichi and Chloe had switched yet again to a private channel. They'd been doing it more and more frequently over the past hour.

Time passed. A few pebbles of concrete went tumbling past, followed by a chunk of rebar. Nadia took a firmer grip on the girder, waiting for the tremor to subside.

It took her a moment to realise there had been no tremor. Another pebble skittered past, and she glanced upwards, craning her neck.

Someone was standing on the ledge above her, looking down from what remained of the basement's floor.

Nadia blinked rapidly, like something had got in her eye. When she next looked, there was no one there. But she had *seen* a figure in a blue pressure suit, crouching right at the edge of the broken basement floor. She thought of the bootprints in the dust.

Dammit, she *hadn't* been seeing things!

'Hey!' Nadia shouted over the radio. 'Who are you?'

No answer.

She heard a *click* as the others came back online.

'Uh, Nads?' Yuichi's voice sounded wary. 'Who were you talking to just now?'

'I swear to God we're not alone down here,' Nadia insisted. 'I saw someone else up above me, in the part of the basement that hasn't fallen yet. They were in a blue pressure suit, Yuichi.'

'Can you see them right now?' asked Chloe.

'No, they're gone,' Nadia replied. 'They pulled back out of sight as soon as they realised I'd seen them.'

More clicks sounded in Nadia's helmet as Yuichi and Chloe switched yet again to a private channel. More than a minute passed before they switched back to shared comms.

'Nadia,' said Yuichi, 'can you check your oxygen levels for me?'

'Dammit, Yuichi, I'm not seeing things!'

'Either way, you still need to conserve your air,' Chloe insisted. Nadia had the sense she was working hard to sound calm. 'We're going to try something else. There's climbing gear back in the truck. Yuichi's going to keep working at moving the rubble while I go and get it. We'll get up on the roof and rappel down to where you are.'

That sounded like far from a good idea. 'Don't you think that's a little dangerous?'

Yuichi laughed sourly. 'It's *all* dangerous, Nadia.'

Nadia glanced across the width of the pit to its far rim. The sun was sinking towards it. She checked her oxygen levels, then wished she hadn't. She had less than thirty minutes of air left.

She tried to relax. Yuichi and Chloe were working as hard as they could to save her. Even so, she could feel each second as it flew by. It wasn't long before another vibration shook the girder—and then another. More of the floor above broke away, but a largish chunk of concrete remained attached by a tangle of cables still embedded within it. The chunk swung to and fro, then gradually slowed to a halt.

The cables led up to what little remained of the basement floor. From what Nadia could see, she might be able to reach out and snag one of them. And if she could do that, *and* the cables held, she might then have the opportunity to pull herself up to safety.

Her throat became dry at the thought, but she'd faced worse odds. Possibly.

She carefully manoeuvred herself upright until she was standing somewhat precariously on top of the bent and twisted girder to which she had clung for too many hours. She steadied herself with one gloved hand against the rough concrete wall from which the girder protruded. The girder wobbled very slightly beneath her, and for a moment Nadia thought her heart might give out.

She let herself stand like that for a couple of seconds, feeling the protest of tired and aching muscles. The pain was worst in her joints.

The tangle of cables was close, but she saw that she would have to lean some way out from the girder in order to grab hold of the nearest of them. Far enough that if she missed, or if the cables couldn't take her weight, there'd be nothing to stop her falling.

Nadia steadied her breathing as best she could, working hard not to think of the nothingness beneath her. She began to lean out, her fingers grasping for the cable, but just before she could reach it another strong tremor shook the girder hard enough that she crouched back down, a scream stalled in her throat. Dust pattered down onto the curved plastic of her helmet visor.

She turned to look at the concrete in which the girder was embedded, and saw a hairline crack growing slowly wider right before her eyes.

There was no more time to think. Nadia stood back up and leaned out and away from the girder, reaching out for the nearest of the cables—far enough she couldn't possibly recover her balance.

She got hold of a fistful of cables first with one hand, then the other, until they were taking nearly all of her weight. They held, and she felt the girder shake more than it ever had.

*Now.* She gritted her teeth, all the air escaping from her lungs as she finally stepped off the girder, her body swinging wildly to and fro. When she glanced back, she saw that the hairline crack now yawned wide, and she watched with horror as a huge chunk of floor, along with the girder, went tumbling into infinity.

Fear gave her the strength she needed to pull herself up the cables, hand over hand, all the way up to the floor above. She scrabbled at broken tiles, the muscles in her arms and shoulders feeling like they were going to tear apart as she ascended. She found just enough purchase with her boots to push herself the rest of the way on top of what little remained of the basement floor.

Nadia's lungs thundered like pistons. She rolled onto her back, her legs and arms threatening to cramp, sweat drenching her skin inside the pressure suit.

*I did it.*

She rolled onto her front and somehow found the strength to struggle upright. She surveyed the stairwell before her. Rubble filled it from top to bottom.

No way Yuichi or anyone else were ever going to dig their way through all *that*.

To her left lay the storage room where they had found the containment units, now dark and silent. By contrast, a faint glow still issued from within the second storage room to her right. The collapse of the basement floor had wiped away all trace of the bootprints she had seen earlier.

She switched on an open channel. 'Hey, guys?' she croaked. 'I managed to climb back up. I'm standing at the bottom of the stairwell and it's completely blocked. There's no way you're getting down here.'

'Holy *shit*,' Yuichi exclaimed. 'You did *what?*'

'Nadia!' exclaimed Chloe. 'You're all right? You still have air?'

Nadia tongued the internal display of her helmet. She stared at the numbers and licked her lips. 'Maybe ten minutes.'

She heard Chloe swear under her breath. 'Okay, listen—I've got the rappelling gear and spare tanks of oxygen. We're both up on top of the building right now. We're about to climb down to you. You stay on channel, hear me?'

As Chloe spoke, Nadia glanced towards the storage room to her right in time to see the light grow dim, then bright again, precisely as if someone were moving around inside it.

'Nadia,' Chloe repeated. 'Please respond. Did you hear me?'

'I hear you,' Nadia replied, making her way over to the storage room entrance. The basement floor had settled at a slight angle, making walking awkward.

She stepped inside. The same figure in a blue pressure suit stood with its back to her, apparently struggling to remove a containment unit from its wall-slot.

Nadia tongued on an open channel. 'I'm in the second containment room,' she said. 'I can see them right now. Whoever they are, they're wearing a blue pressure suit, just like I said. We're not the only ones after the EM.'

'That's imposs—' Yuichi started to say.

'Don't move,' said Chloe, her voice urgent. 'Just stay right where you are.'

*Who are you?* Nadia wondered. *And where the hell did you come from?*

She heard Chloe scream just then, and turned around in time to see widening cracks race across what was left across the floor of the basement. The cracks reached up the walls, growing yet wider, and then Nadia was surrounded by dense clouds of dust and rock and dirt.

The ground slipped out from under Nadia's boots and she fell into the darkness. She covered her visor with her arms as best she could against the tumbling wreckage.

This time, she knew with a terrible finality, there would be no rescue.

Nadia crashed into something, then span away from it. She caught a glimpse of the nearest wall of the pit, illuminated by the setting sun.

The facility—or what little remained of it—was already far

above her, and receding fast. Its ruins fell along with her, appearing motionless from her perspective.

Her oxygen readout told her she had less than three minutes left. The inside of her helmet already felt too warm and close. She spread out her arms in an attempt to slow her spinning. The dirt and rubble had spread out into a great cloud all around her. The nearest wall of the pit appeared smooth, like glass.

She managed to look up. The further she fell, the more pronounced the curve of the edge of the pit became. How long, she wondered with a thrill of horror, before it shrank to a tiny dot, and then nothing?

Perhaps it was a mercy that she would be dead by then.

She became aware of Yuichi and Chloe frantically calling to each other over their radio links. By the sounds of it, neither had been caught up in the collapse. They were beseeching Nadia to speak to them, to tell them whether she was still there.

*I guess there's no better time to way goodbye*, she thought, tonguing the comms channel on.

# Rozalia

It took Rozalia more than an hour to walk all the way from the compound to the fishing hut further up the coast. At first she stayed away from the road, but the lack of any traffic suggested the raggedy-men had given up their search for anyone else.

Inside the hut, she pulled a hammer from a rack and got to work prying up several floorboards. Beneath them lay a grey metal chest set into concrete foundations. Inside were two boxes of shotgun shells, a pair of sawn-off double-barrelled shotguns, half a dozen hand-guns, a similar number of boxes of .22 ammunition and a rucksack.

*Something for a rainy day*, Yuichi had called it. The stockpile hadn't been placed there for any specific reason, or with any specific threat in mind. It was more that stockpiling weaponry bordered on instinct for every one of the Pathfinders.

She shoved all of the pistols into the rucksack, along with the two boxes of shotgun shells and as many rounds of ammunition as she thought she could carry. She lashed one shotgun to the back of the rucksack with a bungee-cord and carried the other. Then she dropped the floorboards back in place and headed towards town, grunting under the weight of the rucksack.

She had no illusions about being able to carry out a one-woman resistance to the invasion, but logic dictated at some point the Authority would respond to the sudden breakdown of communications with Alpha Zero. She wanted to be ready for that counter-invasion if and when it happened—and there was still a chance she wasn't the only one who had avoided capture.

She left the road once the compound came into view, circling around low hills and making her way towards the northernmost part of town. Her skin was damp with sweat, and she couldn't stop thinking about the food in her and Nadia's kitchen and how hungry she was: the military rations she'd eaten hadn't been nearly enough to sustain her.

She crept through the streets, passing deserted house after deserted house and making her way to several residences occupied by Pathfinders. They were all empty, and there were signs, particularly at Winifred's, of there having been a struggle. Lastly she checked out the basement of an abandoned school they'd jointly agreed to use as a hide-out in case of some unspecified emergency, but it, too, was empty.

That left only the Mauna Loa to check out.

She dropped into a crouch behind a tree on the opposite side of the road from the hotel-bar and waited to see if anything moved. The Mauna Loa functioned as a cross between an informal drinking club for the Pathfinders and a town hall, and if anyone on the island was still free, it was the last place left they might be hiding.

She was glad she'd waited when one of Greenbrooke's

raggedy-men emerged from around a corner, tugging his flies back up. He picked up a rifle that had been leaning against the far side of the front porch, where Rozalia couldn't see it. He remained out front of the building and appeared to be guarding it.

Which, of course, meant someone inside was being guarded.

She didn't have anything that could pick the guard off from a distance, and there was no way of knowing yet whether there were more raggedy-men inside the building. She waited until he lit a cigarette and looked the other way before making a move.

Making a low dash across the street, Rozalia threw herself into the long grass out front of a former dentists three doors down from the Mauna Loa, then carefully made her way around the side of the building to the back yard. She climbed over several fences at the rear of the properties until she was round the back of the Mauna Loa.

Creeping up beside the building, she hurried towards its far corner, peering around it and back towards the street. The raggedy man was still standing there, still smoking his cigarette.

Rozalia slid the rucksack down from her shoulders and took a moment to catch her breath. Listening, she caught the low murmur of voices from within.

Standing carefully, Rozalia peered in through a narrow window and inside the Mauna Loa. Selwyn and Winifred sat next to each other in the rear bar, partly obscured from Rozalia's sight by a tangle of rubber hoses and kegs that constituted one of Yuichi's stills. Their faces were drawn and worried-looking, and Winifred sat with her fingers twisted together in a knot.

Rozalia stared at Selwyn, experiencing a powerful rush of cognitive dissonance. Then she lifted herself high enough she could gently rap on the glass.

Selwyn and Winifred both looked up. Selwyn's eyes in particular almost seemed to pop out of his head when he saw who it was. He hurried over, flattening his face against the glass and angling his eyes to one side. 'Cellar doors,' he said, his voice muffled.

Rozalia took a step back and saw a pair of trapdoors set into the ground to her left. A length of wood had been pushed through the pull-handles of both doors, preventing them from being opened from the inside. Rozalia slid the plank out and eased one of the cellar doors open before retrieving the rucksack and carrying it down the steps into the cellar. Pulling the door shut again, she made her way up to the Mauna Loa's kitchen, which was half-filled with all the other accoutrements of Yuichi's home-brewing.

Selwyn came to the door of the kitchen, a look of childlike delight on his face. 'I saw one guard out front,' Rozalia said in a low voice. 'Are there any more?'

'Not that I know of,' Selwyn replied in a loud stage-whisper.

She nodded and followed him through to the rear bar, where Winifred wrapped her up in a hug that felt wonderful. Rozalia glanced over Winifred's shoulder and saw a toasted cheese sandwich sitting half-finished on a plate. She stepped away from Winifred and snatched up the sandwich, consuming it in a couple of bites.

'Hungry?' Winifred asked with a wry smile.

'Thorry,' Rozalia said around a mouthful of bread and cheese. God, but it tasted wonderful. She let the rucksack slide off her shoulders and it landed with a thud.

202

'What happened to you, honey?' asked Winifred. She caught Selwyn's eye. 'Go keep an eye out front in case that guy comes in again.'

Selwyn nodded and turned towards the front bar.

'One second,' said Rozalia, wiping sticky fingers on her jeans. Then she grabbed hold of Selwyn, pulling him into an even tighter bear-hug than Winifred had given her.

'You're the best, Selwyn,' she said, her voice muffled by the thick wool of his jumper. 'I know that doesn't make much sense right now, but I'll explain later.'

Selwyn's cheeks pinked. 'Well,' he said, in a mock-gruff voice, 'what's all *this* in aid of?'

She let go of him and looked between him and Winifred. 'I have *the* most incredible story to tell you. But why is it just the two of you here?'

'We got rounded up by people like that young fella out there in the middle of the night,' Winifred explained. 'They stuck a couple dozen of us in here while three of them stood guard out front and threatened to shoot anyone who so much as hollered.' She shuddered. 'We sat around for several hours and then they started pulling people out and taking them away in jeeps, but in dribs and drabs—sometime one, sometimes two at a time. Selwyn and me are the only ones left.'

Rozalia felt a wave of fatigue wash through her and slumped into a seat. Selwyn had moved into the front bar, keeping a watchful eye on the street entrance. 'What's in the rucksack?' asked Winifred.

Rozalia opened it so she could see inside. 'We need to get out of here,' she said, 'before they come for you and Selwyn.'

Winifred responded by reaching into the rucksack and pulling out a hand-gun. She pulled the slide back and looked inside the chamber, then peered over the gun at Rozalia. 'You came prepared.'

'I—' Rozalia paused, hearing the sound of an engine from the street.

Selwyn came back through. 'Someone's coming,' he said with sudden urgency.

Winifred looked back at Rozalia. 'Looks like you were just in time,' she said, handing the gun to Selwyn and taking hold of the other sawn-off shotgun and a box of shells.

# Nadia

Two minutes of air left and counting. Nadia wondered why she didn't have the guts to crank her helmet open and get it over with.

She'd once read about people who achieved a kind of serenity in the face of apparently inescapable death. Now that she found herself in much the same situation, it came to her that every last one of those stories was worth so much horse-shit.

*Serenity my ass.* It took all her strength to keep from just screaming herself hoarse.

Mostly, though, she was just numb.

She'd fallen far enough by now that the mouth of the pit had indeed shrunk to a point. She could still just about see it whenever her long, slow tumble turned her the right way up. She tried not to think of the pit as something living, because that would mean she was tumbling down its gullet...

The next time she rotated the right way up the mouth of the pit disappeared for a single brief instant, then reappeared

205

again—precisely as if something had passed in front of it.

More rubble, she assumed. Her body span slowly around until she saw only darkness. It was getting hard to breathe, like she had to work more and more for every lungful.

Right way up again: this time, she thought she could just about make out the faint outline of a figure between her and the mouth of the pit. She stared, slack-jawed, as it drifted closer, revealing itself to be clad in a blue pressure suit.

Nadia waggled her arms in an attempt to slow her gradual spin, then cursed as the figure slid back out of sight regardless.

Seconds passed, each breath harder than the last. If anything, her speed of rotation had increased. Sooner than she expected she once again found herself facing upwards.

The figure was closer now—a lot closer. Nadia saw a puff of mist emerge from some point on their suit, pushing them towards her.

*Hey Blue*, thought Nadia. *Your suit is holed.*

More puffs of gas emerged from the stranger's suit, rapidly closing the gap between them. Nadia realised Blue was doing it deliberately. Suddenly they collided, and Blue reached out, taking a tight grip on one of Nadia's arms.

Now they span as one, the pit revolving around them at an increased rate.

Nadia gasped at air that was hardly there. What little starlight found its way this far down was just sufficient for her to glimpse the face inside the helmet opposite hers. She saw a dark-skinned woman with close-cropped hair and wrinkles around her eyes.

*It isn't possible*, thought Nadia, recognising the face inside the helmet. The easiest explanation was that she had lost her mind.

If it was an illusion, it nonetheless felt very, very real.

'Rozalia?' asked Nadia, her voice trembling. Had she come to rescue her? And if so—how in hell were they going to get out of this?

Rozalia—although some part of Nadia's mind insisted this was someone else who just really, really *looked* like Rozalia—shook her head to show they couldn't hear what Nadia was saying. Nadia tongued her comms, switching through channels to try and find one by which they could communicate.

Rozalia's twin pressed her visor against Nadia's own and shouted something. The sound carried through the point where their helmets came into contact.

'How much air do you have left?' the other woman demanded.

Nadia stared at the other woman. The face was undoubtedly the same as Rozalia's, she saw now, but there were subtle differences that made her sure that this was not *her* Rozalia, starting with the hint of a tattoo below one ear and just about visible through her visor.

'What does it matter?' Nadia yelled back. 'Either way we're dead!'

Not-Rozalia frowned inside her helmet. 'Nobody's dying here.'

She held onto Nadia by one shoulder and used her other hand to make some space between them so she could reach down to a panel embedded in the front of her suit. She tapped at the panel, then pulled Nadia close to her in a tight hug.

Light enveloped them, growing incandescent within seconds. There was something overwhelmingly familiar about it, and it hit Nadia that it was precisely the same hue of light she witnessed every time a transfer stage was activated.

In the next instant the pit was gone. They were both still falling, but through rich, golden sunlight. Nadia's senses struggled to make sense of the transition, and she fought the urge to vomit.

Air battered at them, threatening to pull them apart from each other. Nadia caught a glimpse of buttery clouds stretched across an evening sky, and a sea that spread from horizon to horizon.

They hit the water with sufficient force that Nadia was almost stunned into unconsciousness. Despite this, not-Rozalia managed to keep both her arms locked around Nadia's waist.

They sank quickly, Nadia in her suit sucking at air that wasn't there. Above her, sunlight reflected through the waves, something long and sinuous darting out of their way as they descended.

Not-Rozalia was fumbling again with the suit panel and the light swallowed them both a second time. Now they were falling again, but it lasted barely a moment. They landed much harder this time around, and with sufficient force to drive out what little air remained in Nadia's lungs.

Nadia floundered, pain radiating through her ribs. Not-Rozalia rolled to one side and struggled upright. With some effort, Nadia pushed herself onto all fours, and took a look around.

The Gamma Three monitoring station, light glowing from within, stood just metres from where she crouched amidst the ruins of a car park. Which was completely and utterly impossible.

Nadia tried to stand up and heard a rushing sound in her ears not unlike a waterfall. Her lungs ached more than she could ever have imagined possible, and she pitched forward, her knees giving way beneath her. She was at best distantly aware of being dragged through the monitoring station's airlock and of her helmet being removed.

She came to suddenly, gasping at the air flooding into her lungs. It felt like drowning in cotton candy.

'Rosie,' she managed to gasp. 'It's you. How…?'

Not-Rozalia stared down at her, her helmet held by her side. Nadia saw a tiny red rose tattooed on the woman's neck, just below the left ear.

'Do you know me?' asked not-Rozalia, a look of befuddlement on her face.

'Of course I do,' said Nadia. 'You're—' she caught herself. 'Don't you know *me*?'

One corner of the other woman's mouth twitched with apparent bemusement. 'I'm afraid not.' She lifted her helmet back up and re-secured it to her pressure suit. 'I have to go,' she said, her words now muffled.

'No, wait,' said Nadia, struggling to stand upright.

'I'm sorry,' not-Rozalia added. She touched the panel on the front of her suit and vanished in a blaze of light.

Nadia blinked at the empty air where the other woman had been. Then she stared around the interior of the monitoring station, at its storage units and two-way airlock. Just seconds before and she'd been falling to her death, and now—

—now she was here. And the woman who looked so much like Rozalia was gone, as if she had never existed.

Static squawked from inside Nadia's helmet, which lay nearby, startling her. She grabbed hold of it and managed to stand, although it was enough to make black spots dance at the edges of her vision.

'I don't think it's going to do us any good staying around here any longer,' she heard Yuichi saying when she pulled the helmet back on, his words swollen with grief. 'She's gone. She had a few minutes of air left, if even that.'

'I know,' said Chloe. Her voice sounded still and small. 'I just can't quite believe—'

Nadia couldn't listen to any more. She tongued her comms on. 'Uh, hey guys?'

'N-nadia?' Chloe stumbled over her name. 'Oh my God, you're—'

'I need you to pay attention,' Nadia interrupted. 'I'm in the monitoring station. I got out of the pit.'

'You did…you did what?' asked Yuichi, his voice sounding strangled.

'I got…' Nadia swallowed, not quite sure if even she believed what she was about to say. 'I don't know how else to put it, Yuichi. I got rescued.'

'Rescued? How?' His voice became flat and disbelieving. 'By who?'

'Just get back here,' she said. 'I don't know how to explain it to you, I really don't.' She drew a shuddering breath. 'But I guess I'll have to try.'

# Randall

'There it is.' Danks pointed through the windscreen with evident relief. 'Thought we'd never make it.'

The EV truck rolled to a halt a couple of metres from an open-air transfer stage, its field-pillars shrouded in heavy plastic to help protect them from the elements. The wreck of an ancient and huge flying machine built by the same creatures that had constructed the city and its caverns lay close by, much of its shell half-hidden beneath twisting vines.

Something heavy thudded onto the roof of the truck, making it wobble from side to side. Danks muttered darkly under his breath, and turned to give Randall a hard stare. 'Please tell your damn pet not to do that.'

'I don't know if I can,' Randall admitted. 'She's kind of like a cat. She doesn't always listen.'

Major Howes pushed open the inner and outer airlock doors and stepped outside. 'If you can't control it,' asked Private Young, 'then what the fuck were you doing all that time when you were supposed to be practicing with that bracelet?'

'I can tell her to do specific tasks,' Randall explained, 'like *guard this* or *kill that*. Jumping up and down on top of trucks is a whole other thing.'

'Anything else you can't stop that thing doing?' asked Danks, one arm still hooked over the driving wheel. 'Like randomly disembowelling one of us for the heck of it?'

'That won't happen,' Randall reassured him.

From behind them, Satsura laughed scornfully.

'You'd better be able to control that beast,' said Howes, leaning back in through the open airlock door, 'otherwise we're dead meat if we can't get it to take out the hostiles back home.'

'That won't happen either,' Randall insisted, surprising himself with how certain he sounded—although in truth, he probably needed at least a couple days more practise before he could be absolutely sure Betty would obey his commands instead of doing exactly what the Major feared.

Okay, he admitted to himself. Maybe a couple of *weeks* practice was more realistic. But current circumstances meant it had to be now or never.

'Right.' Howes sighed heavily. 'I guess we'd better get to it. Satsura, you're first.'

The plan was to send Satsura back to the Authority in order to raise the alarm. That left the rest of them to transfer over to the island in order to reconnoitre and, if it looked feasible, regain control of the compound.

Randall watched out the windscreen as Satsura made his way inside the circle of field-pillars. The light built and built and when it faded, Satsura was gone. Howes turned towards the rest of them watching from the truck and jerked a thumb in the direction of the stage.

'What about the truck?' asked Young when they stepped outside.

'We'll leave it here,' said Howes. 'The experimental stage back on the island is just a little itty-bitty thing. It's not nearly big enough to take a truck.' He gave Randall a nod. 'You got the co-ordinates there?'

'Sure,' said Randall, pulling a battered, leather-bound notebook from a back pocket. He turned it to a page dotted with long strings of numbers and letters and passed it over.

Howes took it from him. 'Listen up,' he said, looking at each of them in turn—Randall, Young and Danks. 'This is reconnaissance *only*, until I say otherwise. We're unarmed, unless you include that thing over there.' He nodded at Betty, who prowled around the wrecked airship. 'Keep close, and don't do anything stupid.'

'At least they won't be expecting us,' said Danks.

'You'd better hope they aren't,' said Howes, before he turned towards the stage controls.

They stepped inside the circle of field-pillars. Randall touched the control bracelet and felt the Chimera respond. Increasingly, he had the uncanny sense that his mind and that of the Chimera had somehow...*merged*. He remembered how Oskar had talked about the creature as if he knew exactly what was going through its head. He'd assumed it was just the usual crazy Oskar talk, but now he wondered.

Even so, he couldn't help but feel a touch of apprehension when he called Betty to join the rest of them inside the circle of field-pillars. The Chimera moved away from the wreck, loping over to join them, the sun glistening on the spikes jutting from its back.

Danks muttered a curse and averted his gaze from Betty. As

if sensing his fear, the Chimera leaned towards him, sniffing at the top of his head with its blunt snout like a chef inspecting a meal. Then it moved closer to Randall, settling down behind him before curling its broad, whiplash tail around his feet.

Randall felt its warm breath on the back of his neck, and pictured its diamond-sharp fangs just millimetres from his skin. However much practice he'd had, it took all the will in the world not to break into a run.

'It makes one wrong move,' Young muttered to him, 'I put a bullet in *your* head before I die.'

\* \* \*

The light faded to reveal a much smaller transfer stage than the ones in the island's main hangar—and two surprised-looking hostiles, who had apparently been studying the stage controls.

One of them shouted something and both raised their rifles. Then they saw Betty, her spines nearly scraping the ceiling, and their eyes grew wide with horror.

'*Now*,' Howes hissed at Randall.

'I'm trying,' Randall muttered, his fingers tingling where they touched the bracelet. Betty wasn't responding the way she should. He sensed a mixture of apprehension and confusion. What the hell was there to be confused about?

The Chimera reared up, her head thudding into the ceiling. Danks, Young and the Major had all thrown themselves flat on the stage: only Randall remained standing.

God damn it, he'd practiced this enough times! 'Come on girl,' Randall muttered through clenched breath. 'Just kill the bad men, will you?'

The hostiles fired several shots at Betty, and that seemed to kick her into action.

*Of course*, Randall realised. The beast had been entirely dis-combobulated by the transfer process, something it had never experienced before. But it had no problem understanding when it was under attack.

The creature flowed off the stage, and would have flattened Private Young if he hadn't scurried out of its path. The Chimera's skin shimmered as it moved, its flesh and bones becoming translucent.

In the next instant, it had one of the ragged hostiles in its teeth, shaking him the way a dog shakes a rat. Then it dropped him and surged towards the second invader before he could escape through a door. Betty took the man's head in her jaws and twisted.

'Jesus,' Howes croaked, averting his eyes.

Randall meanwhile fought to retain his control over the Chimera. It had smashed its way through the door, taking most of the frame and the surrounding wall with it. Bright sunshine spilled in from outside the domed building.

Then came the sound of more shots, followed by a long, drawn-out scream.

'I have a feeling,' said Randall, 'that we've lost the element of surprise.'

'Danks, Young,' said Howes, 'take those men's weapons and search this entire facility. From this moment on, we're on the offensive.'

The two men seemed to snap out of a trance and hurried down the ramp, snatching up rifles from the two bodies, one of which Betty had decapitated. Randall ducked out to find the Chimera sniffing around the exterior of the building, which had been liberally sprayed with blood from the corpse of a third invader lying nearby.

Randall touched the bracelet, his breath shaky when he remembered to exhale. The Chimera seemed calmer now, which was good, because it meant it was easier to control.

He glanced at the body of the third man, seeing that his skin was oddly glossy and stretched-looking. It reminded him of something, but he was damned if he could place it.

Danks emerged from another building. 'Sir?' he said to the Major, 'I think you need to see this.'

Danks ducked back inside and Randall followed the Major inside what proved to be a machine shop filled with worktables. Schematics were pinned up on the walls. A duffel bag full of what looked like clay bricks had been opened on one of the worktables.

'Explosives,' said Howes, carefully picking up a brick and studying it for a moment before putting it back down. 'Looks like they were planning to blow something up.' He looked at Danks. 'See any more of these?'

Danks nodded. 'Those two hostiles were placing them next to the stage when we materialised, sir.'

Randall started. 'They were?'

'Most likely their plan was to slow down any reinforcements,' said the Major. 'In which case we have to assume they're planning to do the same thing with the other two stages as well.'

'So then we'd be stranded on this island?' asked Young with considerable alarm.

'No,' said Randall, shaking his head. 'Reinforcements could still get here using portable stages, but blowing up the main stages could delay them by a few hours.'

'Then it's a good thing we're here,' said the Major. 'Let's see if we can re-secure the compound before they do any more damage.'

'Hey,' said Young from outside. 'What's wrong with this one's skin?'

Randall exited the building to find Young standing over the body of the third invader. Then it hit him.

'Do *not* touch that body,' Randall warned, a band of fear tightening around his chest.

'Why?' asked Howes.

Randall pointed at the body without getting any nearer to it. 'You've seen something like that before, Major. Remember where?'

Howes stared at the corpse for several more moments, then turned pale. 'That's not possible,' he muttered.

'It's got to be,' said Randall. 'That's what a body infected with the bee-brain virus looks like. Don't ask me how in hell any of these guys have it.'

Howes sucked in a breath. 'It's starting to feel,' he said, 'like there's a lot going on we don't understand.'

'What now?' asked Young.

'The compound,' said Howes. He nodded towards Betty, who had by now climbed onto the roof of one of the clustered buildings to stare out at the ocean. Probably, thought Randall, it was the first time she'd ever seen one.

'I have never come so close to shitting my pants as when I saw what that thing did to those men just now,' said Howes. He turned to Randall. 'You had me worried for a while there, but you pulled it off.'

'Thanks. But I'd still feel happier if I had a gun in my hand before we go near the compound.'

'There's a pair of gun cabinets in another building,' said

Danks. 'I know, because I restocked it a couple of months back, assuming these fellows haven't emptied it in the meantime. If they haven't, chances are there's more than enough firepower for all of us.'

'And even if there isn't,' said Major Howes, 'it still makes sense to send that...*thing* in first. Maybe the sons of bitches'll end up so demoralised by it we don't have to fire a shot.'

# Rozalia

Rozalia froze at the sound of a jeep pulling up outside the Mauna Loa.

'They're coming for us,' said Winifred, loading shells into the sawn-off shotgun she'd taken from Rozalia's rucksack. She stuffed spare shells into the pockets of her khakis. 'They don't know you're here—or that you brought weapons. That gives us a *big* advantage.'

'They'll be coming in the front,' said Selwyn, his voice low and urgent. 'We could just make a run for it round the back, now the cellar doors are open…'

'No way,' said Winifred. 'We can't let these assholes alert the rest of their buddies.'

What Selwyn had said gave Rozalia an idea. 'There's another way,' she said to them both. 'I'll head back out and try and circle behind them. With any luck, we can take them prisoner.'

Winifred regarded her with clear scepticism. 'You sure about that?'

'Yuichi's got enough rubber hosing lying around tying them

219

up won't be a problem.'

Winifred laughed under her breath. 'Personally I think you're being optimistic. But if you want to play it that way, fine.'

Rozalia pulled the hand-gun out from the waistband of her jeans and loaded it, then made her way back through the cellar and eased one of the metal hatch-doors open. She climbed up the steps, then ran to one side of the building in a low crouch, her gun at the ready.

She peered towards the street out front of the Mauna Loa and saw a jeep that hadn't been there five minutes before. A second raggedy-man, also armed with a rifle, stood talking with the first. Rozalia ducked back when they turned towards the Mauna Loa, banging the front door open.

She ran along the side of the building and towards the front, then walked in through the open front door with the gun held in a two-handed grip. Both men were facing away from her, the one furthest from the entrance hammering loudly on the door to the rear bar with his fist. She watched over the shoulder of the second man as the door swung open to reveal Winifred pointing a sawn-off shotgun at the first.

'Don't make a fucking move,' Winifred growled.

Instead of dropping his rifle, the raggedy-man closest to Winifred took a step back, raising his weapon. Winifred shot him in the chest and he reeled backwards.

Rozalia ducked back out of the front door, not wanting to get hit by a stray slug from Winifred's shotgun. She saw the second raggedy-man run out of the front entrance and take cover behind the jeep. He raised his own rifle to his shoulder and aimed inside the Mauna Loa.

Only then did he notice Rozalia in a half-crouch next to the front door. His rifle twitched towards her and chunks of brick went flying out of the wall inches from her head. She raised her hand-gun and returned fire. The third shot struck home—luck as much as anything else, she figured, given he was several metres away and mostly hidden behind the jeep—and he fell back and out of sight.

Rozalia ran forward, still in a half-crouch, and with the hand-gun extended. She peered around the side of the jeep and saw the raggedy-man, his face covered in blood, sprawled on the road. His fingers twitched, as if reaching for the rifle lying nearby, and then he stopped moving.

'So much for taking prisoners,' said Selwyn when Rozalia stood back up. He looked flushed, standing at the front entrance with a hand-gun pointed to the ground.

Rozalia leaned against the side of the jeep, feeling a sudden urge to go home and sleep for a week. Nadia had always been far better at this kind of thing, and she'd seen enough death in just the last twenty-four hours it was starting to take a toll on her psyche.

Winifred walked both ways along the street for a short distance, cocking her head as if for listening for something. 'We should get moving,' she said, 'before they start wondering what happened to their buddies.'

'What now?' Selwyn called after her.

'Get to the Authority and raise the alarm,' suggested Winifred.

'They've surely worked out that something's wrong by now,' said Selwyn.

'Then why aren't they here?' Winifred asked him. She looked at Rozalia, who had returned to join them. 'Are any of the transfer stages still under our control?'

Rozalia shook her head. 'They've got them all under guard, far as I was able to see. Sneaking back in is an option, but I don't think we can pull it off a second time without being caught.'

'Almost as important,' said Selwyn, 'is how many of them there are.'

Rozalia remembered seeing them huddled together outside the fishing hut. 'They started out close to two dozen,' she said, then nodded at the body in the road. 'More like seventeen, eighteen by now, maybe less.'

Selwyn's eyes widened in shock. 'I'd have thought there were a lot more of them than that.'

'Well, there aren't,' said Rozalia.

Winifred was staring into space, clearly deep in thought. 'I figure we should scout out the experimental stage by the runway. Could be they don't know about it yet.'

'I think they do,' said Rozalia. 'But I had the impression most of them were sticking around the main transfer stages.'

'Then here's a plan,' said Winifred. 'We'll reconnoitre the experimental stage and see how heavily guarded it is. If their security's light enough, we take control of it, then transfer over to the Authority and call in the cavalry.'

\* \* \*

Winifred took the wheel of the jeep for the simple reason that, despite being quite possibly the biggest hard-ass out of all the Pathfinders, she looked relatively harmless—a pencil-necked woman with a perpetually drawn face and the outward demeanour of a grandmother. She was also small enough she had to raise herself up on her seat to see clearly over the top of the wheel. Nobody was going to look at her and perceive an immediate threat.

They hoped.

Rozalia and Selwyn meanwhile crammed themselves into the rear footwell and out of sight of any casual observers, dragging the rucksack full of weapons after them. They sat facing each other, their knees pulled up to their chins and the two sawn-off shotguns in easy reach on the back seat. Rozalia felt every single one of the pebbles the jeep bounced over as Winifred drove it back towards the runway.

They heard shooting barely five minutes into their journey. Rozalia tensed, her eyes meeting Selwyn's.

'Whatever it is,' said Winifred from up front, her voice calm, 'it's nothing to do with us. But it's definitely coming from up ahead.'

Rozalia cautiously raised her head and looked past Winifred's shoulder. They were close to the edge of town, the island's extinct volcano rising up dark and steep a few kilometres to the south. Another, distant shot echoed through the air, followed by what might have been a drawn-out scream.

'It's coming from the compound,' said Rozalia.

Winifred nodded. 'Something's definitely up.' She pressed her foot down on the accelerator. 'Maybe the Authority's finally pulled its collective finger out of its ass.'

The jeep lurched forward and Rozalia fell back. She stayed low without getting all the way back in the footwell. The jeep bounced and rocked as it picked up speed and before long the experimental facility hove into view next to the runway.

They pulled up next to the dome housing the transfer stage and stared at the eviscerated corpse lying there.

Selwyn extracted himself from the footwell and stared at

the body. 'I give up,' he said. 'I have *no* idea what's going on any more.'

Winifred got out and knelt by the corpse. The ribcage had been torn open, the dead man's internal organs glistening beneath the sun. She stood back up, her face pale. 'I've never seen anything like it,' she said. 'What the hell could do *this*?'

Rozalia saw what might be claw-marks on the dome's outer shell and felt her blood grow cool and sluggish. 'The Chimeras,' she said. 'The ones Oskar learned to control. One of them could do this.'

Selwyn shuddered. 'Nasty buggers—but it can't be. The one that didn't get blown up is still on Delta Twenty-Five, isn't it?'

'I'm not saying it makes sense,' said Rozalia. She nodded at the door of the building, which had been ripped out of its frame. 'I'm just telling you what it looks like.'

Winifred retrieved one of the shotguns and held it pointed towards the ground before peering into the dome's darkened interior. Rozalia followed her inside. It smelled like a charnel house, but nothing moved.

'More bodies,' said Rozalia, looking around. They had also been savaged. 'Someone must have brought the last surviving Chimera here.'

'But who?' asked Selwyn, appearing at the doorway. 'Oskar is dead.'

Rozalia and Winifred exchanged a glance. 'Randall,' they both said at once.

Selwyn touched the stage controls, peering at the screen. 'The last-used coordinates are for Delta Twenty-Five,' he said, giving them both a significant look.

They heard more gunshots from the direction of the compound, followed by more terrified screams.

Winifred stepped to the ruined door and listened. 'I have a feeling,' she said, as if to herself, 'the party's already over.'

# V

# Doomsday Game

# Randall

'Here you go,' said the medic, handing Randall an orange plastic wristband. 'Be sure not to lose it.' He turned his head inside the hood of his hazmat suit and nodded to the next table along. 'Get yourself something to eat and stay hydrated. If you start feeling dizzy, either tell someone with a medic lanyard or come straight back here.'

'Sure,' said Randall, walking away from the table and rolling his sleeve back down. His shoulder still stung slightly from the shots they'd given him. He slipped the wristband onto his right arm and grabbed a bottle of water and an egg sandwich from the next table, wolfing it down in seconds. All around him the compound buzzed with activity, the number of people in hazmat suits outnumbering anyone who actually belonged on the island by about three to one.

A lot had happened in just the last several hours, starting with Betty charging through the compound fence like it was made of smoke. Randall, the Major and Privates Danks and Young had followed behind in a jeep. Even then, they'd barely

229

been able to keep pace with the beast as it charged ahead.

*Better than any John Wayne movie,* Randall had shouted when they heard the first terrified screams coming from within the compound. Then came the sound of a whole lot of shooting.

They'd hardly had to fire a shot themselves. Indeed, it took far less effort than Randall expected to regain control of the compound. For one thing, only half a dozen of the hostiles had been left to guard the transfer hangar. The rest were nowhere to be found.

The six remaining hostiles had fought hard, but their bullets were useless against a diamond-skinned monstrosity from another dimension. Two were killed outright, but the other four were smart enough to hole up inside the transfer hangar.

They weren't in there for long, however, before Randall sent Betty smashing through the doors. The biggest effort Randall had to make was persuading Betty not to chow down on one of the hostiles when she got him in her jaws. Once they saw that, the rest dropped their weapons and surrendered.

Then the real cavalry arrived: a dozen heavily armed Army Rangers materialised on a stage, all wearing hazmat suits. More followed within seconds, all of them clearly expecting a fight. It didn't take a genius to sense their disappointment at arriving too late. Even so, the Army Rangers started by searching every building and basement in town, then spread across the island in a chain, investigating every square inch of land. Drones meanwhile flew into every hollow and cove.

For all their efforts, they found no remaining hostiles. In the meantime, Winifred, Rozalia and Selwyn got busy retrieving island staff from the various alternates they'd all been dumped on.

Randall helped out too, visiting remote outposts on alternates that had been largely abandoned for months and, in some cases, years. It was astonishing none of the Authority's staff had died, but they worked hard to bring them all back home so they could get their shots and something to eat.

After his fourth round trip that day, Randall walked into the transfer hangar in time to see a single figure come strolling down a ramp wearing a hazmat suit. At first he couldn't see who it was inside the hood, but whoever they were, they had the bearing of a Roman General surveying a newly conquered city.

Then he looked closer, and saw it was Preston Merritt.

Randall stared at Kip's former second-in-command with trembling rage. Merritt, however, hadn't seen him.

Randall watched, stupefied, as an orderly walked up to Merritt, handing him a clipboard just as if he'd been expected. Merritt studied the papers clipped to the board, then signed something before passing it back to the orderly with a nod.

He did it, thought Randall, exactly as if he still held a position of authority on the island.

His hands formed into fists at his sides and he started to make his way towards Merritt.

'Stop.'

A hand grabbed Randall by his shoulder, whirling him around. He found himself facing Major Howes.

'What the hell are you *doing*?' Randall demanded, trying to shake Howes' hand loose. 'Don't you *see* who that is?'

'Don't do anything,' the Major warned him, his expression grim. 'Things have...' He let out a deep sigh. 'Things have changed.'

Randall made a noise from deep within his chest and tried again to wrench himself free of the other man's grasp. Howes responded by twisting him around and slamming him face-first up against the side of a crate, drawing curious stares from some of the people passing by.

'Don't make me throw you in the brig,' Howes hissed in his ear.

'We don't have a brig,' Randall spat back.

'We have a disused latrine with a lock on it,' Howes replied. 'Close enough for me.'

'That son of a bitch is a *murderer*!' he shouted. 'And he's walking around in here like…like he's in *charge*!'

That got them both a few more sideways looks. 'He *is* in charge,' Howes explained. 'And I'm sorry.'

'But…!'

'I know.' Howes cast a baleful glance towards Merritt. 'I *know*. But until we figure out where the hell Kip is, Merritt's been put in charge. Believe me when I say it was *not* a decision I supported.'

Howes finally let go of him and Randall regarded him with undisguised shock. 'And you're going to just stand back and *let* him piss on us like this?'

'Until I understand precisely what's going on back home, Randall, that's exactly what I intend to do. I have my orders, whether I like them or not.'

Randall's right hand drifted towards the bracelet on his left.

'Goddammit, Randall!' Howes slammed him back up against the crate. 'Where is the damn animal, anyway?'

'Around,' Randall snarled back.

Howes let one of his hands touch the brown leather gun holster attached to his hip. 'Am I going to have to take that bracelet away from you?'

'You wouldn't—'

'You harm one hair on Merritt's head, they'll make me arrest you. If I don't, someone else will arrest both of *us*. Next thing you know we'll be transferred over to Washington on my own alternate and, the way things have been going over there, chances are we'll both just...disappear. That's not going to get Oskar any justice. Do you understand?'

'I guess,' said Randall. It wrenched his heart to see Merritt swanning around. 'But when they find Kip, he's back in charge?'

Howes hesitated just a moment too long for Randall's comfort. 'I hope so,' Howes said at last. 'The thing is, we've got no idea where they took Kip.'

'So we still don't know where the remaining hostiles went?'

'If anyone knows,' said Howes, 'they're not telling me.'

Randall stared at him. 'Why not?'

'Maybe this mess was just the impetus Merritt's backers needed to take over the running of this island.' Howes spoke in a low voice, darting a look around to see if anyone might be listening in. 'I've tried to find out what's going on, but they're keeping me entirely out of the loop.'

'We could check the transfer records,' said Randall, nodding towards the nearest stage. 'There's no reason we couldn't go and look right now.'

'Don't,' said Howes, his voice firm.

'Why not?'

'Because we're not allowed to,' Howes warned him.

'Who says?'

Howes gave him a long look, then nodded at Randall's chimera bracelet. 'I need you to promise me you're not going to do something stupid.'

Randall's jaw worked. 'Nothing stupid. Sure.'

'I'll find out what I can,' said Howes. 'And once I know anything, I'll tell you. But until then, try and stay out of anyone's way. For *all* our sakes.'

'Okay.' Randall nodded. 'I got it.'

Howes let go of him, giving him one final look that said *you better mean it.* Randall watched the Major walk away, then headed outside, feeling sick and hot in his guts.

\* \* \*

He spent the next couple of hours brooding on the cliff above the beach behind the hangar. He'd set Betty to keep clear of the compound, partly to avoid scaring the bejesus out of the new arrivals and partly because the image of her snapping Merritt's head off his shoulders was just too tempting.

*Gotta bide your time*, he imagined Oskar saying.

Sitting staring out at the poisoned ocean got to be too much after a while and Randall went to get something more to eat. He caught sight of Danks standing guard in front of the laundry building where the four surviving hostiles were being held for interrogation. It occurred to him that they might have let slip something regarding where Kip had been taken. If so, maybe Danks knew where it was or had overheard some useful piece of information.

He queued up with some island staff recently returned from some alternate or other, all of them still looking shell-shocked, and grabbed another sandwich and a coffee, carrying them over to where Danks stood.

'Hey,' he said to Danks, handing him the sandwich. 'You eaten yet?'

Danks took the sandwich and tore into it. 'Haven't had

anything all day,' he said around a mouthful of bread before chewing and swallowing. 'Thanks.'

Randall could hear muffled voices from within the laundry as Danks ate. Once Danks finished the sandwich, Randall passed him the coffee and nodded towards the laundry door. 'Those guys we captured saying much?'

'Singing like canaries, judging by what I heard last time I was in there,' said Danks. He sipped the coffee and grimaced. 'Uh, listen, maybe you shouldn't be here, man,' he added, his expression growing uneasy. 'Merritt is in there interrogating the prisoners and if he comes out and finds you here…' He shrugged. 'Just saying.'

Randall stared at him and felt a rush of blood to his head powerful enough he rocked slightly on his feet. *'Merritt?'* He nearly shouted. *'He's* in charge of the interrogation?'

'Jesus!' Danks exclaimed, shooting another look at the door. 'Take it easy, okay?'

'He's the son of a bitch that killed my best friend! He—'

'I know it's bullshit,' said Danks in a half-whisper, 'but I have my orders. Right or wrong, he's in charge.'

Randall's hands worked at his sides and for a moment he allowed himself the fantasy of breaking into the laundry building and throttling Kip's former second-in-command with his bare hands. Instead he took a deep breath and focused on an increasingly worried-looking Danks. 'Then can you at least tell me if Merritt's managed to get anything out of them? Did you hear anything when you were last in there?'

'Uh, yeah,' said Danks, dropping his voice even further. 'For a start, they've got a nuke.'

*Oh, for…* Randall allowed himself a moment to absorb this information. 'You have to be shitting me. A *nuke?'*

'The backpack variety, what they call a SADM,' Danks explained. He glanced again at the laundry building. 'They're saying the other hostiles took it with them to the Old Horse Springs facility, and if we interfere or lead any kind of attack to stop them they'll detonate it and blow the whole place up.'

'So they're holding the Authority to ransom.' Randall's thoughts raced. 'Do you think they're telling the truth?'

'Some of our people saw a SADM sitting right out in the open next to the transfer hangar while the hostiles had control of the place,' said Danks. He glanced yet again at the door behind him. 'I told you enough. You gotta get away from here.'

'Just tell me if you've heard anything else,' he asked. 'Please.'

'I know they took the Director and the Russian woman with them as well.' Danks leaned in towards him. 'Don't do anything crazy, Randall. I'm begging you.'

Randall squeezed the other man's shoulder. 'I owe you one.'

'Sure,' Danks muttered. 'Now get the hell out of here.'

Halfway back to the transfer hangar, Randall heard a series of muffled thumps—four, in all—come from the laundry building behind him. He turned and watched from around the side of a research lab and after another thirty seconds the door of the laundry swung open. Merritt emerged, still wearing his hazmat suit. He beckoned Danks to follow him inside. The door shut again, but not before Randall noticed the pistol Merritt held by his side.

Randall started walking again, this time with renewed urgency. He pushed through the crowds of people inside the transfer hangar until he found Rozalia standing at the bottom of a stage ramp.

'I need to talk to you,' Randall said urgently. '*Now.*'

'Just one second, Randall.'

The stage flared with light, then faded to reveal a battered-looking open-top truck. Long lines like claw-marks had been dragged across its hood.

Selwyn and Winifred emerged from the truck, followed by a half dozen civilians who'd been riding in the back. All of them were grimy with dirt and perspiration. The two Pathfinders led them down the ramp to a pair of hazmat-suited orderlies with stretchers at the ready.

'Any problems?' Rozalia asked Winifred.

'Pretty much what you'd expect for Delta Seventy-Nine,' she replied. There was a sheen of sweat on her filthy skin, and her eyes were rimmed with red.

'That's all the staff and military personnel accounted for,' Rozalia said with evident satisfaction. She turned back to Randall. 'Shoot.'

Randall's gaze flicked towards the hangar's rear entrance, then back to Rozalia. Her expression didn't shift one iota, but she nodded. 'Let's talk outside.'

Randall leaned towards Winifred. 'You and Selwyn are going to want to hear this too.'

All four of them headed out back of the hangar. The wind carried the smell of brine and rotting fish. 'Did you know Preston Merritt's been given Kip's job?' Randall asked Rozalia.

Rozalia sucked in her lips and stared out across the ocean. Winifred stared at Randall in shock. 'I was aware that he was marching around like he was in charge, yes,' Rozalia said at last, turning back to him. 'I didn't hear anything about Kip losing his job.'

'Seriously?' asked Selwyn, looking equally as shocked as Winifred.

'I already talked to Major Howes and he said it was just temporary until they found Kip,' Rozalia told Selwyn. 'Although to be honest, he didn't sound much like he believed what he was saying.' She turned back to Randall, her expression full of worry. 'I was going to talk to you about it first chance I had.'

'Well, guess what,' said Randall. 'Merritt already knows where Kip is, and Katya too. And I think he's keeping Major Howes in the dark about it. I talked to him earlier and he didn't seem to have any idea where the hostiles might have taken the Director.'

Rozalia frowned. 'That can't be.' She glanced at the others, then back at Randall. 'Can it?'

Randall told them everything he had learned from Danks, including the gunshots he had heard.

Selwyn looked even more horrified. 'Why would he just...*execute* them like that?'

'Did you actually see any bodies, Randall?' asked Winifred, her voice carrying a hint of skepticism.

'No,' he admitted. 'But I know what a gunshot sounds like just as much as any of you.'

'That still doesn't explain *why* they would shoot them,' said Selwyn.

'Why else,' suggested Randall, 'except to make sure we *don't* find out where Kip is?'

'Don't you think that's stretching it?' asked Rozalia.

'Merritt murdered Oskar, didn't he?' said Randall. Just saying the words was enough to bring a flowering heat to his chest. 'He'd have killed me as well if I hadn't managed to get away. Think about it: with Kip off the map, Merritt stays in charge. He could lock us all the hell up and go hunting for more Hyperspheres.'

'If they did that,' said Rozalia, her words slow and careful as she thought it all through, 'they'd lose Katya as well. Who else are they going to get to build stages for them?'

'She's not nearly as hands-on as she was at the beginning,' Selwyn pointed out. 'She's trained dozens of engineers and scientists in everything she knows. Most of what she does these days is administrative. I don't see them having too much trouble building stages without her.'

'I think it's possible Jerry was taken along with Kip and Katya,' said Winifred. 'I talked to Chloe and Yuichi and they said he transferred back here long before they did, and while the island was still under occupation. Nobody's seen him since.'

Randall looked at them each in turn. 'The way I see it, we're going to have to go and rescue them ourselves.'

Rozalia looked at him like he was crazy. 'The four of us, against a whole gang of plague-infected maniacs armed with a *nuke?*'

'We have Betty,' Randall reminded her. 'That makes things a whole lot more equal.'

'We're *under quarantine*,' Rozalia insisted. 'They're not letting anyone who came into unprotected contact with Greenbrooke and his men transfer over to the Authority. And what if they make good on their threat and blow that damn nuke?'

'As far as the virus goes, we were exposed to it for a couple of hours, tops,' said Randall, 'and we all got immediate treatment. Even putting the nuke aside, Greenbrooke and the surviving hostiles are far more of a danger to the Authority if they manage to escape, and Merritt's too busy playing power-games to take action. That leaves us to do the job.'

'We could still get ourselves blown up along with the

facility,' Rozalia said in a tone that suggested she wasn't quite convinced by her own argument.

'Even losing the facility is better than risking the alternative,' said Winifred. 'And you've *seen* the alternative, Roz.'

There was a brief silence, and Randall knew he had won. 'Even so,' said Selwyn, 'they're not going to just let us all walk onto a stage and disappear.'

'Why not?' Randall countered. 'We've been doing it half the day, rescuing people. How are they going to know where we're transferring to, or why, unless we tell them?'

'You'd have to leave Betty behind,' said Winifred. 'Her, I think they'd notice.'

Randall grinned. 'We can put her in the back of a truck with the rest of you. She'll fit.'

Selwyn blinked. 'If you think I'm actually going to sit *next* to that thing—!'

'She's as good as an army,' Randall insisted, 'and you all know I can control her. You'll be fine, Selwyn. You all will. You have my word.'

For a moment, Selwyn looked like he might offer further protest, but instead he harrumphed and folded his arms, his mouth set in a thin angry line.

'You do realise what it means if we do this?' said Rozalia, looking around at them all. 'I don't see any way we can ever come back here whether we succeed or not, especially not if Merritt remains in charge.'

'Was this ever really home for any of us?' asked Winifred.

'For me it was,' said Rozalia. Her voice took on a wistful quality. 'I really liked our house. It took me and Nadia a long time to get it just right.'

'What about Nadia?' asked Selwyn, 'not to mention Yuichi

and Chloe. We can't make this choice without including them in it.'

'Is anyone here *not* in favour of Randall's plan?' asked Rozalia.

The rest of them regarded each other silently and Rozalia sighed. 'Fine. The three of them are still getting their physicals in the clinic. Go over there and tell them everything you told us, Randall. Then we see where we go from there.'

\* \* \*

Randall headed first to the compound armoury, a single-story concrete building, and found its door was open. Inside, a hazmat-suited figure studied a clipboard while a second, similarly attired, sorted through the shelves.

He saw Merritt's experimental rifle with its weird coils and gizmos wrapped around the barrel leaning against a wall. He hadn't really expected to find it, considering it was damning evidence of direct interference in the stage-building program.

*Thank God for the incompetence of the wicked*, thought Randall. Ignoring the two hazmat-suited men, Randall picked the rifle up like it was the most natural thing in the world to do.

'Hey,' said the man holding a clipboard as Randall turned back towards the door. 'What do you think you're doing?'

'We're still rescuing people from different alternates,' Randall told him. 'We can't go unarmed.'

'You can't take anything until it's all been checked against the inventory,' said the man in an officious tone.

'So file a complaint,' said Randall, again turning towards the door.

'I said you can't—!'

'You got a problem,' said Randall, looking back over his shoulder, 'take it up with Major Howes if you don't mind walking around with his boot stuck up your ass all week.'

Once he was back outside, he slipped around the side of the building and out of sight of anyone passing by. He studied the rifle's underside and found a magazine flush with the stock. He pulled it loose, seeing it still had the two antimatter-laced cartridges inside it. He slid the magazine back home, making sure as he did so that the safety was on.

He took a moment to study it closely. It sure was an ugly looking thing: at heart it was a bolt-action rifle, or had been until some scientist frankensteined it all to hell. The choice of a bolt-action rifle, however, made sense. They were slow to load and re-sight, but incredibly accurate in the right hands. His, for instance.

He still couldn't make any sense out of the tangle of conduits and coolant pipes and other whatever-the-hell-they-were doohickeys wrapped around the barrel, although it was immediately obvious they made the barrel heavier than it should be, ruining the weapon's balance. But he could compensate for that, assuming he ever got a chance to use it.

And with just two cartridges in its magazine, he'd better make them count.

His next stop was a supplies shed. He stole some cord and a piece of tarpaulin, wrapping the tarpaulin around the rifle and tying it all up, partly to disguise it and partly so he could make a loop out of the cord and sling it over one shoulder. None of the people hurrying by while all this was going on so much as batted an eyelid.

Randall's next destination was parked around front of the

transfer hangar—the same open-top truck in which Selwyn and Winifred had recently returned from a rescue expedition. He'd noticed the truck's rear bed had an overhead steel frame, with a waterproofed canvas tonneau sheet that could be rolled down over the frame to protect any cargo from the wind and weather. By the looks of it, he figured it was probably just about large enough to take Betty as well as several Pathfinders.

He took a look around to make sure nobody was paying him any particular attention, then climbed into the truck's cabin and started the engine before guiding it slowly out through the compound gates. The bracelet told him Betty was still prowling the empty grasslands just north of town.

*C'mon girl*, he thought, and felt the brush of the creature's mind. *Come to Pappy.*

Barely a minute or two passed before he pulled over, seeing the immense beast bounding across the grass towards him. He got out and dropped the tailgate at the rear of the truck so the Chimera could climb aboard. Then he climbed up next to her and got to work rolling down the canvas sheets to keep her out of sight.

The truck swayed and its suspension creaked and groaned as Betty settled on the floor of the truck. Diamond-faceted eyes watched him as he worked, and Randall discovered that whatever residual fear he'd still felt towards the creature had entirely vanished: being scared of Betty made about as much sense as being scared of his own right hand.

He grinned to himself and jumped back down, pushing the tailgate shut before climbing back into the cabin. He got the truck rolling again, although with Betty riding along the chassis practically scraped against the tarmac.

\* \* \*

Randall drove back into town, parking the truck outside the clinic. Inside, he found the downstairs office deserted, although he couldn't help but notice some bloodstains on the carpet that looked like they were of very recent vintage.

When he made his way upstairs to the main ward he found Yuichi sitting on the edge of a bed with his shirt off. His upper torso was skinny-lean, with grey hair speckling his upper chest. Bandages had been wrapped around one of his ankles. A medic in a hazmat suit stood by his side, taking his blood pressure with a plastic cuff. Nadia and Chloe sat huddled together side by side across the clinic, drinking what smelled like instant coffee.

'Hey,' said Randall, raising a hand in greeting. 'How are you guys all doing? What happened to those soldiers they had in here?'

'Shipped back home,' said Yuichi, his expression flinty. 'And as to how I'm doing, nothing a beer couldn't fix.'

The medic unwrapped the inflatable cuff from Yuichi's arm and packed it away. 'Everything's fine for all three of you, far as I can tell,' he said. 'We still need to do some blood-work, but as long as the serum does its job I don't have any serious concerns right now.'

'But we're still under quarantine?' asked Yuichi, a hopeful edge to his voice.

'Until you hear otherwise, yes,' said the medic, picking up his bag and heading for the door.

'Yeah,' said Nadia, 'but how long is that going to be exactly?'

The medic just shrugged his shoulders and headed down the stairs.

'Got some news for you,' said Randall, once the medic was out of earshot. He told them about Merritt and the prisoners, as well as his conversation with the others.

'This is kind of a lot to take on board,' Chloe grumbled. 'You're talking about making a decision that changes all of our lives forever, and you're asking us to make it *now*?'

'I think Randall's point is we can't wait on this one,' said Nadia, her gaze fixed on Randall. 'Not to mention I can't ever picture any of us taking orders from Preston Merritt.'

'Every second counts,' said Randall. 'And believe me, I know it's a lot to take in. But the fact is, Greenbrooke and the other hostiles have managed to stay a step ahead of us ever since they turned up. If we don't act, then it's the same as washing our hands of Katya and Kip—and maybe even Jerry, if he's with them.'

'So say we go along with all this,' asked Yuichi. 'Where do we go after it's over?'

'Nova Terra is the only really viable choice,' said Randall.

'Yeah.' Yuichi looked down at his hands, his expression glum. 'That's what I figured.'

'It's still chaos out there in the compound,' said Randall, nodding with his chin at the door behind him. 'But it won't be for much longer. A lot of the personnel that transferred over earlier today are already getting shipped back home to the Authority. We need to take advantage of the confusion while we still can—and while we're still allowed near the transfer stages.'

Randall waited. After a moment Yuichi let out a loud sigh and clapped his hands on his knees. 'I...guess there's really no alternatives. If the rest of you are in, I'm in.'

'I'm definitely in,' said Nadia.

245

'Me too,' said Chloe. She pointed at the tarpaulin-wrapped rifle slung over Randall's shoulder with her chin. 'Is that what I think it is? Preston Merritt's nuke-gun?'

'Damn right it is,' said Randall.

Chloe nodded with evident satisfaction. 'We're going to need weapons for the rest of us,' she said, standing.

'Maybe you ought to take it easy,' said Nadia, watching her with concern.

Chloe shrugged her off. 'I'll be fine,' she muttered, clearly annoyed.

'What's up with Chloe?' Randall asked Yuichi as the two women headed down the stairs.

'She's pregnant,' said Yuichi, pulling his shirt back on.

Randall gaped at the door of the ward as it swung shut.

# Randall

*Alternate Alpha Zero, island military compound*

'No way,' said Chloe once she realised what was lurking in the back of Randall's truck. Her voice trembled as she spoke. 'For Christ's sake, Randall,' she spat. 'Jerry was nearly killed by one of those damn things, and you want me to, to…'

The truck rocked slightly as the Chimera within shifted. 'We need Betty with us,' Randall insisted. 'She's like a tank with legs. I can't just walk her up onto a transfer stage and hope nobody notices—so she's got to ride in the back of the truck. And so do some of you, if we're going to pull this off.'

'I think,' said Nadia, picking her words with care, 'that you should be a little more aware of the history some of us have with that creature.'

'You never had a problem with the Chimeras when Oskar was in control of them,' Randall insisted stubbornly.

Nadia rolled her eyes, the muscles of her jaw tight. 'Yes, but that was when they were *still on Delta Twenty-Five*, Randall. Now one of them's on the *island*, it's *different*. Don't you see?'

'I…' Randall scratched the back of his neck. 'Look,' he said to Chloe, his tone a touch more conciliatory, 'how about you ride up front with me?'

'So the rest of us are stuck in the back with that thing?' asked Yuichi, clearly appalled.

'I don't know what else to do,' said Randall. 'You got any better ideas?'

'Fine,' Yuichi grumbled. 'Just…just promise me the damn thing won't so much as twitch.'

'She's fully house-trained.'

Yuichi glared at him, then stalked around to the back of the truck.

'I have an even better idea,' said Nadia. 'How about *I* drive, and *you* get in the back with that damn beast of yours?'

Randall put his hands up. 'I got no objections to that.'

He made his way around to the rear of the truck and found Yuichi peering nervously into its darkened interior. Betty peered back out, a pair of glowing slit eyes like something out of a carnival horror show.

'After you,' said Yuichi, taking a step back.

Randall shook his head and climbed aboard. In truth, with a beast the size of Betty in there, it made for a tight squeeze. He took a seat on one of two wooden benches set against the sides of the truck's rear bed and leaned back out. 'C'mon in,' he said, holding a canvas flap open.

Yuichi climbed aboard, his movements stiff from his injured ankle and his gaze firmly fixed on the Chimera's massive bulk. He sat down carefully, his body rigid and his hands clasped on his knees. Up front, Randall could hear Nadia and Chloe talking. Then the engine started and the truck lurched slightly as it pulled away from the clinic.

'Did you really just say Chloe's pregnant?' asked Randall.

Yuichi laughed softly. 'What can I say? It's been a day of revelations.'

'How so?'

Yuichi quickly summarised everything that had happened on Gamma Three, including Nadia's escape from the pit.

'You're shitting me,' said Randall. 'She was saved by...by another version of Rozalia?'

'So she claims.'

'It's impossible,' Randall insisted. 'She must have been hallucinating.'

'Maybe,' said Yuichi. The way he said it made it clear he didn't think that was it at all.

Randall nodded at Yuichi's bandaged ankle. 'So I guess you got that when the building on Gamma Three came apart?'

Yuichi grimaced. 'Nope. Tripped and fell on my damn ass about five seconds after we'd finally transferred back here.'

Randall laughed. Before he could say anything else, Betty shifted slightly, making the truck again rock on its suspension. Yuichi leaned back, his face increasingly pale, until the creature had settled back down. Without thinking about it, Randall reached out to pat the creature's armoured hide, then caught the other man staring at him with a kind of horrified fascination.

The truck jerked to a halt. After a couple of seconds a hand pushed aside the rear canvas flap. 'All good?' asked Rozalia, peering in at them.

'I haven't been eaten,' said Yuichi, his voice fraying slightly around the edges. 'Does that count?'

'Here,' said Rozalia, lifting a rucksack over the tailgate and dropping it inside. From the look of strain in her face, Randall guessed it was heavy.

'Weapons,' Rozalia said in reply to Randall's unspoken question. 'Nadia's going to drive the truck up onto the first stage. The rest of us are going to follow on foot.'

'It sounds quieter,' said Randall.

'There's fewer people around now,' Rozalia confirmed. 'It's like you said—they're starting to send people back home.'

'What about Kip's staff here on the island?' asked Yuichi. 'Are they staying or going?'

'I'm not sure,' said Rozalia. 'Nobody seems much inclined to talk to me or even look at me.'

Randall and Yuichi exchanged a look.

Rozalia let the canvas flap back down. After another moment, the truck once again rolled forward at a crawl, and then they waited.

It occurred to Randall now might be an excellent time to take a closer look at Merritt's antimatter rifle. He unwrapped the tarpaulin from around it and saw Yuichi looking at it bug-eyed.

'Is that what I think it is?' he asked.

'Sure is,' said Randall. 'Saw this same thing being used to blow an almighty hole in a cavern door back on Delta Twenty-Five.'

The truck lurched forward and it suddenly became darker. Randall guessed they were now inside the main transfer hangar. Voices boomed and echoed all around, and the truck turned to the left before ascending a gentle slope.

Yuichi bent down and peeked under the edge of the canvas. 'We're on one of the stages,' he confirmed.

They sat and waited. A minute passed, and then another.

'We should have transferred by now,' said Yuichi, his voice taut.

'I know,' said Randall. He had a bad feeling swirling in his belly. 'I'd better see what's up.'

He lowered the tailgate, stepped out of the back of the truck and took a cautious look around. There were still a lot more people milling around the hangar than he was used to seeing, but significantly less than there had been just an hour before. It was hard to tell who was who what with most of them wearing hazmat suits, but his gut told him Preston Merritt wasn't in the hangar.

He walked to the front of the truck, where Selwyn and Winifred had come to stand by the open door of the cabin. He saw Chloe still seated inside. 'What's going on?' he asked.

'Nadia's talking to someone,' said Winifred, nodding down at the stage controls. 'Something's up.'

Randall's gaze settled on Nadia, who appeared to be in a heated conversation with one of the hazmat suited figures. Judging by the look on her face, it was growing more heated by the second.

Randall made his way down the ramp and walked towards her. 'I don't *need* authorisation,' he heard her say to the other person, her voice pitched higher and higher. 'This is a *rescue* mission!' She batted at the clipboard clutched in the hazmat-suited figure's gloves. 'You do *not* know how things run around here, sonny.'

'I'm sorry,' said the man, his tone suggesting he was anything but. Now that Randall could clearly see his face through the visor of his hazmat suit, he realised the man wasn't much more than a kid. 'I need signed authorisation before I can let you go anywhere.'

'What about earlier?' asked Randall, stepping up beside Nadia. 'We've been running missions all day, and nobody had us sign any forms.'

'Yes, but I wasn't here earlier,' said the kid, as if that answered everything.

Randall felt a muscle in his forehead twitch. 'If there's a form needing signed,' he said, 'we'll sign it.'

The kid stood his ground, his expression becoming firmer. 'You don't have the authority,' he insisted, then glanced at Nadia. 'And neither does she.'

Randall's face grew warm. 'Who the hell told you to stand around here causing—'

'What's going on here?'

Randall turned to find Major Howes approaching from the hangar entrance and felt his blood turn cold. 'These people are trying to transfer out of here without authorisation, sir,' the kid informed him.

Howes looked up at the stage to see Chloe sitting in the truck's passenger seat. Selwyn and Winifred still stood next to the truck with worried expressions. Yuichi had also emerged, having perhaps grown tired of sitting all alone next to an alien killing machine. Howes' gaze next shifted to the screen of the stage's control unit, into which Nadia had already punched in the coordinates for the Old Horse Springs transfer stage.

Howes' gaze moved from the screen and back to Randall and locked eyes with him. 'Another rescue mission?' he asked dryly.

'Yes,' said Randall, his throat suddenly hot and sticky.

Howes held his gaze for several more seconds, then took the clipboard from the kid. 'Think you're going to be gone for long?' Howes asked Randall.

'Could be a while,' Randall mumbled.

Howes signed a sheet on the clipboard then handed it back

to the kid. 'Let them go.'

The kid looked down at the clipboard with uncertainty, then back up at Howes. 'But the regulations say—'

The Major gave him a look that would have stopped a wild elephant in its tracks. The pencil-pusher clutched his clipboard to his chest and scurried away without another word.

'Thank you,' said Nadia, her voice small and still.

'I guess it's obvious that…things have changed around here,' said Howes.

Randall licked his lips. 'Major—'

Howes put up a hand. 'Stop. Don't tell me what you're about to do.' In that moment, he looked infinitely weary. 'But whatever it is, you should go now.'

Randall turned to walk back to the stage, then stopped, looking back at the Major. 'Maybe,' he suggested, 'you could come with us.'

Howes said nothing for a couple of heartbeats, then shook his head. 'Thank you, but no. My duty is here. Randall, Nadia…good luck, whatever it is that you're planning. The same goes for all of you.'

He turned on his heel and walked back out of the hangar. Randall realised it was likely the last time any of them would ever see him again.

'Let's just get this over with,' said Nadia. She reached for the stage controls and activated the transfer process. They hurried up the ramp just as the hangar began to fill with light.

# Jerry

'*Pregnant?*'

Katya gaped at Jerry with open-mouthed surprise that soon gave way to delight. She tipped her head back and let loose a laugh that echoed around the narrow confines of the storage room she, along with Jerry and Kip, were locked in.

Jerry's neck flushed red. 'The usual response is "congratulations".'

She brought her head down again but still couldn't suppress her grin. 'Congratulations!' she cried. 'It's just—'

Jerry's eyes narrowed. 'What?'

'It's quite a place to be bringing a child up in, no?' said Katya. 'On an island neither quite one universe or the other…'

'But not for much longer,' said Jerry. 'Not now you've given us Nova Terra.'

'I wish I knew how long we'd been here,' said Kip. He sat with his back to a wall, a high barred window above him.

'Two, maybe three hours,' said Jerry. 'That'd be my guess.'

He pushed himself upright from where he had been sitting and stepped towards a window set high in one wall. Kip shifted out of the way as Jerry reached up, grabbing hold of the window bars and pulling himself up high enough he could glimpse the world outside.

He dropped back down again. 'Well?' asked Kip.

'They've still got that plane parked on the tarmac,' said Jerry. 'It looks like they're loading it.'

Katya shook her head. 'I wonder where they're going.' She shuddered. 'And if they're taking us with them.'

'I think they are,' said Kip, 'otherwise I don't think any of us would still be alive.' He cocked his head, listening. 'Did either of you hear that?'

Jerry had indeed heard the grumble of an engine somewhere just outside the door of their improvised cell.

Kip stood as they all heard a rapid shuffling of feet from the other side of the door. Then came muffled shouts followed by several gunshots, one after the other in rapid succession.

Jerry, his heart beating wildly, jumped back from the door at the same time that Katya also leapt unsteadily to her feet, flattening herself against a wall. Kip helped her steady himself, since their captors had made sure to leave her crutches behind.

They waited. Jerry realised in the silence that followed that the gunshots had lasted hardly more than a moment.

On the other side of the locked door he heard what sounded like an asthmatic struggling for breath.

Then came a final choking noise, and then nothing.

Keys rattled in the lock, and the door swung open to reveal two more of Greenbrooke's men standing at the threshold, both of them armed with submachine guns.

Jerry guessed they'd looted the weapons from elsewhere in

the facility. They also looked, he realised, nearly as scared as he felt.

'Out,' one of them commanded, taking a step back and nodding over his shoulder. His voice shook slightly. 'All of you.'

Jerry went first, followed by Kip and Katya, Katya's arm flung around the Director's shoulder as she hobbled along.

Glancing to one side, Kip saw Svenson slumped on the corridor floor with several entry wounds in his chest and neck, a pool of blood growing ever wider beneath him.

Or at least he assumed it was Svenson, since the man was barely recognisable. His skin had taken on a glossy, papery quality, and his head and facial features were horribly distorted.

'What—' Katya paused to swallow '—happened to him?'

'He's carrying the bee-brain virus,' Kip muttered under his breath. 'The virus lies dormant for hours and days, sometimes weeks or even longer. Then it…turns you into that.'

The armed men pushed all three of them towards a military jeep parked at the far end of the corridor. Kip looked back at the corpse, then gave Jerry a look that was pregnant with silent meaning. *We can't allow these people to get away.*

'I demand to know where you're taking us,' Kip protested as he helped Katya into the jeep before climbing in the back beside her.

He got no answer. Jerry boarded last and the two invaders got in front.

The jeep quickly picked up speed. One of the two men turned to keep a watchful eye on all three of them, the barrel of his submachine gun resting on the back of his seat in case, Jerry assumed, he had a sudden urge to kill all of them.

The driver swung hard around corners as he navigated his way through the facility's labyrinthine interior. Tall windows appeared at the end of one passageway, and Jerry again glimpsed the same passenger jet he'd seen earlier, still parked on the tarmac near the airstrip north of the facility. It looked big enough to carry a hundred people.

'You're flying south, right?' Jerry asked the one with the gun.

Still no response. 'I hear things are pretty lawless past the border with Mexico,' he continued regardless. 'I figure that's why it's taking you so long to fuel that plane—you're going to try and put as much distance between you and the Authority as you can possibly manage.'

Still no answer, although the guard's mouth curled in undisguised contempt.

'You know,' Jerry persisted, 'it doesn't matter how far you travel. You can't outrun a virus that's already infected you.' He nodded back the way they'd come. 'And from what I've seen, there's no amount of serum that's going to save some of your friends.'

'Jerry's right,' Kip added. 'I told Greenbrooke the same thing. There's maybe a couple like yourselves who have a chance at surviving the infection, but not if you're out in the middle of some jungle with no medical facilities.'

The driver turned towards his companion. 'If Beche says another word,' he said, meaning Jerry, 'shoot him in the fucking head.' He snapped a quick, menacing look at Jerry. 'We only need you to keep the other two in line, and it's questionable if we really need you at all. So shut the hell up.'

He returned his attention to the steering wheel and Jerry twisted his hands together in his lap. For a while they rode in silence, and he wondered if their luck, if they'd ever had any, had finally run out.

# Randall

*Old Horse Springs Experimental Facility, Authority Home Alternate*

As soon as they had materialised in the Old Horse Springs transfer hall, Randall jumped down from the rear of the truck, swinging a hand-gun he'd taken from Rozalia's rucksack around in a wide arc. He'd anticipated they might walk straight into a fire-fight with the hostiles, but the transfer hall proved to be entirely deserted.

That surprised him: he'd thought they'd have left *somebody* behind to guard against possible retaliatory actions.

Unless, he thought, worry deepening the lines on his forehead, they weren't here any more. Or had never been here in the first place.

Nadia was next out of the truck, and similarly armed. 'Look over there,' she said, pointing.

He followed the direction of her hand and realised he'd missed a cluster of bodies near the entrance to the hall, partly tucked out of sight behind a row of electric carts.

'I see it.' He adjusted the improvised strap by which he had slung the antimatter rifle over his shoulder. The tarpaulin stayed in the truck now he no longer had a need to disguise it.

Nadia swallowed, her skin pale, and nodded towards the bodies. 'You don't think…?'

'Only one way to find out,' said Randall, his voice grim.

Yuichi was next to disembark, cursing and muttering as he hobbled rapidly away from the truck, favouring his injured ankle, and casting fearful looks behind him. Betty followed him out, the truck rocking violently on its suspension as the Chimera dropped to the stage floor.

'Hey,' Yuichi shouted at him, 'keep an eye on this damn thing! I can't tell if it's coming or going.'

Randall touched his bracelet and Betty responded immediately, dropping down the side of the stage and prowling around the walls of the transfer hall.

'Nobody's here,' said Winifred, glancing about as she checked the magazine on her automatic pistol. She frowned, catching sight of the crumpled forms by the entrance. 'Nobody alive, anyway. We'd better check them out and see if it's anyone we know.'

Randall followed her down the ramp and towards the bodies, afraid that they would see familiar faces amongst the dead.

Once they got closer they saw that there were four of them, all men, all wearing maintenance uniforms. The wrists of each of them had been bound with twine, and each had a single entry wound to the back of the head.

'Looks like they were executed,' said Randall.

'They wouldn't have known what hit them,' Winifred murmured. 'But then, neither did we.'

'Callous bastards,' Randall muttered. 'Why couldn't they have just locked them up someplace?'

The rest of the Pathfinders had by now followed them over. 'We need to make some decisions before we go charging off,' said Rozalia, looking around at them all. 'Yuichi, you're in no fit state to go anywhere with that busted ankle.'

Yuichi glowered at her. 'I can still drive, can't I?'

Rozalia gave him a firm shake of the head. 'Bad idea. I recommend you transfer straight over to Nova Terra and wait for us. There's a guy called Jamieson at Entry Control in charge of new arrivals. When you find him, tell him to expect the rest of us soon.'

Yuichi's eyes narrowed. 'Jamieson is an Authority bureaucrat. Why should we trust him?'

'I know him better than you do,' said Rozalia. 'He's on our side, believe me. Plus, we're going to need supplies if we're to have any chance of making a life for ourselves over there. You can get a head-start on sourcing what we need. The sooner we're able to set up someplace out of the way where Merritt can't find us, the better.'

Yuichi conceded defeat with a shrug. 'I think you should go with him too, Nads,' Rozalia added.

'What?' Nadia looked scandalised. 'Why?'

'You've been through enough, sweetheart. You came close to dying. You shouldn't be putting your life at risk again so soon. You too, Chloe,' she said, turning to her. 'Now that you're expecting...'

Chloe's hands flexed by her sides. 'Just promise me you'll bring Jerry back in one piece.'

'I promise,' said Rozalia.

'I think you should go to Nova Terra as well,' Randall said to Rozalia. 'None of us can put our case across as well as you do. Plus, I think out of all of us you're the one who's spent the most time there. I don't know *anyone* on Nova Terra.'

'That,' said Yuichi, 'would leave just you, Selwyn and Winifred against a horde of heavily armed and highly contagious maniacs armed, so they claim, with a nuke.'

Randall nodded across the hall at the Chimera, which sniffed the air by the hall's exit. 'I'll remind you once again,' he said, pointing at Betty, 'we have that.' He patted the improvised strap holding the antimatter rifle to his shoulder. 'And we have this.'

Rozalia shook her head with evident uncertainty. 'I still don't know...'

Randall stepped up close to her. 'We haven't always seen eye to eye, you and me, but we've both been through worse times than this together, Rozalia. You know I've got this.'

Her nostrils flared. 'It's a bad idea.'

'No,' said Randall, 'we're already past the point of no return. You've got a responsibility to go with the others and help keep them safe on Nova Terra. Like I said, you know that place better than any of us. You sure they'll be able to manage on their own if anything happened to you?'

Rozalia's mouth worked for a moment, her gaze drilling into Randall's. 'Fine,' she said at last. 'We'll take the truck. Don't be long, Randall.' She turned to Selwyn and Winifred. 'Same goes for you. Make sure you come back in one piece, whatever happens.'

'We will,' said Winifred.

Yuichi had hauled the rucksack full of weapons out of the truck and passed a hand-gun each to Winifred and Selwyn. Then Randall watched with Winifred by his side as Selwyn stepped up to the stage controls.

Moments later, the truck and its passengers vanished in a

burst of light.

Selwyn rejoined Randall and Winifred. 'Where now?'

'The control centre,' Winifred replied immediately. Selwyn nodded. 'We can view the entire facility from there through CCTV. If our friends are here, maybe we'll be able to find them that way.'

They boarded one of the electric carts, Selwyn taking the wheel. Randall touched his bracelet and the Chimera came lumbering along in their wake.

Selwyn guided them through long, high-ceilinged corridors until they arrived at a room marked PRIMARY CONTROL AND SYSTEMS MAINTENANCE. The Chimera kept pace with ease, its claws clattering loudly on the corridor tiles.

Winifred went inside the control centre first, swinging her hand-gun around, but the control centre proved to be as deserted as anywhere else they had seen in the facility.

Randall stared around at multiple banks of screens. The seats before them were empty, coffee cups and print-outs scattered across desks a silent testament to how quickly the facility had been evacuated.

Then he saw something that looked out of place: a drum-shaped object like an oil barrel, about a metre tall and partly hidden within a thick burlap sack. Randall stepped over to where it stood against a wall, his skin tingling, and found himself looking at an angled control panel set into the drum's upper surface.

Randall tried to swallow, but couldn't. 'Hey,' he said over his shoulder. 'You need to see this.'

He heard the others come up behind him, Winifred drawing in her breath sharply and muttering an oath. 'Is that what I think it is?'

'An SADM,' said Selwyn, shouldering Randall aside. 'I know how these things work.' He gazed down for a moment at several readouts embedded in the control panel along with numerous rocker switches and dials. 'It's armed,' said Selwyn, reaching out towards a rocker switch.

Winifred's hand shot out and grabbed hold of Selwyn's wrist before he could touch it. 'Don't do anything,' she said, grating the words out. 'We don't know if it's boobytrapped.'

Selwyn laughed under his breath. 'That kind of thing's only in the movies,' he said. 'These things aren't that complicated. It's armed and on a timer, but disarming it isn't that difficult. Pretty easy, in fact.'

'How the hell do you know how these things work?' asked Randall.

'They had me use one a couple of years back so we could blow open a concrete bunker on an alternate I was sent to,' Selwyn explained. 'Jerry was with me on that mission. As bucket list items go, "detonated a nuclear bomb" makes for a terrific entry.'

'And you're *sure* you can disarm it?' asked Randall, his tone disbelieving. 'Wouldn't it be better to just leave the damn thing alone?'

'Well, I could,' said Selwyn, nodding at the control panel, 'but it's on a timer. As a matter of fact, it's set to blow in less than twenty minutes.'

The words raised hackles on the back of Randall's neck. 'And you're sure you can disarm it?'

'One way to find out,' said Selwyn. He hit a rocker switch and the readouts on the control panel shifted and changed until just one remained active. It also turned bright red.

'Is it disabled?' asked Winifred, her voice edging higher and higher.

Selwyn said nothing and just stared at the control panel. 'Selwyn?' Winifred asked again. 'Did you disable it?'

Selwyn licked his lips. 'Actually, I think it's about to—'

As he spoke, the readout begun to flash on and off, at first slowly, but then with increasing and unnerving rapidity. Then it stopped flashing altogether and died.

'Well, that was unexpected,' said Selwyn in a small, still voice.

'What happened?' demanded Randall. 'Damn it, Selwyn, what did you do?'

Selwyn tapped at the readout, a queasy grin on his face. 'It flashed up an error message,' he explained. 'There's nothing inside it. No fissionables or even conventional explosives.'

'Then it's—?'

'A bluff,' said Selwyn.

Winifred went to sit down nearby, her movements as slow and careful as someone who had just received a last-second reprieve from a hangman's noose.

Randall gripped Selwyn by the shoulder and nodded over at the banks of screens. 'I need your help figuring out where Greenbrooke is, and if he's got Kip and the others with him.'

The screens showed empty corridors and vast stretches of concrete and tarmac, but nothing that moved. Even if Greenbrooke and his men had been here, it seemed to Randall, it seemed increasingly certain they were long gone. If the SADM had been intended only to delay them, then it had surely done its job well.

Selwyn hurried over to a console and started typing rapidly at a keyboard. Randall watched as several screens mounted above a workstation flickered, then changed to show multiple views of a medium-sized passenger jet with a fuel truck parked next to it. Several figures with a familiar ragged look to them milled around the truck.

Randall stepped up close to the screen, watching as the fuel-lines were disconnected from the plane and discarded on the tarmac. The figures—recognisably Greenbrooke's men—moved the ladder they'd used for the refuelling over to the aircraft door before hurrying up the steps and inside.

'We're too late,' said Winifred, her voice taut. She had come to stand beside Selwyn. 'They're getting away.'

'Doesn't mean we can't still try to stop them,' said Randall. 'How do we get from here to there?'

'The runway's north of the facility,' said Selwyn, nodding at a map taking up most of one wall.

'Then there's at least a chance we can get to them before they take off,' said Randall. He patted the antimatter rifle still slung over his shoulder. 'And if we have to, we'll shoot them out of the damn sky.'

'Hey!' shouted Selwyn. 'Not if they've got Jerry and the others with them, you can't!'

'You're right.' Randall felt a hot flush of shame for not having thought of that, then glanced down at the bracelet on his left wrist. 'I have a better idea,' he said, holding his arm up so Selwyn could see the device. 'We'll send Betty after them. I wouldn't be surprised if she could outrun that damn plane. But I'll need one of you to drive me after her. The closer to her I am, the more precisely I can control her.'

Selwyn looked towards the exit. They couldn't see the Chimera, but they could all hear it prowling around outside. 'Winnie's a better driver than I am,' said Selwyn.

'On it,' said Winifred, turning and hurrying back out of the control centre.

Randall and Selwyn both followed in her wake to find Betty outside in the corridor. It was barely large enough to contain the Chimera: her broad, armoured shoulders were hunched, her upper spines raking holes in the ceiling plaster.

Randall felt something very like impatience coming from the creature's mind: it was built to hunt, and it badly wanted to fulfil its purpose.

He stepped up close to the beast. Its jaws opened slightly, revealing diamond-sharp fangs. Warm, sour breath washed over Randall as he patted Betty's snout. 'Time for you to get back to doing what you were made to do, don't you think?'

He turned to see Winifred sitting in the driver's seat of the cart, Selwyn in the back. Judging by her expression, she clearly regarded him as a lunatic. 'What's the plan?' she asked him.

Randall left the Chimera and climbed into the cart beside her. 'You know how to get to the runway from here?'

'I took a good long look at the map,' she said, and hit the accelerator.

The Chimera went rocketing past them when the corridor became wider, the ground shaking beneath the wheels of the electric cart as it passed them. The air filled with broken plaster and dust as its spines raked long grooves in the walls and ceiling.

'I don't know how you can stand to be near that thing,' Winifred muttered, her mouth locked in a tight grimace. Compared to how fast the beast was moving, they might as well have been standing still.

'You get used to it,' said Randall, laying the antimatter rifle across his lap.

When they turned onto one of the facility's main thorough-fares, the Chimera was already gone from sight. Even so, a long, low bellow reverberated through the deserted spaces around them.

'So just to be clear,' asked Selwyn from behind them, 'that thing is on its way to the airplane?'

Randall nodded.

'And then what?'

'And then I'll have her do whatever I can think of to keep that plane from taking off.' His fingers brushed against the bracelet with the lightest of touches.

There was some kind of a feedback loop between him and the beast: he could taste its hunger as if it were his own, feel the rush of the wind against its armoured hide as if they were one.

*I take it all back, Oskar,* he thought to himself. *This beats NASCAR any day.*

He could somehow see, in flashes, what the Chimera was seeing, and the more he pressed his fingers against the bracelet the stronger the impressions grew. His breath caught in his throat as Betty leapt towards broad windows, plummeting to the ground several metres below in a cascade of shards. He felt her forelimbs slam into concrete as if he'd been the one who made the leap. He gasped, drawing a look of alarm from Winifred beside him.

The facility was shaped like a compass, with antimatter stored at underground locations close to the tip of each compass point. The facility was split into quadrants, with the runway crossing east to west just north of the facility.

Betty swung her massive head around until it caught sight of the passenger plane, still sitting next to the runway. Then she began to run, the tarmac blurring beneath her paws.

Randall thought he could hear Winifred saying something

from very far away, but for the moment at least, his senses were almost completely locked in with Betty's. Up ahead, a jeep was racing towards the jet.

# Jerry

The military jeep transporting Jerry, Kip, Katya and the two invaders drove out through broad doors and into sunlight. Jerry saw the passenger jet still sitting on the tarmac half a kilometre away.

*We can't just let them put us on that plane.* His hands twisted at his sides in despair, a sick, hot feeling growing in his belly.

The invader with the rifle was still watching them closely, but when they emerged into the open he briefly turned to look towards the jet.

Jerry glanced sideways at Kip. 'Now,' he whispered.

Kip's eyes grew wide. 'What?'

Jerry reached out and grabbed hold of the invader's assault rifle by its barrel, twisting it hard to one side so that it was no longer pointing at him or Kip or Katya.

'Kip!' Jerry shouted. 'Help me!'

Kip, who had been sitting there frozen, suddenly snapped out of it. He also seized the rifle by its barrel, adding his

270

strength to Randall's own.

The rifle fired, making a sound not unlike a burp. The shot went wide, but at such close proximity the noise was deafening. The jeep slew to a halt hard enough that both Jerry and Kip lost their grip on the rifle. The invader holding the rifle brought it around to bear on them.

Jerry found himself looking straight down the barrel of the assault rifle and knew he was about to die. He could see the man's finger whitening on the trigger.

Then something behind them caught the invader's attention, his jaw dropping in disbelief. Immediately, he swung the weapon towards whatever he had seen.

Something huge smashed into the jeep with sufficient force to send it rocking up onto its side. Jerry fell out of the jeep, landing hard on the tarmac. He scrambled away, afraid it was going to land upside-down on top of him. Instead, it thudded back down onto its wheels, right side up.

When he tried to sit up, he felt a deeply unpleasant grinding sensation in his chest, as if he'd broken a rib—perhaps several, judging by how much it hurt.

Something enormous loomed over him, its jaws full of brilliantly sharp teeth and its back festooned with spines like daggers. Then it stepped over him with a roar that turned Jerry's insides to water.

The jeep's driver had managed to stay behind the wheel while everyone else was thrown clear by the force of the impact. He was able to bring his own weapon to bear on the Chimera, and fired several rounds into it at point-blank range.

In response, the Chimera leaned over the invader, closing its huge jaws around the man's head and shoulders. He didn't even have time to scream before the Chimera bit down. Jerry looked away, sickened, as the beast dropped the man's torn body onto the tarmac.

Something hissed past Jerry's ear, kicking up bits of tarmac inches from where he still lay sprawled. He turned in the direction of the plane and saw sparks of light coming from next to it. Greenbrooke and his men had emerged from the jet and were shooting at the Chimera.

'Jerry!'

He looked around, still dazed, and saw Kip and Katya had taken cover behind the jeep. He crawled across the tarmac towards them. The Chimera meanwhile went racing after the second invader, who had gone running for the plane. It caught him with consummate ease, and he died as quickly as the first.

The pain in Jerry's chest was bad enough it felt like he was dragging himself over broken glass. Kip came out from behind the jeep and grabbed hold of him, dragging him to safety.

'They've stopped shooting,' said Katya, peering over the top of the vehicle. 'And the plane's started to move.'

Jerry took a cautious glance towards the jet, now taxiing onto the runway. He watched as its door was pushed into place by the last of the shooters to board. It soon picked up speed, but not so fast that the Chimera couldn't throw itself forward and sink its glistening talons into the plane's rear fuselage. Bits of debris went whirling in the creature's wake as it pulled itself atop the jet.

'My God,' said Katya, her voice somewhere between awe and horror, 'it's trying to tear its way inside the plane!'

'Someone's coming,' said Kip, turning to look back towards the facility.

# Randall

'Pull over,' Randall said to Winifred when he saw the three figures standing by the jeep.

Winifred slammed the electric cart to a halt and jumped out, hurrying over to join Kip and Jerry and Katya, all three of them clearly confused and frightened. Randall meanwhile grabbed hold of the antimatter rifle and headed for the jeep, throwing himself behind its wheel.

'Hey!' Selwyn called after him in bewilderment. 'Where are you going?'

'Can't let them get away,' Randall shouted, pressing down hard on the accelerator. The tyres shrieked against the concrete.

Selwyn said something else, but there wasn't time to reply, not with the jet already picking up speed now it had reached the runway. Goddamn, but he hadn't thought it would actually work when Betty made that last, desperate leap...! And yet she still clung on, still tearing huge chunks out of the fuselage and scattering them all across the runway.

Even so, Greenbrooke and his men still had a fighting chance of escaping. Once the plane took off, Betty could easily lose her grip and go tumbling back down to the ground.

He drove towards the runway, cursing when the jet disappeared behind the line of buildings that made up the North point of the facility's compass: by the time he drove around the line of buildings, the jet would already have taken off and quite possibly be long gone.

He looked around in desperation for some way through the buildings on his left, but there was no shortcut from the north-east to the north-west quadrant of the facility that he could see.

Then an idea came to him, one so obvious that he cursed himself for not having thought of it already.

He swung the wheel hard to the left, then again to the right until he was right alongside the long line of engineering workshops and research labs that separated the quadrants. He spotted broad glass doors just ahead on his left and pulled over, seeing that beyond them lay a lobby furnished with couches and coffee tables. A sign above one of the doors read VISITORS CENTRE. There were several stories to the building, mostly offices from what he could see.

Grabbing hold of the antimatter rifle, Randall jumped out of the jeep and crouched behind the side furthest from the Visitors Centre. He took off the safety and carefully balanced its barrel on top of the jeep's passenger-side door.

His breath caught in his throat, his heart feeling like it had grown to twice its normal size. He hesitated a moment, wondering if there was something he had to do to the gizmos and doohickeys mounted all around the rifle in order for it to work properly.

It would be kind of ironic, after all, if he just blew himself up.

'This is not the time to vacillate,' Randall muttered to himself. He worked the bolt, chambering one of the two remaining cartridges, and peered through the rifle's sights. He took aim at the far wall of the lobby past the doors, letting the air out of his lungs before he squeezed the trigger.

The rifle jerked against his shoulder, and in almost the same instant, the Visitors Centre vanished amidst a great rolling ball of light and heat that rose quickly upwards.

Randall felt himself lifted up and dropped back down. Purple and green splotches danced across the back of his eyelids and several seconds passed before he could see anything. Fragments of burning paper and bits of wood and glass were raining down all around him, and he yelled out loud when a photocopier came smashing down onto the concrete just metres from where he lay sprawled, the rifle still gripped in one hand.

The day was windy, and the smoke was quickly carried away, revealing the north-west quadrant clearly visible in the gap where, until a moment ago, the Visitors Centre and all of the offices above it had had been.

Randall stared at the destruction in awe. 'That,' he muttered under his breath, 'was fucking awesome.'

He scrambled back up, ignoring the aches and pains in his back and shoulders, and drove the jeep across a smattering of rubble that was all that remained of the Visitor's centre. Within seconds he was in the North-West Quadrant, and he span the wheel until he was driving back towards the runway.

But, he saw, he was already too late. The jet had lifted off, its body angling up from the runway as it rose towards the clouds. Greenbrooke had got away.

And yet, incredibly, Betty still clung on. He could just about see her as the jet angled over the facility, turning as it rose to fly south towards Mexico.

Randall's stomach churned. Could the Chimera even survive a fall from so high? He could almost hear Oskar remonstrating with him for having taken so many risks with Betty, especially after he'd been heartbroken over Lucky—

Except, Randall reminded himself, Betty wasn't Oskar's old dog Lucky. And while it had a mind of sorts, the Chimera was more akin to a keen-edged blade—a living weapon designed for a singular purpose.

And if he didn't use that weapon, a whole world was going to die.

He picked up the antimatter rifle and climbed up onto the jeep's hood, settling back against the windscreen with his legs splayed before him. He shouldered the rifle and worked the bolt, chambering the remaining cartridge. Steam curled from the coiled tubes surrounding the barrel, the breath rattling in his throat.

The jet banked, and Randall saw it was going to pass straight above him. There was still a chance he could bring it down. And he had just one shot at it.

The roar of the jet's engine built as it rose higher, towards the clouds. Randall let his mind merge with Betty's long enough to discover she likely couldn't hang on for more than another few seconds, and by that point, the jet would be beyond the reach of either of them.

He puffed his cheeks and blew out his breath, forcing the tension out of his shoulders. 'I'm sorry about this, Betty,' he muttered, tears pricking the corners of his eyes. 'I really, really am.'

He held the rifle at about a forty-five degree angle with the stock tight against his shoulder. He could see the jet's belly through the sights. He tracked it for a moment, steadied his breathing, and gently squeezed the trigger.

The rifle jerked, steam hissing from its coils. A second passed, and then another, and then a new sun came into being above the facility, consuming both Betty and the jet.

Randall lowered the rifle and covered his eyes with one hand, staring up. The heat from the explosion felt like standing next to an open furnace. He peered through his fingers and saw something dark spinning through the air towards him.

Randall dropped his hand and stared up.

'Aw hell,' he muttered, as most of one wing, trailing burning fuel, came crashing down on top of him.

# Jerry

Jerry stared at the second plume of smoke rising high above the facility. The jet had been there one second…and the next it was gone.

He got behind the wheel of the electric cart, drawing a look of alarm from Winifred.

'Oh, for God's sake!' she shouted. 'Where the hell are *you* going now?'

'I need to find Randall,' he said, grimacing from his aching ribs. He'd popped a painkiller, but he wasn't sure it was going to help any.

Winifred looked towards the twin plumes of smoke. 'Fine,' she said. 'Then we'll all go.'

Winifred got in front beside Jerry while Kip and Katya squeezed into the rear beside Selwyn, both of them still looking pale and shell-shocked.

When they arrived at the remains of the Visitor's Centre, they had to abandon the cart and pick their way across the rubble on foot.

They soon saw that the plane had broken into several sections which lay scattered across the concrete and across roads and drainage ditches. Bodies could be seen all over the quadrant.

Closer to hand, what looked like an entire wing of the jet had been sheared off. It rested on top of what appeared to be—

'Oh dear God,' said Jerry, his insides tightening to a hard knot. The outline of a jeep was just about visible amidst the flames.

*Maybe he made it out*, thought Jerry, looking around. It would be just like Randall to come striding out of the smoke with an *aw shucks* look on his face. He yelled Randall's name until he was almost hoarse.

Then he saw something lying on the tarmac and went to pick it up. It was the bracelet Randall had used to control the Chimera.

A hand fell on his shoulder. 'C'mon Jerry,' said Winifred, her voice not unkind. 'We have to go.'

'But—!'

She pulled him around and pointed upwards: far overhead, military jets streaked through the sky.

'*Now*, Jerry. Before someone finds us here.'

* * *

They made their way back through the rubble and Winifred took the wheel of the electric cart. Katya told her where to drive, and they were soon on their way back towards the centre of the facility.

Katya ordered Winifred to pull over next to a fire escape. They disembarked, and Kip helped Katya up the steps and inside a building.

Jerry glanced south through a window and saw tiny figures in white exiting troop carriers that had parked in one of the other quadrants. They were wearing hazmat suits, and they fanned out, heading towards different parts of the facility. A helicopter flew overhead, bound for the wreckage of the jet.

Katya, still leaning on Kip, guided them next to a tall steel door with a sign reading STAGE TESTING PLATFORM. 'I think you can guess what's in here,' she said, sliding a card down a wall-reader.

The door swung open in response. Inside, Jerry saw long benches piled high with manufacturing equipment, and at the far end stood a smallish transfer stage surrounded by measuring devices.

'There are spare portable sets over there and ready to go,' said Katya, pointing to the far wall. Jerry saw modified back-packs clearly intended to carry portable stage components—a design he had never seen before. 'We should grab one each, just in case.'

'Just in case of what?' asked Selwyn.

Katya shrugged. 'Any unexpected eventualities.'

They did as she suggested while Katya programmed the stage. Jerry felt his heart beating ever faster as he stepped inside the circle of field-pillars. It felt like events were moving much more quickly than he felt he could really deal with.

The light built up around them, and Jerry felt a familiar moment of weightlessness before finding himself standing on a much larger transfer stage built from rough-hewn wooden planks.

They were on Nova Terra, an alternate where neither humanity nor any other species had evolved to the level of civilisation, a whole world's worth of untrammelled wilderness.

Jerry breathed in, scenting pine. The stage was open to the air, and he saw dense forest stretching across a shallow valley, A steep-sided mountain rose up into the sky some miles distant.

He followed the others down broad wooden steps. A dirt trail led to Newtown—a settlement already twenty-thousand strong, much of it built from native wood.

It was approaching dusk, and most of the buildings were lit from within. Woodsmoke rose from multiple chimneys, while farther away, close by a river that wound down from the mountain's steep slopes, stood a foundry.

Trucks and SUV's were parked side by side fifty metres or so from the stage, accessible by a gravelled path bordered on either side by long grass.

They found the rest of the Pathfinders waiting by one of the trucks, Chloe amongst them. Jerry walked towards her, and then suddenly they were in each other's arms.

The others made their own greetings, and he heard them telling each other their stories. Then they stopped talking as Rozalia clapped her hands and got their attention.

'Here's the plan,' she said. 'We're going to take some of these trucks along with whatever supplies they can carry and get the hell out of town. I figure our best option right now is to make our way to Splitsville.'

'Splitsville's a good hundred kilometres from here,' said Kip. He looked dazed, like he hadn't quite caught up with events himself.

'But it *is* on the Normandy coast,' said Nadia, standing by Rozalia's side. 'They have boats there—even a couple of schooners.' Jerry couldn't miss the excitement in her voice. 'Me and Roz are damn good sailors. Beg, borrow or steal one, I don't care. We won't be safe from the Authority until we're in open water.'

'And go where?' asked Kip.

'South, of course,' said Winifred. 'I figure we can head for Portugal. We'll put in some place along the coast and set up for ourselves. There'll be other people there eventually, once the evacuation really gets underway. But maybe by then the heat'll be off us and they'll leave us alone.'

'Or maybe we'll spend the rest of our lives running from them,' said Jerry.

'What's *your* plan?' asked Selwyn. 'Go live on some post-apocalyptic and see how long it takes before something eats, poisons or irradiates us?'

'Okay, okay,' said Jerry, raising his hands defensively. 'I hear you. I'm just saying nothing about this is going to be easy.'

'Jerry my lad,' said Selwyn, a gleam in his eye, 'would you have it any other way?'

Somehow, Jerry couldn't find an answer.

He followed the others towards the line of trucks, and the more he walked, the more he felt the past falling away.

He realised suddenly that his life as a Pathfinder was over.

He looked at Chloe and took her hand, feeling her fingers tighten around his. *There's three of us now*, he realised with a shock.

'Listen,' Jerry said to her as they climbed into the cabin of one of the trucks, 'we should at least consider naming it Randall.'

She regarded him slyly. 'And if it's a girl?'

Jerry opened his mouth, then closed it again.

'Why don't we just wait,' she said, 'and see what the future brings.'

# VI

# Eight Years Later

# Nadia

*Nova Terra*

She watched the kid pick his way down the tumble of rocks on one side of the waterfall, moving from boulder to boulder, one hand tucked in close against his chest.

She squinted against the light and saw he was carrying something in his hand. Whatever it was, he was taking great care not to drop it.

'Hey,' Nadia called up. 'Careful there, Randy. I'm the one who's in trouble if you break your neck.'

'I found something!' His voice betrayed excitement. He reached down to a slippery-looking boulder with one booted foot, his one free hand braced against the rock behind him.

Just watching the kid make his way down such a precipitous slope one-handed was enough to age Nadia by a year for every minute he took to get back down to the ground. Every day with Randy was a reminder of why she could never have been a mother.

Randy reached the last boulder, then gently hopped down to the flat, muddy soil next to the creek. He was awkward and gangly-looking, a collection of barely-held together sticks granted sentience and set to the task of terrifying any adults within a twenty-mile radius by risking his life climbing up the side of goddamn waterfalls.

He came towards her, both hands cupped around something she couldn't see.

'Show me what you've got there,' she said, and he showed her a tiny grey-green creature that squirmed and made a *ribbit* sound.

'A frog?' She looked up from it and stared at the kid, aghast. 'With all the kindness in the world, Randy, but what the fuck?'

Randy grinned nervously, his cheeks colouring. 'Mom says you're not supposed to say words like that to me.'

'Your *mom* is eighty kilometres away, wondering why in hell your father and I are taking so long to get you back home.' She rapped him on the head with her knuckles, smiling to show her affection.

Randy ducked away, grinning too. 'Now tell me,' said Nadia, 'what in the name of Christ are you doing risking your life for the sake of a damn *frog*?'

'It's not just any frog,' he said. 'It's for Uncle Yuichi.'

She looked at the frog again. 'Yuichi asked you to collect frogs?'

'No,' he replied, as if she were slow. 'He asked me to collect ones with these markings.' He lifted it for her further inspection, and Nadia saw it had yellowish markings on its back. 'It's for medicine.'

'What kind of medicine?'

'Anti…' Randy screwed his face up. 'Antibee…'

'Antibiotics?'

A wide grin spread across the kid's face. 'Yes!' He pulled the frog close to his chest. 'It's because they've got that disease up in New Paris and they need antibiotics.'

'I'm pretty sure frogs don't have anything to do with antibiotics,' she said carefully.

'Actually, they do.'

She turned in surprise and saw Jerry standing grinning a few feet away. 'As long as they're the right frogs,' he added. 'It's some property of their skin.'

'Uncle Yuichi said I should look for more of these frogs and write down where I found them so they can use them for making medicine,' said young Randall, proudly.

'Yuichi's idea?' Nadia asked Jerry.

'Rozalia's, actually,' Jerry replied. 'He's just picking up from where she left off.'

Nadia's own smile became brittle, long-remembered pain twisting it into something closer to a squint.

'Go on back to the camp,' she said, making a swatting motion.

The kid ran ahead of them and she and Jerry walked side by side back to where they'd set up a couple of tents. The horses were grazing nearby while coffee brewed in a pot set over a campfire.

Jerry took the pot off the boil and poured some coffee into a tin mug, passing it to her. He'd let his beard grow out, and it was just about long enough that it brushed against his upper chest.

She drank the coffee appreciatively and they chatted for a while about the trip. Randy went off to feed the horses, having deposited his frog in a plastic container with holes in it for safekeeping.

'I figure we're maybe three days from home,' said Jerry.

'Long as the weather stays clear, anyhow.'

Nadia finished her coffee. 'I should go do some hunting so we've got something for dinner.'

Jerry nodded and glanced towards the sea, visible beyond the trees no more than a kilometre or two away. 'You know, Yuichi told me that Randall Senior once insisted he'd like to be buried at sea.'

Nadia laughed sourly. 'One time, when he was drunk, he told *me* he wanted to have his ashes mixed into a vat of chocolate so he could be eaten by underwear models.' She got up, chuckling to herself, and shouldered her hunting rifle. 'With the greatest of respect,' she added, 'Randall was full of shit at the best of times.'

He shrugged. 'Well, at least we've got him back. It's still better than not burying him at all.'

'Is that what you're going to do?' asked Randy, emerging once more from their tent. 'Throw Randall in the sea?'

Jerry grinned. 'We'll figure out just what we'll do once we've got your namesake home. And it's *burial* at sea, okay?'

Nadia glanced automatically towards the horses grazing nearby, and the saddlebag that contained Randall Pimm's ashes. It had taken most of a decade to persuade the Authority to return his remains to those who knew him best.

Just retrieving them had required a three-week round trip to New Paris. It was some kind of a victory, at least. Oskar's remains had simply gone missing.

It would have been nice, somewhere down the line, for all the hard work the Pathfinders had done for the Authority to be acknowledged, not least by letting them bury their dead properly. But she had long ago reconciled herself to the fact the Authority had no desire to make anything easy for them.

Now they were going to take Randall Senior back to Anywhere, the settlement they had founded, and give him the goodbye he deserved.

* * *

She ruffled Randy's hair and grabbed hold of her hunting rifle, making her way inland before she could change her mind about what she was thinking of doing. She pushed deep into the woods, keeping an eye out for cave bears.

Usually, you could hear them coming from a mile off, although they were getting scarcer as more refugees arrived and Nova Terra's population exploded.

She came across deer tracks and followed them for a while until the light became dim and almost ghostly in its quality beneath the dense forest canopy. She stopped and breathed in the air, thinking: this was the place to do it. Here, they'd never find her.

They'd look for her—she knew that, of course. But in the end they'd figure a bear or a lion or some other primeval critter caught her unawares and made a meal of her. And then they'd get on with the rest of their lives the way they should.

She reached down into her satchel, checking yet again that the bottle of pills was still there. Not that it could have gone anywhere.

She heard a twig snap from somewhere out of sight.

She turned in a circle, looking deep into the trees, her rifle at the ready. It'd be more than a little ironic, she thought, if a bear did in fact choose this moment to maul her to death.

Nothing moved. Birds sang love songs to each other from across the wide glades.

'Okay,' she said, her voice trembling just very slightly. 'Now how about you show yourself, whoever the hell you are?'

*Please don't be Randy*, she thought, listening.

She heard footsteps, to her right. She turned to see a dark-skinned figure standing next to a gnarled and ancient-looking oak, her hair cut close to her scalp.

Nadia's mouth worked for several moments, the rifle very nearly slipping from her grasp. '...Rozalia?' She staggered slightly and caught herself with one hand on the branch of a tree. 'You're...'

'I'm not who you think I am,' said the other woman, a warning in her voice. 'At least, not exactly.'

Rozalia—or the woman who could have been her twin—wore dark green fatigues belted at the waist. There was a device clipped to her belt, and Nadia's mind flashed back years, to when she'd last seen a similar-looking device mounted on the pressure suit of an identical woman.

'I remember you,' said Nadia. 'I remember the tattoo.'

Not-Rozalia reached one hand up to the tiny red rose tattooed below one ear. 'What about it?'

'You were going to get that tattoo on your twentieth birthday,' Nadia explained, her voice hoarse. 'Except the brakes on your shitty little Škoda gave out and you nearly ran me over on my Vespa. That was the first time I met you. I guilted you into buying me a coffee to make up for it.'

A faint smile curled up one corner of not-Rozalia's mouth. 'Or at least, that's how it happened in your universe. Right?'

Nadia nodded. 'Right. So...why are you here?'

For a moment, not-Rozalia appeared indecisive. Her fingers twisted at her sides, and she stared off into the forest for a moment.

292

'Good question,' she said, turning back to look at Nadia. She sighed. 'You must have wondered who the hell I was, after the last time I saw you.'

*Every single night for eight years*, thought Nadia. 'So how long have you been following me?'

'Since a while back,' she replied vaguely.

'I never heard or saw anyone the whole way here,' said Nadia.

'You wouldn't have,' said not-Rozalia. She moved a little closer, then stopped when Nadia took a half-step back. 'I just want to show you something,' she said, putting out her hands in a *don't-run* gesture.

Nadia nodded, both hands still on her rifle, and watched as the other woman tilted her head back as if scanning the forest canopy above them. After a few moments of waiting, something came flitting down through the air towards the woman.

She reached up with one hand, turning her palm upwards. The thing—whatever it was—landed on her hand with fluttering wings that looked somehow odd.

Nadia moved closer, despite her caution. At first she'd thought it was some kind of bird, like a finch or some other tiny denizen of the forest. Instead she saw a drone with gossamer-thin plastic wings that glinted oilily in the sunlight. It hadn't made a sound.

'I've been watching you using this,' not-Rozalia explained with an embarrassed grin. 'You wouldn't have heard or seen it.'

Nadia licked dry lips. 'How long?' she asked, stammering slightly. 'Since when—?'

'I saw you by the river a few days ago,' said not-Rozalia. Her voice was gentle in a very deliberate kind of way. 'You were sitting on a rock and you had some pills in your hand like you were about to swallow them.'

'You *saw* that?'

'Then that kid shouted for you and you put the pills back in a bottle before he could see them.' Not-Rozalia opened a box the size of a pack of cigarettes and put the tiny drone inside it, then grinned apologetically, tucking the box into a pocket. 'I was trying to pick the right time to say hello.'

'There's got to be some other reason you're here,' said Nadia. Her fear and caution had abated, and in their place was a curious longing she hadn't felt in a long time.

But this person was not Rozalia, no matter how much she looked like her. She was someone else, a stranger.

Then it hit her: this was Rozalia as she had been, before her cough grew worse and worse and her cancer shrank her to nothing. It had been so long Nadia had almost forgotten what a healthy Rozalia looked like.

'You took me by surprise when I saw you,' said not-Rozalia. Nadia didn't need to be told she was talking about Gamma Three. 'I didn't know who you were, but I could tell you were someone like me—otherwise, there's no possible way you could have been there. Yet somehow you *knew* me.'

'Are you alone here?' asked Nadia. 'Or are there others?'

'Just me,' not-Rozalia said guardedly. She looked off into the forest, then back again. 'There used to be more than just me. It's...kind of a long story.'

*I'll bet it is*, thought Nadia.

'I fixed the brakes on that Škoda and went and got this tattoo.' One corner of her mouth twitched. 'To my eternal regret. The tattoo, that is. I spent my whole life wishing I had never got it.'

'So why didn't you have it removed?'

Not-Rozalia looked at her like the explanation was more than obvious. 'Well, the world ended. What could I do?'

Nadia grinned and began to laugh. So did the other woman. 'How did you even *find* me?' asked Nadia. 'And why come looking?'

Not-Rozalia's hand reached unconsciously towards the box on her hip. 'There's ways to track a person through n-space, if they're travelling between alternates. And as for the other question…I guess I wanted to know more about you.'

'So what have you found out so far?'

'That you're not happy.'

Nadia flinched slightly at that. She stepped over to a rock just about the right height and shape to sit on and brushed moss from it before taking a careful seat. 'Well, I guess it doesn't take much to figure that out.'

'Why?'

Nadia raised a hand from her thigh then let it drop again. 'There's nothing left for me here. Nothing but growing old and living in a cabin way out in the back of nowhere.'

'Don't you…go places any more?'

'You mean like jaunting around the multiverse? We had portable stages, but they broke down or needed fixing, and the nearest working stage is three hundred kilometres north of here. But after—'

She caught herself. She had been about to say after Rozalia had passed away, there didn't seem any point in anything: Jerry and Chloe's lives were focused around their kid and the others were busy with their own lives.

All but Nadia: poor Nadia, who had to drink herself to sleep every night.

Not-Rozalia gave her a frank look. 'You're pretty good at feeling sorry for yourself, aren't you?'

Nadia scowled at her. 'You're just as much of an asshole as the Rozalia I knew, you know that?'

Not-Rozalia grinned. 'Sounds like I'd like her.' She reached out one hand towards Nadia while her other touched the box on her hip. 'Take my hand,' she said, as the box began to glow blue. 'We're going somewhere.'

'Where?'

'I just want to show you some things.'

Nadia stood, her posture nervous. 'What things?' She glanced back the way she'd come. 'They need me back there. They—'

'Nadia,' said not-Rozalia, her voice gently chiding. 'They don't need you—or not right now, anyway. Or you wouldn't have come all the way out to some place where you were sure they'd never find your body.'

Nadia stepped towards her, keeping her hands by her sides, as if afraid they might reach out of their own free will. 'But *why*?'

'Because I want to get to know you better. And because I want you to tell me about the other Rozalia.'

Nadia muttered an oath under her breath, took one last glance back the way she'd come, then stepped forward, taking the other woman's hand. 'You need to bring me back here. I don't know for certain I was going to swallow those pills.'

'I will,' promised not-Rozalia. 'If you want me to, I'll bring you back.'

By then, the blue glow had grown to surround both women. The light grew, and grew, and grew, and once it had faded all that was left were the trees and the birds singing from their branches, and the rush of a stream across rocks, and the distant roar of a cargo plane somewhere far overhead, on its way to destinations unknown. Eventually there were voices, calling to one another deep in the woods as the day turned to dusk: one young, one older—and with time they, too, departed, and the world moved on, trundling down a new path and following new probabilities into a future that was perfectly, gloriously unknowable.

# About Gary Gibson

Gary Gibson is one of the UK's leading authors of hard science fiction with a career stretching over fifteen years and ten books, including STEALING LIGHT, FINAL DAYS and most recently EXTINCTION GAME, which received the coveted "starred review" from Publisher's Weekly. His work has been translated and published around the world, including Russia, Brazil, Germany, France and others.

For updates and notifications of new releases, as well as more information about him. either visit his website at **www.garygibson.net** or subscribe to his newsletter: http://eepurl.com/b1ma4L.

BOOKS BY GARY GIBSON
  Standalones:
  ANGEL STATIONS
  AGAINST GRAVITY
  GHOST FREQUENCIES
  DEVIL'S ROAD (forthcoming)

Shoal Sequence:
  STEALING LIGHT
  NOVA WAR
  EMPIRE OF LIGHT
  MARAUDER

Final Days Duology:
  FINAL DAYS
  THE THOUSAND EMPERORS

Apocalypse Trilogy:
  EXTINCTION GAME
  SURVIVAL GAME
  DOOMSDAY GAME